CHAPTER 1

AZURE ROARED AS blood spattered across her flank. Hooves thudded on the earth as the small herd of bulls scattered in the opposite direction. Their terrified snorts filled the air as the scent of iron hit her snout.

No!

What a dick!

Growling low, she watched as the elk crumpled onto the forest floor, dead before it hit the ground.

She shifted quickly, breathing hard. "You bastard!" Azure yelled. Her voice was thick; her vocal cords still remembering her dragon form.

A cracking noise filled the clearing as Ice's bones and tendons reformed themselves. His scales pulled back into his flesh, as did his wings and tail. Within a second, he was in his human form as well. "You're getting slow." The male grinned.

"Slow?" She snorted. "You wish!" She knocked him hard with her shoulder. "You're an asshole!" she yelled, feeling slightly better when Ice staggered back from the blow. He was laughing hard, crunching slightly over his middle.

Deep rumbles behind them had her turning towards the others on the team, where they hovered just above the ground. The earth shuddered as elk carcasses dropped, brought down by the others earlier that day. Three more dragons landed in the clearing. They shifted as well. "Who brought the elk down?" Fog asked.

"Who do you think?" Ice lifted his chin, a smirk on his handsome face.

Azure made a noise of irritation. She rolled her eyes and snorted again.

"Really?" Fog frowned. "You missed?" He spoke to her. "I can't believe you missed. You're the fastest—"

"Azure is not the fastest!" Ice folded his arms.

"She is!" Fog shot back. "You're stronger, but she's just that little bit faster." He sniggered.

"I am the fastest person in this team, and you know it!" she told Ice, keeping her voice even. "And no, I didn't miss." She looked at Fog, shaking her head.

"Azure is getting slow," Ice chided, still grinning. "How old are you now? You refused to say at your birthday last week," Ice teased, his blue eyes dancing in the late morning sun. They were glacial, like his name suggested.

She put her hands on her hips and leveled him with a stare. "My age has nothing to do with it." She sounded shocked because she couldn't quite believe what she was damn well hearing. *The nerve of this male!* He was supposed to be her friend. *As if!*

Dragon
HEAT

AIR DRAGONS BOOK 1

CHARLENE HARTNADY

Fog laughed. Avalanche and Sun joined in as well. They were all laughing at her.

"Ice wing-cuffed me just as I was about to dive in for the kill," she told the group. "I almost flew straight into that outcrop of trees." She pointed in the general direction of the small pine forest. "I was ahead of him. That's cheating!" she told Ice. "You cheated, you dick!"

His grin widened, and a whole lot of dimples popped out on his cheeks. Two on the left and one on the right. He was too darned cute for his own good. "It was an accident. You flew too close to me," Ice smirked. He had done it on purpose, and they both knew it. "It's you who should be more careful," he jibed.

The nerve! "You're an ass!" Azure was smiling, too. She couldn't help it. This was great. It had almost been six months since she'd joined the hunting team. Months of hard work and determination. Months of being treated… differently, just because she was a female. Not badly, just different. The guys weren't rude or obnoxious. In fact, the opposite was true; they were too careful. Too nice. Too well mannered. It had made her work that much harder. Six months of trying to prove herself, and it was finally working. Ice had wing-cuffed her, just like he would have done one of the others.

Yes!

"Yeah, you're a dick, Ice!" Fog added. "You could've hurt Azure."

She rolled her eyes, getting ready to retaliate.

Ice didn't give her the chance. "I *am* a dick," he retorted. "I also happen to have one, and I know how to use it." He laughed, cupping his junk in one hand.

Azure shook her head. "Whatever, Ice." She laughed

as well. "Then again, you've told us countless times that you want a big family, so a dick is important."

"In that case, your balls are more important." Avalanche rubbed his chin.

"Enough about my junk." Ice choked out a laugh.

"I think you owe Azure. You stole that kill out from under her." Sun folded his arms, looking serious.

Here we go again!

"Bullshit!" Ice put his hands on his hips. "I won fair and square. With that in mind, it's payback time." He looked her in the eyes. "You need to carry the carcass back, and I believe you'll need to gut and skin it as well." He jerked a thumb at the fallen elk. "Not just that one… all of them." He glanced at where the other four elk lay.

Azure tried not to show her surprise. Ice would normally expect this of one of the males, but never of her. "I should make you do it, since you cheated, but… you're right, I need to be more careful. Know that I won't be making that particular mistake again." She narrowed her eyes on him to show she meant business. It looked like there would be no more going easy on her. She was finally one of the team, and it felt good.

Fog looked down at the fallen elk and then at her. For a moment, it looked like he might offer to help her by carrying it.

Don't!

Don't you dare!

Azure willed him to shift. The other three were talking about the upcoming weekend away. Their team was off duty for a change. Just when she thought he was going to offer to help her, he licked his lips. "I'll help you if you agree to have dinner with me." Dinner was code for sex. They all knew it.

So much for thinking things were finally improving. Azure sighed. "For the last time. No! Not happening. Not ever." She shook her head.

"It's only dinner." Fog made puppy dog eyes.

"That's it!" Ice growled. "The next person who propositions Azure during shift will gut and skin all of the game for the rest of the goddamned year. Am I clear? Do this kind of shit on your own time."

"Yes, Ice." Fog looked down at his feet. "I apologize, Azure. It's just that I've never had such a sexy teammate before." He smiled at her. Fog was a big old teddy bear. She wished he would drop it already.

Ice rolled his eyes. Azure could see that he was trying not to laugh. "On your own time," he told Fog.

Azure had to bite back a smile, even though she was a little annoyed at Ice. She could fight her own battles. She knew he meant well, so she left it alone.

"I'm sorry!" Fog put up a hand. "Really sorry." He directed it at her.

She nodded once.

"It won't happen again," Sun said.

"Ever," Avalanche added.

Fog looked down at her carcass. This time it definitely looked like he was planning on offering to carry it. It was sweet, but maddening.

"See you back at the lair," he finally said. Then he shifted, and she felt like she could breathe again. She watched him pick up one of the other carcasses.

Yes!

Azure smiled as she shifted. Six whole months and she was finally going to be one of the males. Plucking the elk from the ground in one of her claws, she rushed to catch up.

Just over half an hour later, they landed on the top of the mountain. Their lair was beneath them, carved into the side of the sheer cliff face. She dropped the elk and shifted.

"Here." Ice handed her a hunting knife and chuckled. "Have fun." He winked at her.

As much as Azure loved her job, she hated this part of the process. They all did, although hate was a strong word. It wasn't as much fun as the hunt. Her dragon loved the thrill of the chase. She was wired that way. They all were.

Azure sucked it up and smiled. "It'll be your turn tomorrow if you're not careful." The rule was whoever didn't make a kill had to skin and gut all the game themselves. Ice's wing-clip had ensured that she was that person today. Thankfully, all of them were successful on most days.

Ice snort-laughed. "Not a chance. I plan on making a kill or two *again* tomorrow."

"Let's wait and see," she retaliated.

"Sun is due for a no-kill day. It's been a while since your last one," Ice said.

"I'm bringing down a prime bull, don't you worry. I'm excellent at my job and know all of your tricks," Sun threw at Ice. "I'm not gutting and skinning multiple animals, since I'm saving these hands for the weekend." He held them up, opening and closing them several times. "Thank the gods tomorrow is Friday!"

They all cheered. Everyone except Azure.

"If you need your hands, you're doing it wrong," Ice jibed.

Sun tilted his chin up. "I use everything. My mouth, my hands, my cock, my—"

"Spare us!" Fog grunted.

"For the love of all things scaly, please spare us. I'm

with Fog on this one." Ice shook his head. "I definitely don't want any kind of visual that involves you rutting." He pointed at Sun.

"Not cool, dude. Not cool!" Avalanche chipped in; he was grimacing.

"What about you?" Ice asked, turning to her.

Azure moved the hunting knife from her left hand to her right one, feeling the weight of it in her palm. She frowned. "What about me?"

"Are you coming with us?" Ice hung his carcass on a nearby hook, turning to look at her once he was done.

What?

They were inviting her to town on their stag run? Couldn't be. She snort-laughed because she was so shocked. "To do what exactly?"

"To rut like the rest of us." Ice shrugged.

"Who or what exactly am I rutting?" She knew it wouldn't be one of them because when human females were around, she-dragons disappeared. At least it felt that way. Particularly if a female was infertile... as she was. Besides, she didn't want to rut with anyone on her team. It didn't feel right. Too close to home. There would be other dragon males at the stag run, but back to her first point. It had been an age since she last rutted, and yet she couldn't think of anyone she wanted. Okay, perhaps there was one male, but he was off limits.

"A human," Ice said. "There are plenty of males in the bars and clubs we frequent." He shrugged again.

"The hunting grounds." Sun bobbed his brows.

She choked out a laugh, moving the knife back to her left hand. Azure was eager to start skinning and gutting the elk. The kitchen would be waiting for fresh meat. They also imported food items nowadays, but still, the bulk of the food offering this evening would be elk. She shook her head. "Why would I want a human male? Where the females of the species are soft and delicate… you males seem to find those qualities attractive, which is great. Those same qualities are not all that attractive in the males."

"Yeah." Sun nodded, making a groaning noise. "Humans are very soft and so fucking tight."

Fog clouted Sun on the back of the head. The male bellowed, clutching his scalp, his face contorted in pain. "What was that for?"

"We told you that we don't want to hear about it," Fog admonished the male. "You were saying?" he said to Azure.

She shrugged. "I'm not looking for soft and weak. I hear human males have tiny cocks and that they don't know how to use them. Not eager for that either, thanks."

All of them broke out into fits of laughter. "It's true." Ice nodded, still chuckling. "Human females are always complaining about the males of the species."

"Yeah." Sun nodded. "They actually look shocked when they come— Hey!" He ducked, just missing another slap from Fog. "Stop that, dickhead!"

"Why the hell would I want a human male, then?" she deadpanned.

"Good point," Ice said.

"Totally understandable." Fog nodded.

"You should come anyway." Ice shrugged. "It's fun. Have a couple of beers with us."

"For five minutes?" She raised her brows. "Then you'll all disappear to go and rut your humans for the night?"

"Jealous?" Ice smirked.

"No!" she snorted. "I could have rutted with all of you at least ten times by now."

"All of us?" Ice cocked his head.

"Ten times?" Fog gave her a similar look.

Ice was right. Out of all the males on the team, Ice had never tried to get her under him. Not once. Then again, he was technically her superior, and they'd become friends over the last couple of months. As for the rest of the team, they'd offered on plenty of occasions, but none of them would have rutted her more than once or twice. That was the way of things. Fun with no strings attached. Any more than once or twice, and she might become emotionally attached. Heaven forbid. "What I meant to say..." she gave Ice a dirty look, "is that although I've had plenty of opportunities to rut with *most* of you, I'm not interested in your sorry asses. I'm *not* jealous." She narrowed her eyes on Ice's. "I have better things to do with my time than watch you pick up human females... thanks for the offer. Now, if you'll excuse me, I have a job to do." She picked up the carcass at her feet, hanging it on a nearby hook. Azure made the first incision.

The guys started moving. They shouted their goodbyes.

"I'm sure you have something better to do than watch me work." Azure turned to Ice, who was still standing there.

He pushed out a breath through his nostrils. "Not really. I like watching you work."

"Really now?" She'd just pulled the entrails out of the animal when he picked up an elk, hanging it on the hook next to hers. Ice grabbed himself a knife and started on the carcass. Azure turned to him. "What are you doing? I didn't make a kill today, which means that I am responsible for processing *all* of these elk."

"It'll take you hours, Azure. The kitchen needs the meat within the next three, or there won't be dinner tonight. I'm doing two. I did wing-clip you, after all."

"No, you didn't. I was clumsy," she countered.

His eyes flared with something that looked like admiration. He nodded once. "That may be so, but I'm still cleaning two… for the kitchen. This isn't me helping you. I want steak for dinner." He gave her a half-smile that made her look away for a moment.

"Right, the kitchen." She smiled at him. That meant that she had three to do. "Thanks," she mumbled.

"Don't thank me." He shook his head. He cut through the ribcage, using upward strokes with the knife. "I mean it. These elk won't be ready on time, and that would reflect badly on my team. I can't have that."

"No, I mean thank you for today." Her cheeks heated. She realized that she had stopped working and got started on cutting through the ribcage of her own elk.

"It's been long overdue," Ice said. "I should've set them straight a long time ago."

"That would've been special treatment. You were right to wait."

He nodded. "You've more than proven yourself, Azure. You're an asset to my team. Your only flaw is that you can't see a wing-clip coming." He laughed.

"Fair enough, but you need to know that I'm a fast learner." She grinned at Ice.

"We'll see about that." He chuckled, then quickly sobered up. "You should reconsider coming with us on the stag run. It would be good for the team morale. We could have some fun."

She shook her head, turning back to the job at hand

and getting busy. "Nah! I appreciate the offer, but for all the reasons I already listed, I'm going to have to decline. Besides, I know you're on the list to find a mate, and I wouldn't want to mess with that."

Ice frowned. "How would you mess with that?"

She made a face. "I'm a female. Not sure you noticed, but I am." She grinned. "I might scare them off… if I'm there with *all of you* males." She quickly added the last. "I'm tall, and I know how to give a scathing look. Human females do tend to irritate me."

"I noticed that you're a female." Ice chuckled. "It might be fun watching you intimidate the humans. If you're trying to give me reasons why you shouldn't come along with us, you're doing a bad job." He had made all of the required incisions and was preparing to start skinning the carcass.

"Back to the part about you being on the mates' list. I was at your birthday party just last month, and you're not getting any younger either, buddy." That wasn't true at all. It was females who had a shelf-life. "Is your mom still bugging you about starting a family?"

Ice rolled his eyes and groaned. "Only every week when I visit. It's worse after a stag run, especially now that I'm on the list."

"She wants her grandbabies." Azure laughed.

"Don't you know it." His eyes flared, and he turned serious in an instant. "I didn't mean it like that."

"I know how you meant it." She waved a hand. "Don't worry about it." Her own mother had died giving birth to her. Sure, there had been plenty of times growing up that she wished she had a mom, but that was what fate had dealt her. It was how it was. "My father has always said that it's a blessing I can't have children." She didn't see him very often since he lived and worked at one of the mines on the outskirts of dragon territory.

"I don't know about that." Ice frowned. "Although I understand why he would feel that way."

"For sure," she mumbled. "Who knows, maybe you'll meet someone perfect this weekend, and you won't have to worry about your mom giving you a hard time." She decided to steer the conversation away from her dormant womb.

"You never know." Ice started skinning his elk. "We'll have beers when I get back. I'll invite the team. We'll need to set up a wager as to who's buying."

"Sounds like a plan." Azure should be happy that Ice had invited her to join them on the run. Perhaps she was wrong to turn down the offer. Then again, it didn't feel wrong. It was one thing wanting to be treated the same when it came to work; it was another being treated like one of the males after hours. She wasn't one of the males. Azure was very much a female. It was normal that she didn't want to sit there and watch… No, she wasn't going to dwell on it. She'd stay home this weekend. The others could all go on their stag run. It would be business as usual on Monday. Thankfully Ice didn't push it.

CHAPTER 2

The next day…

TAKING LONG STRIDES, Azure walked down the hallway that led from her apartment. She still had plenty of time to make it to the balcony, where the rest of her team would be assembling soon.

Azure pulled some hair behind her ear. It was getting too long. She needed to cut it off again. She could use one of the hunting knives. They were sharp and could do the job just fine. She smoothed a hand down her dress. It was plain cotton, easy to take on and off when required. The garment was practical. She owned several more just like this one in various sensible colors.

Azure slowed as she caught sight of the human. *No! Not today!* Talking about impractical, everything about this human was impractical. Her strides slowed, and she contemplated turning around and going back to her room. She could pretend that she'd forgotten something. It probably wouldn't help; the irritating human would probably still be there when she came back out.

"Hi, Azure." The female smiled brightly.

"Hi, Melina." Azure tried to smile back. It more than likely came across as a grimace. It couldn't be helped. She was feeling ratty this morning. Azure didn't know why. She should be excited about having a weekend to herself.

"You look well," Melina said. "My order finally arrived yesterday." Her eyes were bright. "Don't you love my bodysuit?" She looked down at herself.

"It's very pretty." Azure nodded. It was tied around the human's neck in a knot at the back. It was a good thing that she didn't need to shift. It must take forever to get in and out of that thing. "What do you do when you have to go to the bathroom?" She frowned.

The other female laughed. "You have such a great sense of humor."

Azure frowned harder. She hadn't meant to be funny. "No, really." She couldn't see a zipper or any buttons. Why Melina needed high heels here at the lair was beyond her.

"I undo this." Melina pointed at the knot at the back of her neck. "And then pull the whole suit down. Not that difficult."

Azure nodded, even though she didn't agree at all. She was trying to be polite. Melina was irritating, but she wasn't a bad person. The last thing Azure wanted was to hurt her feelings, hence needing to be on her way.

"I don't mind." Melina shrugged. "It's not like I'm naked under here." She laughed, even though what she had just said wasn't funny in the least. Azure didn't get why humans were so appealing to her kind. Okay, perhaps she did. They were highly fertile, but they were also… strange creatures. "I'm wearing a bra," Melina felt the need to add. "It's not like I can afford to let the twins free."

"I can imagine." On that note, Azure agreed with the human. Her own breasts might be large for a dragon shifter, but they were small next to this female. Azure was thankful, too. Breasts like that would get in the way of everything.

"I don't know how you humans wear undergarments. I tried a bra once; it made me itchy and half suffocated me."

"I'm sure you were wearing the wrong size," Melina said. "You should come over. I'll help you pick the right size. You can try on some of my stuff. I have a dress that would really suit you. It's a gorgeous purple that would match your eyes… which are amazing, by the way."

"I doubt any of your clothing would fit me. I'm about twice your height."

"Twice?" Melina snorted. "Not hardly. You might have legs that go on for miles, but you're lean otherwise. There are a couple of things that would fit you just fine. I could even do your makeup." Her eyes brightened.

"Um… thank you. Um… yes, sure… that sounds like fun." *Not!* She would rather poke her eyes out or stand on hot coals.

"What about tomorrow? I hear that your team is on the stag run. That means you're not working, right?"

"I'm pretty tired. It's been a grueling week. Can I let you know tomorrow morning?" She didn't want to be rude to the female.

"Of course. I hope you'll come. Freeze can hang out with his friends. It can be a girl's night. We'll drink wine, and—"

"Sorry, Melina, I'm going to stop you there. I need to get to work." Azure winced, pointing down the hallway.

"Of course." The human nodded. "Let me know… okay? You have my number." She lifted her brows, rubbing her shiny lips together. Whatever she had plastered on them smelled nice… like berries. Not that she was interested in doing that to herself. Makeup? *Hard pass!*

"I have your number. I'll call you." It seemed like the human was eager to make friends, which made sense since she was about to mate a dragon shifter. Freeze was a sweet guy. They made a cute couple. Next would come the mating. Then it wouldn't be long before Melina was heavy with child. Azure felt a pang but quickly pushed it aside. Children tied you down. There was so much she wanted to do. It was better that she couldn't have them.

They said their goodbyes. Within minutes, Azure arrived at the balcony. Fog was already there. He wore a pair of black cotton pants. They were lightweight, like her dress. "Hey!" Fog said as she approached. "I have to say, the elk was delicious." He patted his abs. "The steaks were perfectly cut. Not too thick and not too thin." He rubbed his hands together. "I'm thinking that we should look for wild boar today."

"That's a crapshoot. We'd be lucky to come across a boar." She pulled her dress off, hanging it on a hook on the wall for when she returned. "It needs to be bison. We can bring a couple down. Enough to feed the—" She stopped talking because she noticed how Fog was looking at her. The males on her team might have offered her a rut from time to time, but they had never ogled her before. "You okay?" she asked, frowning.

Fog snapped his eyes up to hers and even gave a small

shake of his head. It was like he was trying to clear his mind. "Um, did you do something to your hair?"

What?

She groaned internally. Just when she thought things were going well. "No!" she pushed out.

"Oh!' He rubbed his chin, giving her the once-over again. "Maybe… maybe it's your scent." He sniffed the air. "Are you wearing perfume? A different shower gel, perhaps?"

"Stop your shit, Fog!" she snapped. "What's up with you?" She gave him a shove.

Fog stepped back. "Nothing. I was just wondering what changed. You have this air about you." He shrugged. "Ignore me."

"I do not have an air about me, and nothing has changed. Drop it!" She was worried the others would pick up on the vibe and join in. Just when she was starting to feel like one of the team. Just when they were accepting her.

"Ready to watch me take down our dinner again tonight?" Ice yelled across the wide balcony. He was already naked. Avalanche and Sun were with him. They were all smiling. Fog was taking off his pants.

"In your dreams." She shifted quickly and took to the sky. From the sound of wings flapping behind her, she knew that the males were close on her heels. They were headed northwest today. Hopefully, they would pick up the scent of a bison herd, or perhaps another elk or two. She flew hard. Ice could forget about making the kill today. He could forget about pulling a cheap shot, too. *Bastard!* If she'd been in her human form, she'd have smiled right then. Instead, she roared.

They flew for nearly three hours. Ice was just about to call for a break when Azure made a rumbling noise. She was still ahead of them and moving fast. The rumble meant that she had spotted something up ahead. Ice picked up the pace, and sure enough, there they were, a herd of bison. It was a big herd, too.

He gave a rumble as well. There were many young males in the herd. It wouldn't be long before they were kicked out. Young bulls happened to be their main target. Hunts were always strategic. Never a female during the birthing season. Big male bulls in herds of females were also left alone. Young males were the best option, or females just before breeding season. There were a whole lot more rules. It was all about making sure their hunting didn't affect the number of game adversely. Ultimately, about sustainability.

Ice felt his blood quicken. It looked like they would bag a couple of kills today. The tribe would have fresh meat for days. Bison were huge.

Ice enjoyed messing with Azure yesterday. She was their 'newest' team member, after all. Truth be told, they'd all gone far too easy on her in the early days when she had first joined them. They had treated her differently because she was a female. No more! It was time that she was initiated and properly accepted. That meant that she would have to eat some dirt on their next couple of missions. It was only fair. Then, and only then, would she truly be part of the hunting team.

Azure dove toward the herd; they all did. Only he went after her instead of picking a bison to take down. He wanted to take her kill... again. Next week, the others could give her shit, and then they'd ease off. Azure could take it. The female was strong and fast. More importantly, she was strong-willed. She'd proven herself over and over again during the last six months. It was time to cut her some slack by treating her exactly the same as any of the others. He felt ashamed for thinking less of her as a hunter simply because she was a female. It had been wrong of him. It wasn't just her beauty that had affected how he thought about her; it was how sweet she was. What he hadn't realized was that there was just as much heart and grit as there was kindness. Ice would be the first to admit that his initial assessment of her wasn't fair. Well, it was time for her to be initiated by him, good and proper.

Ice spotted a large young bull. It looked like Azure had her sights on the creature. He made a soft rumble. Azure was so intent on her prey that she hadn't noticed him directly behind her. She slowed slightly, bringing her claws forward to deliver the killing slash.

This was his opportunity. Had the female learned nothing after yesterday? Just as he was about to clip her again, she ducked, and he got air. His mind instantly clouded with... lust. His cock filled. His snout twitched, pulling in great lungfuls of air. Then he crashed into a large boulder... hard.

Ice fell on his back with a crash of scales, wings, and limbs. He lay there dazed for a good couple of minutes. When he blinked, he saw her... Azure standing over him. Her legs were a little apart, and her hands were on her hips. Her arms were splashed with blood, and she was smirking at him.

Ice shifted back into his human form. He growled loudly, the sound rough and raw and filled with pain.

Sure, he'd hit his head hard. Hard enough to leave him reeling, but that wasn't the reason for his discomfort. Shifting with an erection was always painful. Certainly not recommended.

What the hell?

He groaned again, this time deep and hard. His stare was focused between her legs. At her pussy. Such a pretty cunt.

Where had that come from?

What was wrong with him?

By everything that was scaled and winged. What the hell was he thinking? He breathed in deeply, his mouth filling with saliva. Fuck, but she smelled good. So good! His balls pulled tighter, and his cock gave a twitch.

"You're getting slow, Ice." Azure laughed. Her tits bounced a little. Big enough to bounce, but small enough to fit in his mouth. He was sure that by now, he was drooling. He wanted to rut… with Azure… now.

What the…?

"Fuck!" Avalanche groaned, drawing Ice's attention. The male was looking at Azure strangely. He sniffed openly at her, which irritated the fuck out of him. It made him want to hit the male. He had to force himself to release his fisted hands.

"What are you doing?" Azure asked, sounding unsure.

"Azure… holy shit!" Fog muttered. The male had blood dripping down his chest. He must have killed a bison as well. He was breathing heavily. Ice doubted it was from the exertion.

Ice clambered to his feet, noting that the rest of the herd had scattered. There were four carcasses on the churned-up ground. Then he caught her scent again. "Holy crap!" he murmured.

"Can someone tell me what the hell is going on?" Azure's eyes were narrowed, and her face was flushed. She was beautiful. Her dark hair fell about her shoulders in a wild tangle. Utterly breathtaking. Why hadn't he noticed before? He'd seen her as beautiful, but not like this. Not sexy. Not alluring.

Ice had never tried to rut her. Besides not being attracted to her in that way, it wouldn't have been right. She was his subordinate. Right now, though... all he could think about was pushing into her tight heat. Of rutting her hard and fast, and more than once. This was all kinds of fucked up.

"You are all making me nervous." She looked at them each in turn. "What is it? Do I have guts on my...?" She looked down at herself. At her soft skin. At her— This needed to stop. He took a few steps back, downwind of the female. "You're in heat," he choked out.

"Me? What?" Azure shook her head. Then she started laughing. "Good one, asshole. You got me there, for a second." She slapped a hand on her upper thigh, laughing harder.

"It's true." Fog's voice was just as choked. "It won't be long, and you'll start to feel it too."

"Feel what? What are you talking about?" Her voice was shrill.

"You'll..." Avalanche swallowed thickly, moving back as well. Then swallowed again.

"You'll get turned on. You'll start to crave sex," Fog told her.

"Okay." Azure shook her head. "That's enough. I don't mind you clipping my wing or trying to steal my kill, but this has gone too damned far." Her amethyst eyes were glowing. A gorgeous contrast with her dark hair and bronzed skin.

"It's true," Ice said. "You're seriously and very definitely in heat, Azure." He forced himself to breathe through his mouth. He could taste her. Delectable! He wanted to— *Stop!*

Fog put a hand over his fully erect cock. "Your scent is maddening," he growled. "If you need someone to share your heat with—"

Ice roared, and Azure gave a small jump. He'd never seen her look nervous or back away from anything, ever… until now. She backed away from them a few steps, her eyes wide with shock. She shook her head slowly in disbelief. "It can't be," she whispered.

"You should pick me." Sun stepped forward. "Better yet… I think you might be the female for me. Let's go find a cave and make some whelps. We could have a long, happy life together." The male looked like he meant it, and Ice was inclined to agree with the whole sentiment. It was his testosterone talking. Thankfully, he had the good sense to realize that.

"Fuck you!" Azure spat.

"That would be the idea… yes." Sun nodded. "We could fuck a whole hell of a lot."

"Stop this," Ice growled at the males. "Go!" he told Azure. "You need to go straight to your chamber. Fog was right; your scent is maddening. I… we can't think straight, and it's going to get worse."

"You too?" Azure looked at Ice like he had lost his mind, which he had. His dick throbbed. His balls tightened even more, making him grit his teeth. He felt sweat bead on his brow. She looked down at his cock, and her eyes flared as she quickly looked away. He was sure he heard her curse softly.

Ice nodded as she turned back, and he swallowed hard. "Go! Don't stop. Stay clear of any males. I thought you were... That..."

"I'm infertile." Azure looked shocked. "I've never come into heat before. Not once in all my years. It can't be. It must be some kind of mistake." She looked down at herself again, her nipples pebbled, and she made this little noise he felt at the base of his cock. It was starting to hit her. The need. It affected females differently. Some could handle it better than others. Azure might end up begging for relief. He wasn't sure he could turn her down. They would probably end up fighting over her if she stayed. Ice knew that he would win, but although he wanted to be a father, he didn't want it to happen like this. This was a mess.

"Go!" he growled. "I will send a healer to your chamber."

He watched as she shifted and took to the sky. Thank the gods. He could finally breathe.

"Holy shit!" Fog turned around, his hand working his cock.

"At least go behind a tree," Ice growled. The need to ease himself rode him hard, too, but Ice ignored it. A moment later, Fog grunted loudly; a thick spurt of seed erupted from his cock.

Avalanche grunted from behind the boulder. Sun made this noise in the back of his throat and ran off, his hand holding the tip of his cock. He groaned, hunching over his middle. The male was a lightweight. No wonder he needed his hands during sex.

Fog turned back to him. "What the hell was that?" He was breathing deeply. "I've been around females in heat before. It's always been uncomfortable but never like that." He shook his head. "It was insane."

"I'm not sure," Ice said. "Then again, this was probably a good example of zero to hero. From never coming in heat to the mother of all heats."

"You're right," Fog remarked. "That sounds like a good explanation."

"Nothing, and then an explosion of hormones and pheromones," Sun groaned. "I can still taste her on my tongue. I don't think I'll ever be able to look at Azure the same way again."

"Don't be an asshole," Ice told the male. "This is Azure we're talking about. Of course, we'll look at her the same. Nothing has changed."

"Everything has changed," Sun groaned. "I think I'm in love. I never noticed how plump her—"

Ice cuffed him on the back of his head.

"Hey!" Sun yelped. "What was that for?"

"For being a dick to Azure. She's Azure, not some random female. We need to try to respect that. We also need to follow her in case she runs into trouble on the way home." Ice felt everything in him bristle and tighten. He was feeling possessive all of a sudden. It was the hormones. Just the hormones. "Let's go." He roared as he shifted. It hurt like hell, since he was still fully engorged. All he could think of was keeping Azure safe. That, and rutting her. He worked hard at dismissing the second thought. It wasn't going to happen.

CHAPTER 3

A ZURE PACED FROM one side of her chamber to the other. She felt on edge. She felt needy. Her skin felt too tight. There was this throbbing between her legs. Her heart pounded inside her chest. The soft cotton of her loose-fitting dress rubbed against her skin, her nipples. It was all too much.

She was in heat.

In heat!

How?

Why her?

Why now?

Back to how?

It was going to be okay. It was going to be alright. Every instinct in her told her to find a male... any male. She could have a whelp of her own. She could be a mom. This was really happening.

No!

No way!

Her whole life would be upended. Besides, who would she choose? Her mind instantly went to Ice. To his bright blue eyes. Like shards of glass, only warm and bright. He was cocky, arrogant, and— What the heck was she thinking? Ice was their team leader. He was technically her superior. Not a chance! They were friends. This was just the hormones talking. She paced faster. Her skin felt so tight it almost hurt. She couldn't do this on her own. Days of need and pain. She'd have to pick someone… anyone.

The only problem was that there was no one she wanted to pick. No one she wanted to actually father her child. Then again, she didn't need to breed. They could just rut. Condoms! The humans used them. The males used them on the stag runs. She needed to choose someone to help her through this. They wouldn't need to make a whelp. A young, innocent life. *No!* She'd never had thoughts like these. She'd never had to think along these lines. It was all so confusing. She needed someone to rut. That was all. Once again, her mind went to Ice. To his sexy smirk.

No!

No!

No!

Not if he was the only male left in their tribe. Even then… no!

She paced faster. Perhaps she should take another cold shower. It was supposed to work for males. It hadn't worked for her. She needed a cock deep inside her. She needed sex. Hard, sweaty sex, and she needed it now.

Azure sat down in a nearby chair. *Breathe!* She needed to breathe. She could get through this. She didn't need a male. Azure had never needed a male before; she didn't need one now. There would be no sex and no whelps. Her chest tightened with longing.

No!

Her brain wasn't working right now. She had to remove that thought, and quickly. Her future depended on it.

There was a knock on her door, which opened seconds later. "Summer!" Azure yelled when she saw her friend, still dressed in an apron.

"I heard," her friend said.

Azure's phone vibrated on the coffee table where she'd left it. She ignored it. "You left during your work shift, didn't you?" she asked, although she had been stating more of a fact.

Summer nodded. "You needed me, so here I am."

Azure nodded. "I did." She smiled at Summer. "Thanks for coming."

"I can't believe this," her friend squealed. "How does it feel?" Summer looked at her with big, bright eyes. Also infertile, the other female had never experienced a heat.

Azure used the word that Fog had used. "It's maddening. Every instinct is screaming for me to take a mate… to breed… and to do it now." Her phone vibrated again.

"Who will you choose?" Summer raised her brows, looking excited.

"No one." Azure shook her head. "I will wait for this to pass, and then I'll get on with my life."

"Azure," Summer's eyes widened, "what are you saying? You have a chance at a family. Don't throw it away. You're so lucky." Her friend clutched her hands together, pulling them up against her chest. "I would give anything to have what you have right now."

Azure's phone vibrated a couple of times in quick succession.

"I know! It's so confusing. I don't know what to do. I had resigned myself to a simple life. I enjoy my job. I have great friends. I—" Her phone vibrated yet again.

"Someone is trying to get ahold of you."

Azure pressed her lips together, feeling her cheeks heat with anger. She wasn't sure why she was so angry. Only that the emotion was there in full force. "It's another proposition."

"Proposition?" Summer frowned.

"Suddenly, every male in this tribe wants to mate with me."

"That's great." Summer smiled brightly. "You can have your pick. Choose someone and—"

"No!" And there it was. The reason for her anger. The reason she was so averse to choosing a male. "I wasn't good enough for any of them before I went into heat." She shrugged. "They can all go to hell. Every last one of them." She picked up her phone, scrolling through the messages, and noted that none were from Ice. There was a part of her that was happy about that. And another part that was disappointed.

"Don't say that, Azure. You may never have this opportunity again. A baby of your own," Summer half-whispered; her eyes had a faraway look. "This kind of thing doesn't happen very often."

"I know! I'm so confused." She covered her face with her hand and sighed.

"Give it some thought."

Azure's phone vibrated with yet another message, and she growled, turning the device off completely. They could well and truly go to hell. All of them. She *was* good enough. She had *always* been good enough. Just as good as the human females. Just because she couldn't reproduce before did not make her defective. And yet, that's how she had been treated. That's how she had felt.

There was nothing anyone could say to change her mind. It was done. She would brave her heat alone, and that was that.

There was a knock at the door. Azure rolled her eyes. "Leave it," she told Summer. "It's probably one of the males. They're all trying to seduce me, and *I'm not interested!*" she yelled in the direction of the knocking.

The door opened. "Forgive the intrusion. I am mated." The male held up both hands. "I'm not here to seduce you," he added. Mated males were not affected by another female's heat… thank the gods.

"Who are you? Why are you here, then?" Azure asked, folding her arms.

"I am Cloud. You have been summoned by the king. I am to be your guard as I escort you to him."

"The king?" This didn't make any sense. Why would the king summon her? Because of her heat? Why?

"Thunder has asked me to give you this." It was a parcel wrapped in brown paper. Azure couldn't tell what it was by its smell. "It's a special soap to help keep the heat scent under control. You need to shower with this as quickly as you can, and then I will take you to him," the male said, handing her the package. "He's waiting for you."

Crap!

Azure met Summer's gaze. Her friend's eyes were wide, and her face pale. Much like her own, she would imagine. Azure nodded once, taking the soap. She couldn't refuse an invitation from the king, now could she?

CHAPTER 4

Huge wooden doors stood before her. They were carved with intricate designs. All Azure could think to herself was that behind that door was the king.

The Air King himself.

Thunder.

Holy dragon wings. Her mouth felt dry, and her eyes felt wide. She was about to have a meeting with the king.

Her heart raced. Her hands felt clammy. The guard at the door growled low, snagging her attention. "Did you get my text, Azure? I'm Sleet. We have met before. I was wondering—?"

"Not interested," she pushed out, feeling relieved that she meant it. That despite the hormones that raged through her right then, she was still in control. There would be no males. No mating. No breeding. None of that. She could do this.

Another male was standing on the other side of the door. He inclined his head. "Good afternoon," he announced.

"Um… hi!" She waited for him to sniff at her or come onto her, but it never happened.

"This is Skarn. He is from the Earth tribe," her guard, Cloud, announced.

"Oh! Nice to meet you," she mumbled. The male must be mated. He didn't scent of another female, though. It didn't matter.

"You, too." He dipped his head and gave her a kind smile before looking away. All she'd had today were leering males trying to proposition her; this was a refreshing change.

The door to Thunder's office opened. "His Highness will see you now," a male from inside the room announced.

Cloud gestured to the door. "I will wait here," he told her.

She pulled in a deep breath and stepped over the threshold. Aside from the guard who opened the door, there were four people inside. She recognized two of those people. The king was one of them. *By scales and claws, it was him!* There was also an Air healer. Azure inclined her head at Thunder, giving a small curtsey. "Your Highness."

"That won't be necessary," Thunder said curtly.

She frowned, lifting her gaze. There was a large male dragon she had never seen before, and a human female. They stood close together, their scents intermingled. They were a couple.

"Welcome," Thunder said. "This is Druze." The king

pointed at the male dragon. "He is a healer from the Earth dragon tribe. This is his female… Dr. Baker."

"You can call me Britt," the female said, holding out her hand.

What was going on here? Azure took her hand and shook it. "Nice to meet you," she said, sounding uncertain.

"We're excited," Thunder announced. "You've gone into heat for the first time. This is truly wonderful news."

Azure nodded once, feeling like an experiment. Something in a petri dish. All eyes were on her.

"I think it's fantastic," Thunder went on. "This rarely ever happens."

"It is, indeed," Britt said. "I am a fertility specialist. We would like to run a couple of tests… if that's okay with you?" The human healer went on. "Perhaps we can figure out what triggered you to go into heat all of a sudden. We might be able to use these findings to help others in the various tribes. Women just like you. Women who are desperate to conceive."

"You must go with them," Thunder said. "Let them run these tests."

"Whether you come with us and help us is up to you," Britt said.

"We aren't going to force you," the Earth healer added.

"You could help others. Even if what we discover helps one other dragon female," Britt went on, "it would have been worth it."

"You will do this!" Thunder pushed. "We do not have many she-dragons, and most of those are infertile. Human mates give us male offspring, but we need female dragons to be born. That can only happen if more of our kind go into heat."

"I will accompany you, my child," the Air healer said. "Like our King pointed out, it is important that we examine you. Perhaps we will be able to figure out how it is you came into heat so suddenly after being barren all this time."

Heat infused her cheeks. Azure nodded.

The elder made a strange noise at the back of her throat. "Unusual, indeed. I, for one, have many questions for you, my child."

"Azure will go with you," Thunder insisted, his piercing eyes on her.

Although Azure felt her anger rise, she pushed those emotions aside, thinking of her best friend, Summer. Not just her best friend, but all the other she-dragons desperate for a family of their own. Azure nodded. "I will go with you. You can conduct your tests."

The human healer sighed. She smiled at Azure. "Thank you!"

"Inform me as soon as you are done," Thunder said to the healers. "I need Azure in the great hall by this evening. I am making an announcement that concerns her."

It irritated Azure that Thunder spoke about her like she wasn't even there. Worry made her frown deepen and her stomach churn. What announcement? She didn't like the sound of that at all.

The human healer nodded. "Of course."

"I wish to extend my gratitude to the two of you for dropping everything to fly to our lair." He looked at a watch on his wrist. "You made it here in under two hours. Very impressive."

"We couldn't miss out on this opportunity to explore how it is that Azure suddenly came into heat," the human female told Thunder while smiling at her.

"It is important that you investigate this thoroughly," Thunder went on, "but don't take too long. As per our earlier conversation, this is time-sensitive. Do your tests, ask your questions and then release our female," he said to the healer. Then he turned to her. "I am so proud of you," he said, as if she had actually had a say in why this happened. "Today is a wonderful day." He smiled. The king smiled at her. Azure felt nothing but unease.

CHAPTER 5

P OKED, PRODDED AND harassed. That's how Azure
felt. They had taken her temperature. The speed of
her heartbeat. The pressure of her blood. She hadn't even
known that blood had a pressure. They'd finally taken her
actual blood from her vein using a silver-infused needle.
It had stung, and she'd felt slightly ill for a few minutes
afterward. Thankfully, the effects hadn't been lasting.

What she hadn't known was that the seriously
embarrassing tests were yet to come. They had taken body
fluid samples from her. How disgusting. What could they
possibly glean from her urine? It made no sense. Then the
human healer had put her on a special bed. She'd strapped
her legs open so that she could examine her... down there.
It was the most uncomfortable moment of her life. Only it
had lasted longer than a mere moment. Azure had gritted
her teeth, her hands so tightly fisted that there were half-

moon crescents on her palms from her nails, when it was over. Part of her discomfort was because she was in the middle of a raging heat. The other was that a female was touching her so intimately. A human, at that. Nudity had never worried her, but she'd never been happier than when the healer gave her permission to get dressed.

Then came the questions. From all three of them. Where had she been? What had she done? Who had she done it with? So many endless questions were fired at her, one after the other.

Finally, Cloud had knocked and entered, announcing that their time was up.

"Thank you for doing this, child," the healer told her.

Azure inclined her head. She didn't say anything.

"This is a rare occurrence. The older a female is when she comes into heat for the first time, the less likely she is to have a heat again. This more than likely will be the only heat you will ever have." She smiled. "I want you to be aware of that before making any decisions regarding your future."

"Thank you," Azure muttered. She knew this. Of course she did. It didn't make it any easier. This was probably her one and only chance at a baby. Why wasn't she happy? Why wasn't she jumping at the opportunity?

Azure pondered on all of this while Cloud and the Earth guard took her back to her chamber. It was eerie how quiet the hallways were. "Where is everyone?" Azure asked her guards.

"Everyone is assembled in the great hall," Cloud answered. "I have been instructed to take you there once you are showered and dressed. You will need to wash with the soap again, please."

Azure swallowed thickly. "The king is expecting me. He's going to make an announcement. Do you know what this is all about?"

They both shook their heads. "No, I'm sorry, I have no idea." They arrived at her chambers. "Please don't waste any time, Azure. Everyone is waiting."

"We will be here in case you need anything," the Earth guard told her.

Her stomach churned. Her hands felt clammy. Azure nodded once. "What is your name?" she asked him. "I know you told me earlier, but I can't remember." It was weird. The male didn't scent like he was mated, and yet he didn't seem interested in her. He was nothing but polite.

"I am Skarn," he replied deferentially.

"Thank you, Skarn. Thank you both." Azure turned towards her door and gripped the handle. She could deal with whatever was about to come her way.

All she wanted was to hide out in her apartment. She was in heat. In a perpetual state of arousal. She felt wet. Her breasts felt tender. Her nipples pulled tight. The last thing she wanted was to have to go to the great hall. Her eyes widened when she saw what was waiting for her in her chamber.

What the heck? She groaned internally.

There were three females looking her way. All elders. That wasn't all. Her mouth fell open when she saw what they had with them.

"Come inside," one of the females said. "We have much to do to get you ready, and not much time."

Azure shook her head. "Is this really necessary?"

"Come now, child," the second elder insisted. "We must prepare you for the ceremony."

"You must bathe and get dressed." The second elder held up a dress. It was long and nothing like the dresses she normally wore. "Why am I needed in the hall?"

"There is no time to talk," another elder said. "You will find out soon enough. You are very lucky, child."

Lucky? She didn't feel lucky. Did that make her a bad person? Then there was this business of a ceremony.

What ceremony?

This was worse than she had ever imagined. Way worse!

CHAPTER 6

*B*Y ALL THAT *had scales and claws.*

Ice could hardly breathe. He certainly couldn't take his eyes off Azure as she walked down the aisle of the great hall. His cock hardened, making him feel like a total asshole. The female was his subordinate; more than that, she was his friend. He shifted from one foot to the other, trying to get himself under control. His body would not listen. It didn't matter that her scent was muted; it was still there. *Fucking delicious!*

A murmur went through the great hall. Some of the males even growled. Every unmated male stood taller. Every eye was on Azure. Every unmated cock was hard. He could scent the testosterone. The arousal. The excitement. It angered him. Infuriated him. Why exactly that was, he could not say.

Her eyes flashed about the hall. From one male to the

next. Azure looked unsure; he would even go so far as to say that she looked afraid. He'd never seen fear in her eyes. Not in all the time he'd known her. Not when they'd come into contact with human hunters in helicopters. Not when they were shot at. Not when she'd taken down large prey. Never! Right then, she looked it. It didn't detract from her sheer beauty, though. He was totally a prick for noticing.

Fuck!

Her hair was half up and half down. Delicate white flowers were threaded through the dark strands. Her white dress was long and flowing. It was cinched at the waist. It showcased her breasts and her long legs. He'd seen Azure naked countless times. Yet seeing her covered like this had his mouth going dry. Need surged. Logically, he knew it was the hormones and the pheromones talking. It wasn't real. He wanted her all the same. They all did, only he had more respect. He did!

Ice looked away. Fuck, but he could scent her arousal. Ice could almost taste her pussy on his tongue. Just like every other unmated male in attendance, need coursed through him. The scent of testosterone was thick and cloying. It clouded his mind, making him want to fight or rut, or both.

Instead, he folded his arms. He willed his body to calm the fuck down. Willed his cock to stop its shit. Willed his dragon to shut the fuck up. He lifted his eyes towards her.

Azure hesitated on the stairs leading onto the stage.

"Do not be afraid," the king said. He was smiling broadly. "Come on up," Thunder encouraged her.

Azure walked up onto the dais, moving to stand next

to the king. She clasped her hands in front of her, looking uncertain. He watched as the delicate column of her throat moved as she swallowed, clearly nervous. At the same time, she squared her shoulders, lifting her chin. All he wanted to do right then was to save her. To take her away from all this. Ask her what *she* wanted, because this clearly wasn't it.

"Welcome," Thunder said, and the males cheered.

Ice grit his teeth. Everything about this felt wrong. They were parading Azure like a piece of prized meat.

"It is a joyous day," Thunder went on. "One of our dormant females is in heat."

The males cheered again.

Thunder put his hand up to quiet the crowd. "In six months, a whelp will be born to our tribe." Thunder smiled broadly. "Perhaps even a female of our species."

"Sire… I'm not sure…" Azure began to speak. Her voice was soft and hesitant. Not like Azure at all. Ice felt something clench inside him.

"As one of our Air tribe females," Thunder talked over her, "it is your duty to choose a male… any male you see before you, to spend your heat with. To breed. To bring life to our people. To continue our species," Thunder was speaking to Azure, even though his eyes flicked to the crowd every so often. Although females dotted the periphery, there were mostly males in attendance. Then again, their tribe was comprised mainly of males, since females were in such short supply. Fertile females even more so. Still, what Thunder was demanding of Azure seemed wrong. It sat wrong with Ice. From the look on Azure's face, it sat wrong with her, too.

Her jaw tensed as Thunder spoke. Her eyes went from unsure to blazing with anger. Much more like the female he knew and liked. The female he'd come to respect.

"I don't want a mate," Azure announced.

"I'm not asking you to take a mate. I am asking you to fulfill your duty as a fertile female of this tribe. You must choose a male and—"

"I'm not sure I'm ready to become a mother, Sire. It is a big responsibility." Azure cleared her throat. "I wish to spend my heat alone," she pushed out, projecting her voice.

"There are plenty of females who would give anything for an opportunity to become a mother. There are four mated couples who cannot conceive. You can give the whelp to any of these—"

"No!" Azure shouted. "That's not what I would want, either." There was a hint of panic in her voice. "It's my body and my choice. I don't want to—"

"We can't always get what we want, Azure," Thunder spoke softly and carefully. "I'm sorry." His eyes held pity, but it would be a poor consolation to Azure. "My mind is made up. There is an ancient tradition among the dragons, particularly in difficult times, where every female who comes into heat is expected to conceive."

No!

"It's called Kikalla," Thunder went on. He pronounced the word deep in his throat. "The breeding season," he explained. "Any dragon female within any of the tribes who comes into heat will be expected to breed, even those who already have whelps. I am sorry this happened to you, Azure. I am sorry for you, but not for our tribe... or for our people. This is a joyous day for the Air Tribe. We need more such as you. Hopefully, the healers will be able to cure our kind. They can learn from you. From this blessing." The thing about blessings and curses was that they often went hand in hand.

"Cure?" Azure shook her head. "There was nothing wrong with me before."

"Of course not." Thunder's eyes softened with more pity. "You need to be strong, female. You need to do this for all of us. It is up to you who you choose to spend your heat with. Up to the two of you whether or not you mate each other afterwards. You do not have to keep the child, but you must breed. Kikalla is upon us." Thunder held up a fist. "It is the breeding season for the dragons."

All the males cheered.

"This is barbaric!" a female shouted from the side. It was the human healer. Her male pulled her in close, his arm circling her waist. He whispered in her ear, trying to explain. The female shook her head, looking pissed off.

"No, Druze," she said. "I don't agree. I didn't sign up for this," she added.

The male said something else, but Ice's gaze was pulled back to Azure. Her purple irises were aflame. Her hands were tight fists at her sides. Her chest heaved. Her nipples pressed tightly against the thin, gauzy fabric of her dress.

He growled low. This was wrong!

"You must choose," Thunder boomed.

"I can't!" Azure's eyes turned hazy. The fear was back. Both fear and anger. Was Azure afraid to breed because of what happened to her mother? Or was it the manner in which Thunder was tackling this? Azure was fiercely independent. She was a female who made her own decisions. Who stood on her own two feet. Here she was being dictated to and treated like a child. Forced into something that might scare her.

Ice wanted to rush forward. He wanted to… what? Help her. How? What could he do to help her?

Nothing.

Sweet fuck all.

Frustration welled. He hated this feeling of helplessness.

"If you cannot choose, then the males will fight for the chance—" Thunder started to say.

"No!" She shook her head. "No fighting." Her eyes locked with his for a second. Just a second.

"Why not? The last male standing will spend your heat with you," the king went on. "You would breed with the strongest dragon in our tribe."

"No fighting!" Azure shook her head. "I'm not sure why you're doing this. All of our males want human females. None of them is remotely interested in—"

"I'll spend your heat with you!" a male from the front shouted.

"Pick me!" another male shouted.

Different voices rose throughout the hall. Males were trying to snag her attention. Ice wanted to do the same. He was tempted to step forward. To put his hand up. To make his interest known.

Interest?

Fuck! Azure would look at him with horror if he put his hand up. *Shit!* If only they had time. He could approach her and offer to help her. They could talk about it. Perhaps then—

"Me, Azure!" a familiar voice cried out among the others. "You know me! Pick me!"

"We work together, Fog." Azure shook her head, looking irritated. "It's not going to happen," she said.

"Why?" Fog shouted. "We would be good together."

"Thank you for your offer." Azure's eyes were blazing. She pushed her lips together, folding her arms across her chest. "But I can't possibly accept... We're friends." Ice had his answer. It would be no different if he offered.

Fuck!

Azure wasn't going to pick someone she knew well. Someone she worked with. Her superior. Azure would never pick him. It was better that way. What was he even thinking? Ice wanted children. He wanted a big family... but a child with Azure?

No!

No!

He'd almost made a gigantic mistake. Yet the thought of someone else with her made his blood boil. Again, it was the hormones. They worked together for months. He'd never looked at her in that way. He wasn't blind either. He knew that she was a beauty, but he'd never thought of her like that. Not until right then. It was the hormones. It was her scent. Her heat.

It would pass.

This would pass.

"I will give you until tomorrow afternoon," Thunder announced. "I can't give you any longer. Tomorrow midday, you must pick a male and leave immediately for the nearest cave. I will expect you to rut, to breed." He looked down for a second before addressing the hall once more, "The stag run is hereby canceled."

This elicited a commotion from males who were due to spend time on human territory. Particularly for males who were permitted to pick mates. Ice remained silent.

Azure rolled her eyes. There was the female he knew and liked. His lip twitched, and again he felt the need to offer himself as her heat partner. *Not a fuck! Not like this.* He gritted his teeth against the urge. Going against his every instinct. They were wired to breed. Then again, he thought that they had moved on from being such base creatures. Right then, it didn't feel that way. His cock throbbed. His balls pulled tight.

Azure stepped forward and cleared her throat. "I don't need until tomorrow."

"You are ready to pick a male now? Is that what you are saying?" Thunder lifted his brows. He smiled.

She nodded once. "For the record, I think this is bullshit!" Azure announced. "Up until five minutes ago, no one in this tribe was remotely interested in me. I was invisible."

"That's not true, Azure!" A male put his hand up. A male Ice knew well.

"Get lost, Sun!" Azure shot at him. She almost smiled... almost. "I think this is wrong on all levels." Her eyes shimmered with unshed tears. She blinked them away.

"I agree!" the human healer interjected.

"Britt, my love... we need to stay out of this," her male murmured. "This directive was given by the Fire king," Ice heard him say.

"I wish I had this opportunity," a dragon female shouted. He noted that it was Summer, Azure's best friend.

"I wish I could give it to you," Azure whispered, wiping a tear from her cheek.

Fuck! He hated that she was crying. This female was tough as nails. Just as quickly, a look of determination appeared in her gaze.

"I'll take the child," another female shouted. "Please!" There was desperation in her voice.

"You said that I can pick any male in this room." Azure ignored them.

"Any unmated male," Thunder corrected.

"Of course," Azure stated. "I pick Skarn." She pointed at a male at the base of the stairs.

"Skarn is an Earth dragon," Thunder said, a look of irritation on his face.

"So what of it?" Azure put her hands on her hips.

"You can't pick an Earth male." The king shook his head.

"You said any unmated male. Are you mated, Skarn?"

"No, I'm not. I am honored you would pick me." He inclined his head.

What the fuck?

Everyone started talking at once. There were growls and grunts and general displeasure at Azure's choice of male.

"No!" Thunder boomed. "You will need to pick again."

"With all due respect, Your Highness, I have already picked. You said any unmated male in the hall. I pick Skarn."

"What?" Thunder's voice boomed. "You can't be serious."

"I'm very serious. I pick Skarn." Azure narrowed her eyes.

If Ice wasn't so wound up, he would've laughed. *Go, Azure!* This female was something. Forced to take a male to her bed during her heat, she was doing it on her terms. Giving the king what he wanted while giving him the middle finger at the same time. He admired her tenacity. Her grit. Her courage. At the same time, something dark churned and wound around inside him. Something with barbed hooks.

"Why would you pick an Earth dragon over one of our own?" Thunder spat. It was a damned good question. One he would have asked himself. One he knew the answer to.

"He's the only unmated male in this whole lair who's treated me with any kind of respect. I would like the night to prepare. We can leave tomorrow," she said to Skarn.

The male nodded in assent.

"You will leave tomorrow at dawn." Thunder's jaw was set. The king was clearly trying to take back control. His eyes were stormy.

Ice's chest heaved. He couldn't seem to catch his breath. His whole body bristled. He needed to get out of there. His mind was foggy. Her words angered him. Skarn was not the only male who had treated Azure with respect. *Fuck that!* Why would Azure say such a thing?

Ice pushed his way out of the hall. Thunder was speaking, but Ice wasn't listening. He needed air. He pulled in lungfuls of the stuff as soon as he was on the sprawling balcony.

"Hey, boss!" Fog said as he joined Ice outside, jogging over to him. He was grinning. Ice wasn't sure what there was to grin about. "Good news, right?" He raised his brows.

Ice frowned. "What?" he asked, his voice a rough rasp.

"Thunder said that we can go on our stag run after all. Good thing Azure picked a male right away, don't you think? I wish it could have been me, but a soft human will take the sting away." The male shoulder-bumped him. "You have to agree?"

Ice grunted. He tried to force a smile.

"I'll see you bright and early tomorrow." Fog chuckled.

Ice tried to muster excitement for the stag run. "Um... yeah," he told Fog, watching as the male strode away.

All he could think about was Azure. That she was leaving with that male come morning. Ice gave his head a quick shake. He needed to get over it. The best way to do that was to get a female under him. A soft human female. Fog was right. All would be well. Once Azure's heat was over, things would go back to normal.

CHAPTER 7

The next day…

AZURE PACED ON the vast balcony. It was still early. The sun was still hugging the horizon. The sky was colored with streaks of orange and pink. The lair was still sleeping. *Lucky them.* There had been no sleep for Azure. Between the burning need for release and the idea of spending her heat with Skarn, she'd tossed and turned all night.

Holy shit!

What had she done?

Why had she chosen a stranger?

Better the devil you know. She should've picked someone she knew. Someone she got along with. Someone she was at least attracted to. *Ice.*

No!

Shit!

That would be messy. This would work better. They could rut. It wouldn't be too bad. Skarn was a good-looking male. He was polite and kind. He would be a good father. *Hopefully,* he would be a good father. It wasn't like she knew him. Why had she been so foolish? So hellbent on having some control over this... her body... her life. So hellbent on sticking it to Thunder and all the males in her tribe that she'd done a stupid, stupid thing.

"Good morning," Skarn said from behind her.

Azure almost jumped out of her skin, which felt too tight. Too hot. She turned. "You should know that this will just be rutting and breeding," she blurted. "That's all. No more and no less. I don't want to mate you," she told him. "I think it's important that we set boundaries before we leave... Sorry... um... good morning," she mumbled the last, feeling bad.

His nostrils flared, and he took a step back. She had thought him immune to her heat, but it seemed that she had been wrong. "Let's take this one step at a time," he said.

"There is only one step. We have to breed. That's it. What did Thunder call it?"

"Kikalla. The breeding season."

"Yes, that."

"Okay... that's fine." Skarn nodded. "We will breed. It's absolutely fine about all the other stuff. No pressure at all." He held up a hand like he needed to placate her.

Poor male!

Hearing him talk about breeding made her feel panicked. The rest of what he said made her feel bad. This *was* a blessing. Most of the infertile females would give anything to be in her place. She wished for the hundredth time that she could give this away to someone else. Someone with more of a clear-cut idea of what to do and who to do it with. What was she saying? She had already picked Skarn. It wasn't like she could change her mind. That wouldn't be fair to him.

"Azure…" He smiled. "It's a lovely name, by the way."

"Thank you." Skarn was too nice! He was too damned nice. It irritated her. Grated on her nerves. She'd picked him because the others were rude. Assholes even. Now she didn't want him because he was too nice. What was wrong with her? It was *her* and not him who was the problem. That much was very clear. She needed to get over herself. This was a duty, like any other.

"We are going to have a whelp together. That is a big deal." He kept his voice even. "Perhaps we should steer clear of making any kind of big decisions too early."

"I don't want a mate." She shook her head. "I will allow you to be a part of his life, of course. If that's what you want." She touched her belly, even though they hadn't even rutted yet. She could feel the possibilities inside her. All it did was scare her. She was a horrible, terrible person. Azure was going to suck it up. She was going to do this for her tribe. For this male, who was looking at her with such expectation. Such longing. Such desire. Her stomach was in knots. It made her feel ill.

This whole thing felt so wrong.

Why had Thunder made her choose?

Azure knew the answer. She might never have a heat again. This might be her only chance at a child. Her tribe's only chance.

"We might have a girl," Skarn said. "And you might develop feelings for me."

Azure didn't say anything. Skarn was sweet. He was a guard, but she could easily run circles around him. She wanted a partner who challenged her. Someone who interested her. Who made her heart thrum faster whenever he was near. Her mind wandered to thoughts of a certain male with glacial eyes. Just as quickly as the thoughts entered her mind, she shut them down. She'd be over it in a couple of days. She'd be with whelp in a couple of days.

Oh, by the gods!

Her heart beat faster, and she felt ill. Then again, this was the first time in a very long time that she had allowed herself to think about a mate. A partner. Someone to spend her life with. To grow old with. She'd learned to shut such thoughts down as soon as they entered her mind. She'd done so in self-preservation because she knew that a mate most likely wasn't in the cards for her. Not as an infertile female. Things had changed. They'd changed, but she was still the same. She'd had no chance to accept the change and grow from it. Now she'd never know.

Ice.

Was it the hormones talking?

Or was it truly him?

Had she thrown away a chance at being happy?

Ice had never been interested in her in that way, though. Not like that. She'd snuck a glance his way once or twice during the ceremony, and he'd gone from looking indifferent to... angry. Ice hadn't looked remotely interested. He hadn't stepped forward. He hadn't said a word. There had been a part of her that had hoped he would come and see her, but it had been radio silence since she'd raced off yesterday. Since her heat had first started. No! It was time to move on.

Skarn's nostrils flared. "Come, female. Let's make for the cave. Your heat grows stronger. I scent your need. I will fill your womb with my seed."

Part of her wanted to run. To run and hide. Instead, she nodded once, lifting her chin. Azure had never backed away from anything in her life, and she wasn't about to now. She shifted and took to the sky.

Ice clenched his jaw. He watched as Azure shifted. That blasted Earth male followed suit. His mouth twitched when he saw the male struggle to keep up with her as they flew away. That was Azure. Dishing it out every chance she got. Everything swirled inside him when he reminded himself where they were going. What they were about to do.

Fucking hell! He had no right to get angry. No right feeling this way. It wasn't like that between them. Why was he so damned jealous?

Ice wasn't sure he liked what he had seen go on between the two of them. The dynamic had been all wrong. It looked like an argument to him. He'd caught a few words, and he didn't like it. Azure hadn't looked happy.

Fuck! He should have gone to her before the meeting in the hall. Spoken to her. He should've offered to… What, exactly? Father a child? Why did he keep saying such dumb things? A whelp? With Azure?

Not a chance!

"You looked pissed off." Fog scrutinized him. "If I didn't know you better, I would say that you were having regrets right about now."

"Regrets about what?"

"Regrets about not throwing your hat in the game

yesterday. You look sorry to see Azure leaving with that male." By now, the couple were specks on the horizon.

"I *am* sorry," Ice grunted. "Not in the way you think," he lied through his teeth. "She should have picked an Air male." His voice was gruff.

"You look like maybe you think she should have picked *you*." Fog chuckled. "I know… it's her scent. There is nothing like the smell of a dragon female in heat. Her wet pussy—"

Ice wasn't sure what came over him. One second, he was watching Azure leave, jealous as fuck, and the next… he was punching Fog. The male needed to watch his mouth. He'd warned him.

Fog's head snapped back. He put a hand over his mouth, his eyes going wide. "What the hell was that?" He took his hand away and his lip was bleeding. Fog looked down at the smear on his fingers. "I can't go on a stag run with a busted-up lip."

"Your mouth will be healed in an hour… you asshole! I've told you not to talk about Azure in that way."

"She's in heat."

"I don't give a fuck!" Ice growled. "She's still Azure. She's still part of our team. She's a friend."

"Who just happens to be hot as hell."

Hot!

Was Azure hot?

Holy shit! She was hot. She was. From her shiny hair to her long legs. Then there was her full mouth, her breasts that were just the right size, with tight pink nipples that begged to be sucked… He groaned, running a hand through his hair. *No! No!* This was her heat playing tricks on him. Yes, she was hot, but it wasn't like that between them. It just wasn't.

"Let's go already. I'm sorry about hitting you… Actually, I'm not!" Ice added. "Don't say shit like that again. It's not right."

"You're right. Fuck! She's Azure. She's… our teammate. I won't… do it again." Fog wiped his mouth, which was dripping blood. "Let's get out of here."

Ice noted that everyone had arrived. That some of the males had shifted.

"I can already smell human pussy." Fog bobbed his eyebrows.

"Don't be a jerk." Ice shook his head. Is this what Azure had to listen to all these months? Is this how they sounded? How *he* sounded. No wonder she'd been pissed off. No wonder she had chosen an Earth male. They *were* a bunch of assholes.

"I'm going to bag two." Sun held up two fingers. "There's just so much of this to go around." He pointed down at himself. "Too much for just one female." He thrust his hips suggestively.

Ice grit his teeth.

He watched as, one by one, they shifted and flew away.

"Let's go!" Fog shouted at him.

Ice shook his head.

"What do you mean? It's our turn to go on a stag run. You're on the list to pick a mate. Human pussy, bro. I mean," Fog widened his eyes. "Really lovely human females await us, dude. Come on!"

Ice shook his head. "I think I'll sit this one out."

"You can't be serious. It'll be weeks, possibly months, before we get another opportunity to—"

"Go! They're leaving you behind," he urged Fog.

Fog frowned. "You're not thinking of going after Azure, are you?"

"No! Of course not." He shook his head, looking at Fog like he'd lost his mind, because the male *had* lost his mind. He wasn't planning that at all... Was he?

Fog cocked his head, studying him for a few moments. "There are rules to Kikalla. I don't remember what all of them are exactly. Not that there were that many. It doesn't matter because one of the rules was that once a female has chosen, she can't change her mind. Males may not fight over her anymore. Once it's done, it's done. Azure chose Skarn. She—"

"Stop!" Ice held up his hand. "That's not it. I just... I'm not feeling the stag run. That's all."

"Are you feeling pressure about taking a human mate?"

"I don't have to take a mate," he countered. "So, I'm not feeling any pressure."

"We are urged to take a mate when we are eligible," Fog said. "If you stay, it will be frowned upon. You need to at least try to find someone you are compatible with. Also, your mom will have a shit-fit." Fog chuckled.

"My mom will survive, and I don't care what Thunder thinks." Ice realized that he was pissed off at what had happened to Azure. Pissed that she had been forced into this. It wasn't right. Thunder was being unreasonable. This Kikalla bullshit was ancient. It was barbaric. It was plain wrong! "Go already. Have fun!"

"Don't do anything stupid," Fog said just before he shifted. Ice folded his arms, watching as Fog took to the air, his great wings flapping.

CHAPTER 8

I T TOOK THEM forty minutes to get to the heart of the mountain range. There was a natural rocky ledge on the side of the cave. The entrance was high up on the north-facing slope. Azure gripped the stone surface, her claws scraping for purchase.

A moment later, she shifted, stepping to the side to allow Skarn to land beside her. She'd bathed that morning, washing herself with the special soaps that the elders had left for her. From the way Skarn sniffed openly at her, it was clear that the scent of her heat was coming to the fore. The soaps were no longer working. He roared as he shifted, sounding pained. The reason for his pain became obvious as soon as he was in his human form. His erection jutted from between his legs. Azure quickly averted her gaze.

Crap!

Although, if she was honest with herself, her body was ready to be rutted. Her channel felt achy and empty. Her lower belly coiled with the need for release. Her nipples felt tight and her breasts heavy. Azure could feel that she was wet and ready, but she couldn't... she just couldn't face the thought of rutting Skarn.

The male stepped towards her, his eyelids hooded with desire. He reached for her, but Azure took a step back. "I'm not ready."

Skarn sniffed at her again. "You smell ready." His voice was deep.

"Soon," she promised. Why did it sound like a lie? "Let's look around first." She walked inside the cave. Although the entrance was narrow, it was voluminous inside. It smelled musty and damp. Fresh air blew in from the entrance. She could also scent minerals from the rock. There was another scent, one she couldn't place. Plantlife? Creatures who lived deeper in the cave? Azure wasn't sure.

Those kinds of thoughts left her when she spotted the large bed in the center of the space. It had a post on each corner. To the right of the bed was a fireplace. There were candelabras on all the flatter rock surfaces. The only other furniture was a table and chairs, as well as a large chest to the rear. On top of the wooden chest was a basket. She could smell fresh bread, cheese, as well as various other items, such as salted nuts and jerky. The cave looked deep. Water dripped somewhere at the rear. She knew that there were bathing pools back there; that's how the heat caves had been designed. Practical and low maintenance, yet comfortable enough. They had everything they could possibly need for a couple of days. The bedding smelled like it had recently been laundered. Everything had been prepared for them. Everything was ready. Everything except for her. She wasn't ready. Not even close.

Skarn touched the side of her arm, and she jumped half out of her skin.

"Do you want to eat? We could talk." His voice sounded strained. Need would be riding him hard.

Her stomach churned. She was turned on and yet loathed the idea of rutting with this male, even though he was a nice person. They would be making a whelp. This wasn't just a rut. This was serious. She would need to get through the pregnancy… the birth. If that went well and it was a big if, they would be responsible for another life. Tied together for the rest of their lives. This was a huge deal! Food was the very last thing on her mind. She nodded anyway, needing to buy time. "That would be nice." It wasn't Skarn's fault. He hadn't had much choice in this either. She needed to try to remember that. He was a pawn, just as much as she was.

"Go and sit." He gestured towards the table. "Shall I light some of the candles? It might be nice… romantic even?"

Shit! He was such a nice male. What was wrong with her? "I'll light the candles. You get the food," she told him, forcing a smile.

Skarn nodded. His face was pinched, his mouth a grim line.

Azure went through the motions. She found some matches inside the chest and started on the candles.

"I hear you're a hunter," Skarn said as he put plates down on the table.

By claw, his erection was huge. It looked angry. Could

a cock look angry? Seed leaked from the tip. She quickly looked away before he caught her eyeballing him and got the wrong idea.

"Yes," she squeaked. "I'm a…" She swallowed hard. "I changed careers six months ago. I worked in the kitchen before that as a cook. I got to know the hunters. They brought us fresh meat every day. When an opening came up, I applied… and got the job." She was babbling. She couldn't help it, it was the nerves.

"You've lit enough candles," Skarn remarked. "Come… sit."

There were still a couple of candles that remained unlit, but he was right, it was enough. Candlelight flickered all around the bed, highlighting that specific space. The far reaches of the cave were bathed in deep shadow, particularly to the rear. Azure wasn't really thinking about what she was doing. She turned, thanking claw that Skarn was already sitting. He smiled at her. It was brittle. The muscles on either side of his neck were roped, and sweat beaded on his forehead. Azure felt terrible. She felt like the worst person on earth.

"I can't do this," she whispered. "I was just so pissed off yesterday when my king blindsided me. I…" She licked her lips, considering her next words carefully.

"You feel like you might have picked the wrong male?" Skarn offered.

Azure nodded. "I'm sorry. We need to go back. I need to—"

"No!" Skarn shook his head. He pushed out a deep breath through his nose, looking at the table. His hands were flat on the surface. Then he lifted his dark eyes to hers. "I'm sorry. I'm a little on edge."

"I know, and I'm really sorry." She took a step back, putting some space between them. Not that it would help much.

"You don't understand." There were frown lines on his forehead. "It's too late to change your mind."

"It's not too late."

"You can't pick again. You already picked me. The rules of Kikalla state that once a female picks a male, she can't change her mind." His eyes seemed darker, even though the firelight flickered in them. "Thunder made that clear last night. Weren't you listening?"

She shook her head. She'd watched as Ice left the room. There were several other males who left as well, not just him, and yet her eyes had trailed after him from the hall. Her mind was in turmoil. "No, I guess I wasn't listening."

"Then I'll fill you in. When we left that hall yesterday, our fate was sealed. You can't pick another male, Azure. I'm sorry. We are here, and this needs to happen."

"I don't plan on picking anyone else." Her voice was slightly shrill. "I'm not doing this. Those healers can spend the rest of my heat cycle conducting all the tests they want. I need time. I can't bring a child into this world. Not with a male I don't love. It doesn't feel right. I'm sure you're a good person, but none of this feels right. I—"

"This is happening." He slapped his hands on the table… hard. His chest heaved as he fought for control. "I'm sorry. I didn't mean to scare you. We can't go back. The kings have—"

"I don't give a shit about the kings. This is my life… *my* body. It's my—"

"This is going to go one of two ways, Azure. Both will end with my seed in your womb. My suggestion is that we quit wasting time. Get your ass on that bed!" he shouted, pointing at the bed.

Her mouth fell open for a few seconds. She couldn't quite believe what she had just heard. "I suggest that you go outside for some fresh air. My scent has addled your brain. You should think about honor while you are out there. Forcing me against my will would not be an honorable thing to do." She worked at keeping her composure. She knew instinctively that if she lost it, that he would too.

"There is no forcing in Kikalla. I have been tasked with breeding you. I will carry out my duty."

"That's bullshit!" She kept her voice low. "It would be rape!"

"No!" His eyes burned. "You need to do your duty. You will fight me for all of five seconds, and then your body will take me. You need me, female. You are nearing the height of your heat."

Her sex throbbed. Revulsion was at the forefront of her emotions, though. It wasn't true. "Go outside! Better yet, I want you to leave. Know that if you choose to do this, I will fight you and keep fighting you. I don't want you. Although I respect my king, we are no longer in ancient times. Blaze, Thunder, and all the others can stick Kikalla up their asses."

"We are in troubled times. Kikalla was rightly instituted. I'm not going to debate this with you. I am a male. I am therefore stronger than you are. You don't stand a chance against me." He stood up, turning to face her. "This is your last opportunity to keep this pleasant.

I *will* breed you, Azure. I take my duties very seriously. I would prefer that this was pleasant for both of us. I urge you to please do the right thing."

She'd rather take a loud-mouthed, dirty-talking asshole any day over this polite piece of shit.

Where Skarn was strong, she was fast. Azure wished she could shift as she moved, but the exit was small. *Damn!* She needed to try. Azure had meant every word. She'd fight him with everything that she had.

"Screw you!" she shouted as she ran. Her arms pumped.

Azure was quicker than he was, but in his position near the table, he was slightly closer to the exit. With testosterone and adrenaline fueling him, the bastard was faster than she expected. Still, Azure managed to get through the exit first. Within half a second, she was on the ledge, about to throw herself over. She'd shift as she was falling. There was no time right then.

She was pushing back to launch herself when his hand fisted her hair, yanking her back. Azure swore that she was going to shave off every strand when she got out of this mess, and she *was* getting out of it. With a piercing yell, she was hauled back against him. Against his hard body. His throbbing cock. She felt it pulse at her ass and lower back. Azure snarled as his hands grabbed at her, squeezing her breasts, pulling her harder against him. She struggled, but it only caused her body to rub against him, so she stopped.

Skarn growled low. "What an unexpected treat this is."

Raping her was a treat. Is that what he meant? *Fuck him!* She stomped down on his foot and drove her elbow into his middle.

His hold on her loosened, but only for a second. Azure couldn't break free. Skarn dragged her back into the cave, angling them towards the bed. "Don't fight me. Get on your knees... be a good female."

Fuck him!

She needed to think. He had the upper hand. "I prefer my back," she said. "My legs up high." She was panting. It was fear... not arousal.

Skarn didn't seem to notice. She could feel his seed leaking onto her back. *Oh god! Oh god!* "I'm glad you changed your mind. You want me inside you? You want my seed to fill you?"

"Yes," she moaned the word. "I'm aching," she lied. Azure felt nothing but cold.

"I like a female on her knees." He pushed her down on the bed.

Crap! Crap! "The seed finds the womb more easily if a female has her legs in the air," she quickly pushed out, hoping he didn't hear the fear and desperation in her voice. "We have a duty. This is not about rutting; it's about breeding." She used his own words on him.

"Yes, it is," he whispered in her ear.

He moved back, flipped her over. She had half a second. Maybe even less. It was all she needed to pull her knees against her chest and to kick him in the face. She heard something snap. A tooth... bone? It didn't matter. Skarn flew backward, bellowing like a stuck pig. There was a spray of blood. She would have loved to watch him bleed, but she knew she didn't have much time. Skarn was pumped full of testosterone. He wouldn't feel the pain. He'd be angry and still intent on breeding her. She scrambled back, since he was in front of her and already recovering.

Damn!

The entrance looked too far away. She'd heard that many of these old caves had tunnel systems. Tunnels that went deeper down under the mountains and others that led out. If she kept running down the tunnel, he'd track her scent. He'd catch her. There was no hiding… unless. Water. Water could mask her scent. It was also a great conductor of electricity. Of lightning. She'd fry the bastard. She just needed to calm down long enough to be able to harness her power. She was too tense, too highly strung. Also, he couldn't be touching her, or she'd fry herself as well.

Dammit! The asshole wasn't far behind her. She could hear his ragged breathing. He'd be able to see her. One misstep and he'd have her. Azure sucked in a deep breath and turned. She held out her hands, tapping into the energy inside her. There was a crackle and a flash.

Skarn staggered back a few steps. He grinned. "Is that all you've got? As much as I'm enjoying the chase, I'd prefer to be inside your willing body."

"I'm not willing!" she screamed. She hoisted up a fist-sized rock in each hand and threw one at him, using every ounce of anger she could muster.

Skarn hadn't been expecting it. The rock smashed against his face… hard. The prick lost his footing and fell. He roared as he went down. The sound filled with both rage and pain.

Bastard!

Azure didn't hesitate. This would buy her a couple of seconds, at best. The rock would have hurt him. It definitely didn't disable him.

The deeper into the cave that she ran, the more

difficult it became to see. Non-humans could see well in the dark, but it required some light. The moon, stars, reflection from towns and cities… something!

The caves, well, this was something else. This must be how humans felt at night. All she could see were outlines and shadows. There were glints just ahead of her. The pools. She could use the darkness to her advantage. Azure inhaled deeply as she heard Skarn clamber to his feet, and then she heard loud footfalls. *Shit!* The chase was on. Azure did not like being prey. She wasn't a victim. Skarn was going to be sorry he ever took her on. She prayed that this would work. Azure threw the remaining rock further into the cave. She ducked down, then as gently as she could, she eased herself into the cold water.

The water rippled and lapped as she dropped all the way under, taking a deep breath just before the water closed over her. She counted to ten. Enough time to let the male pass her. Her head prickled. She half expected him to grab her out of the water. Perhaps he'd seen or heard her enter the water. This was where his testosterone-flooded body would fail him. He might be stronger, faster, and have a higher pain threshold, but he lacked focus. His senses would be muddled.

As soon as she hit ten, Azure gently surfaced. She pulled in a breath, careful not to make a sound.

"What the fuck!" Skarn yelled from somewhere within the cave. She assumed he had found the rock with her scent on it, and he'd realized he'd been fooled. It was time to slip out of the pool. Skarn would hear her, but she'd have a big enough lead to be able to get to the exit… at least, she hoped she would.

There was a loud hiss, followed by a deep rumble. A hiss? Did Skarn just hiss? It didn't sound like the noise a dragon would make. It didn't sound human either. Not by a long shot. That scent she had picked up earlier was stronger. She couldn't recognize it.

"Who are you?" Skarn shouted. "Let me go." She heard the sounds of a struggle.

What?

Did something have Skarn?

There was more low hissing. It would be too low for a human to hear. It sounded like it was coming from multiple sources. What was that? It was too dark down at the bottom of the cave for her to see much of anything. She heard shuffling of feet and louder sounds of a struggle.

Shit!

Goosebumps rose on her arms. It had nothing to do with the cold water. Her mouth dried. Her breathing hitched. Her heart raced. This wasn't right. This wasn't right at all.

Skarn screamed, "Put me down!" He snarled and growled. It sounded like he might be partially shifted.

There were several loud thuds, as well as hisses and grunts, followed by a snarl. Skarn roared, the noise cut short with another thudding noise. All was silent for a few long seconds. Gooseflesh broke out all over her body.

"*Glan di gom!*" a thick, deep voice sounded.

Fuck!

Holy shit!

Not like anything she'd heard before. A shifter?

"*Sik!*" another one of them said. She had no idea what was talking. The things definitely weren't human.

Azure's eyes were wide. She was panicking. Should she run, or should she—? Someone was coming. If she hadn't been paying close attention, she might have missed it. The footfalls were almost completely silent, even with the loose stones on the cave floor.

Pulling in a small breath, she slowly and carefully sank down into the water. A dark shape appeared at the water's edge. It was a human… Wait a minute, was it a human? It grew in size. Then again, perhaps it was coming even closer and merely looked like it was growing. Either way, the thing was big. It was… She sank down lower as it leaned over the body of water. It was huge, and it was right there.

She saw… She… Icy tendrils of fear wrapped themselves around her when she got a look at the creature standing over her. It was dark, and water obscured her vision, but she could see its outline. If the thing looked down, it would see her. *Crap!* She was in real trouble.

Azure sank right down to the pool floor. Her lungs burned. She closed her eyes and forced herself to stay calm. Azure wouldn't be able to stay below the surface for too much longer.

This was unreal.

She needed to hang on… just a little longer. She needed to survive. She needed to warn her tribe.

CHAPTER 9

I CE FLEW AS fast as his wings would take him. His muscles burned. He gritted his sharp teeth, his tail flicking in irritation as he pushed on. A thousand thoughts were spinning through his head. What if he was too late? He slowed, hovering for a few seconds. Of course, he was too late. It's not like Azure and that Earth male would sit and have a chat or make themselves a nice breakfast. They'd gone to the 'heat cave' to rut… to breed. That's what they were doing right then. That's what the cave was designed for… fucking.

No!

There was this clench deep in his gut. This burning inside him told him to keep going. If they were rutting like he suspected they were, he'd leave. If not… If not, what then? What would he do, knock and enter? Have a chat with them? With Azure?

Ice had no idea why he was there. Why he was flying to see a female who had chosen someone else to spend her heat with. Ice flapped his wings and kept flying, anyway. All he knew was that something drove him to keep going. Something drove him to check up on Azure. Yeah, that was it. He needed to make sure that she was okay. Not physically. He knew that no harm would come to her. There were patrols in the area, and Azure was with a dragon shifter. No harm would befall her. He needed to make sure that she was okay with the situation and to help her out of it if she wasn't. Ice was going to tell her what he thought of Kikalla. He'd help her stand up to Thunder. This was utter bullshit! He knew Azure, and he knew that she was upset about this.

His gut churned. He didn't want to find them rutting, though. If watching them fly away together made him jealous, what would hearing them rut do to him? What if he caught the scent of her heat? It might enrage him. It was a natural instinct for dragons to fight over females in heat.

Fuck!

Ice liked to think that he had some sort of control over himself. He wasn't going to be a yellow-bellied pussy; he was doing this. Not for himself, but for Azure. He couldn't shake the feeling that she needed him. He was going to suck it the fuck up and help her. She'd probably laugh in his face. Or tell him he was an idiot. Then again, she probably would never know he had gone there today. She'd be too wrapped up in her heat... in that male. *Fuuuck!* He was jealous, right to his core. What if the real reason spurring him to that cave was jealousy? What if it had nothing to do with helping Azure? There was no real way to truly tell. He was such an asshole for doing this, and yet he kept on flying. His mouth tasted bitter. It was fear of what he would find. He'd fucking kill that male if he was touching her... His... Azure was—

Holy shit!

He pulled up, giving his head a hard shake. So hard that his whole body shook. From his snout to the tip of his tail. It would be better once he was back in his human form. His dragon was base. It wanted to mate and breed. It wanted... Azure. Her heat was messing with him big fucking time.

Ice took a few deep breaths and carried on flying. He could see the mountain. He could even see the entrance to the cave. If he listened carefully, he might already catch the sounds of them rutting.

Nothing.

He couldn't hear a damned thing. Ice slowed his flapping, wanting to be quiet. He felt like the biggest prick. Like a voyeur. It didn't matter; he was doing this. Once he was satisfied that she was okay, he'd leave. If she wasn't one hundred percent comfortable, he was leaving *with* her. That Earth prick could go to hell.

Ice moved closer. He thought he heard a rustle and a hiss but from deep in the cave. Perhaps it was the wind. He couldn't hear rutting. In fact, there was an eerie silence. His scales prickled.

Ice landed on the rocky ledge, being as quiet as possible. He shifted, still on high alert. The hairs on the back of his neck stood up the instant he did. There was something very wrong. Ice moved quickly and quietly, stopping just short of entering the cave. He heard water dripping and someone gasping for air. He listened, but all was quiet.

Ice walked into the cave. All of his senses were on high alert. He scanned the area. The bed was still made. Aside from indents on the comforter, all was well. He could smell the sweet scent of Azure's heat. His cock filled. He could also scent seed. He couldn't smell the deep musk of rutting. Perhaps they hadn't— He pushed the thought aside. He also scented the coppery scent of blood, but perhaps it was just the minerals in the cave. No one was bleeding, surely?

He heard a whimper from the rear of the cave. Were they there? Fucking? It didn't sound like it. What the hell was going on?

"Azure!" He was done messing around. His voice was a harsh growl.

"Ice." He could hear the barely contained panic. Her voice was small and choked. It made his adrenaline surge.

He rushed to where her voice had come from. Azure was striding towards him. She was deathly pale and soaking wet. Her eyes were wide and fearful. "Skarn," she muttered, looking behind her. "He... um... they took him. I think they have him." She gave a sob. "We have to try to save him."

Ice grabbed her hand to stop her. He gently gave a tug, keeping his fingers wrapped around her icy hand. "Take a deep breath. You're not making sense. Where is the Earth male? Who took him?"

"The creatures... they're not human. They speak this strange language. They'll get us if they come back." She pulled in a deep breath, looking back into the darkness behind her for a second. He could see her working to get herself together, trying to slow her breathing. Her eyes fluttered closed and her throat worked. All he could do was stare at the trail of water droplets as they trickled down her skin. Her nipples were tight, pink buds. The scent of her heat had his balls pulling tight. He felt like the biggest prick alive. Azure was in trouble.

Ice let go of her hand and concentrated on breathing through his mouth. He could do this. Azure was afraid. Something had happened. He needed to stop this. He looked at her face.

"Sorry," she muttered. "I'm… I'm in heat. You're uncomfortable… I…" Her gaze dropped to his very erect cock.

"Ignore it! Ignore me! It's just a reaction. I'm fine." He shrugged. "You're safe with me." He wasn't sure why he said it. Perhaps because she needed to hear it.

"I know." Azure burst into tears. She put a hand over her face. Her shoulders shook. *Shit!* He touched her arm. "Hey." He tried to sound calm and soothing, but his voice was too deep of a rasp for that. "Whatever happened, it can't be that bad. We'll figure this out."

She cried harder, shaking her head. "I'm sorry. I'm not normally this emotional."

"It's okay. It's fine. I know you're not. This isn't a normal situation."

"It's really not fine… not at all." She sniffed, wiping her eyes.

He stroked her arm one more time, stopped himself from pulling her into his arms. That would be too much. Instead, he let his hand drop to his side. "You're scaring me… and only because you're one of the most badass dragons I know. What happened? You said that something took the Earth male."

She wiped her red-rimmed eyes and nodded. "Yes. I couldn't see it properly. There were a couple of them. They didn't speak English."

He frowned. "What do you mean? What language did they speak?"

"I don't know. They hissed and rumbled. They spoke strangely. They weren't human." She shook her head.

He frowned. "Shifters? Not dragons?"

"Possibly shifters. I don't think they were dragons, but I can't be sure. I saw one up close, but the light was bad, and I was under the water, so my vision was blurred. It was big, Ice… really big. I don't think it was a dragon, I didn't see wings. Its face was elongated. I think I saw scales, but I can't be sure." She shook her head, lifting her eyes; it was clear that she was trying hard to recall. "It wasn't like any dragon I've ever seen. It didn't sound like any dragon I've ever heard. All that hissing."

"You're saying they took Skarn? Where did they take him? I didn't see anybody when I arrived."

"Further into the cave." She looked into the darkness. Her eyes were wide. "Down there." She pointed. "That's where they came from."

"You're right. We need to try to get him back. I'm sure you're worried. One more question…" He frowned. "Why didn't they take you?" *Why was she dripping wet?* What the hell had happened that she wasn't telling him? There was definitely more to this.

Her throat worked. "Skarn got angry when I said I couldn't go through with it."

Why did hearing her say that she didn't want to go through with it make him happy? It shouldn't. Not when she looked distraught. It did, though. Something eased inside him. "What happened?" he urged her when she chewed her lip instead of speaking further.

She cast her gaze to the stony ground. "He tried to force me."

"The Earth male?" His voice was soft, although

everything inside him raged. Scales popped out on his chest, and his teeth sharpened.

"Yes," she practically whispered. "He chased me, tried to…" She bit down on her lip so hard he thought she might bleed. "I fought and ran. I hid in the pool."

"We're going," he told her, gripping her hand.

Azure didn't step forward. "We have to help him."

"We don't have to do shit. He tried to rape you. That's what you're saying, isn't it?"

She looked him in the eyes for a long moment, and then she nodded once. "Yes, but I fought him off. He didn't—"

"We're not risking our lives for a piece of shit like that." His voice was a low growl. "That prick tried to force himself on you. Wait a minute… blood! I scented blood when I arrived. Are you hurt?" He looked her over. Were her knees scraped? No. Her face? He tilted her chin up. He turned her around, checking her from behind. Her elbows?

"It's not my blood. It's his." Her voice got deeper, and sure enough, when he turned her back around, her eyes were narrowed with anger. "I kicked him in the face and threw a rock at his head. It hit its mark."

"You don't miss very often." He had to bite back a smile, since it wasn't appropriate in a situation like this. Even though he felt proud of her.

"I *never* miss." Her mouth twitched. "I ran away from him. He was just so strong… so damned fast. Not listening to anything I had to say." She told him what had happened. "I ran deeper into the cave and slipped into one of the pools. That's when I heard them with Skarn. They didn't know I was there. When one of them came over to the pool, I sank down beneath the surface. I was on the verge of passing out, but thankfully, by then, they were gone. I waited a few seconds, just to be sure, before easing myself out of the water. Soon after, I heard you call my name."

"Let's go. We're getting out of here before they come back."

"What about—?"

"I'm not risking anything for that Earth male. As far as I'm concerned, they can have him. We'll talk more about this when we're safe." He pulled on her hand, trying to urge her to go with him.

Worry bled into her expression. "I think they're going to kill him."

"He deserves to die. If he gets out of this, I will kill him myself."

"You'd have to stand in line." Her voice was cold and hard.

That was the female he knew and… liked. "Let's go." This time, when he gently pulled on her hand, she allowed herself to be led. A couple of strides later, and she was letting him go and walking ahead of him. Anger churned in his belly. That fucker Skarn had better stay right where he was. If he put so much as a scale above ground, he was dead.

CHAPTER 10

*D*AMN, *DAMN, DAMN!*
    Azure struggled to breathe. Her skin was far too tight for her body. She felt her pussy flood. Her heat hadn't been this bad before. Not even close. Maybe it was because she felt safe now. Maybe because she wasn't panicking or afraid of being forced into something she didn't want.

Was that it?

Crap, crap, crap!

"Are you okay?" Ice asked.

Azure realized that she was panting. She looked over her shoulder at him. His glacial blue eyes locked with hers. Such a beautiful blue. She made this groaning noise. It was him, too. It was Ice. She was attracted to him. She hadn't been attracted to Skarn. Her clit was throbbing. She felt something trickle down the inside of her thigh.

Shit, shit, shiiiit!

Her nipples were so tight she could use them to cut glass. Her breasts felt bigger. She could feel them jiggle while she walked. Azure looked down and, yep… definitely bigger. This was bad. This was worse than bad. She needed air. "Let's just go outside," Azure told him.

He made a noise of agreement that sounded strained.

Once they got out on the ledge, she noticed that he kept his distance, standing on the far end. Azure gulped air. It didn't help.

Ice's muscles were bulging. His tendons were roped. Particularly the ones on either side of his neck. His face was red. His eyes had this intense look. His erection— *Don't look!* It just made more wetness dribble down her inner thigh. It made her lower belly clench tight with need. She put a hand to her stomach.

"You don't look so good." His eyes filled with concern, even though he kept the pinched look.

"You don't look all that good yourself."

"You smell amazing." His Adam's apple worked. "Not that I would…" He put his hand over his cock, but not before she saw seed leak out. Even that made her mouth turn dry and her clit zing.

"I know you wouldn't… I know that you— Oh god." She bent over at the waist, trying to get this raging need under control. She was on the verge of begging Ice to rut her. It was wrong on so many levels. She wasn't going to do it. No damned way. "You should go," she managed to push out, instead.

"I'm not leaving you."

"I don't think I can shift like… like this." She felt sweat bead on her brow. "I'm… I'm…" She groaned.

"You're in pain?"

She nodded. "It hurts," she whispered, pushing her hand harder into her belly, trying to make it stop. *Please make it stop!*

"You're at the peak of your heat. It'll be bad for a day or so before slowly improving. I'm sorry, Azure. I... I'm so sorry."

"Just go... please." She looked up at him. Seeing him standing there hurt her even more. He was so masculine. So fucking hot. Her mouth filled with saliva and her womb cramped. Her channel felt achy. She was one fucking cliché after another, only the superhuman version of them all. She was in heat, standing in front of the male who made her feel alive. The male she had been trying to impress for months. The male who made her heart beat faster. It wasn't just her heat talking. It was the way she felt. The way she had felt for a while now, only she hadn't allowed herself to feel it. She'd shoved the emotions aside. Put them in a box and put a lid on it. She'd hidden from them. There was nowhere to hide anymore. Not with him standing right there. Not when he looked at her like that. "You need to leave. I'll follow you... in a few minutes... I swear." She choked over her words.

"Not happening, Azure." His voice was gruff. His cock jutted from between his thighs. His pinched look had eased some, now that they were in the open air. "What if those things come back? Even worse, what if that fucker comes back and you're here alone? I'm not leaving you. I'm looking after you. I'm seeing you home safely, and that's that."

"That's going to be a problem, since—" She whimpered as more pain hit. She was so aroused she didn't know what to do with herself. "Since I can't shift. Not unless I— Just go!" She wasn't beyond begging. Either beg him to leave or beg him to rut her. The latter was not going to happen, no matter how much she needed it. She liked Ice. Really liked him. If they rutted now, it would mess things up. Plus, she didn't want a whelp. At least, she didn't think she did. No, she didn't! It was all so confusing, which was even more reason to stay away from him. "Please," she added when he didn't move. Not so much as a muscle.

"I can't!"

"I need to ease myself. Are you going to stand there and watch?" Her voice was a touch shrill, but that was tough luck. It couldn't be helped. Not right then.

His jaw tightened. "I'll look away. I understand. It's not the end of the—"

"You'll look away?" She snorted. "No! Just leave me. I need three little minutes... that's all. I'll ease myself enough so that I can shift. It's that, or you can carry me." She groaned. "We need to hurry. I need... I need..."

"I know what you need, Azure, and easing yourself won't help." His voice was gentle.

"It will! It has to," she threw back at him.

Ice was pacing. "It won't. If I left, you'd feel slightly better, but I can't leave you. I could carry you, but your pain is just going to get worse and worse with each passing minute. It wouldn't be... Fuck it!" He leveled his stare at her. "I'll ease you. I'll do it, if you'll let me."

Yes, yes, yes!

"No!" She shook her head, pushing out a choked noise.

"Unless you can't tolerate the thought of it, after what

happened with that prick. I promise I won't try anything." He held up both hands. "I'll still respect you. I *do* respect you! It wouldn't change anything." He ran a hand through his hair, looking flustered. "I'd use my mouth," he whispered, so softly she could hardly hear him. "I'll make you come a few times. I'll use my mouth and my hands until it's more manageable, and then we'll go." His voice was a rough rasp that caused her skin to break out in gooseflesh.

"I thought you didn't need to use your hands," she blurted.

Ice choked out a laugh. She loved making him laugh. He rubbed the back of his head. "I don't, but since I can't use my cock, we'll go with my hand. Unless it would make you uncomfortable."

He was so sweet. "What about you? It wouldn't…" She groaned as she cramped again. This was insane.

"Forget about me, Azure. I'm fine. You're in agony."

"You're not fine. You'll get worse when—"

"Let me do this already. It'll stay between us. No one needs to know. You're in too much pain to make it home."

"Okay." Her skin seemed to tighten as she said it.

Ice pushed out a sigh. "Good… okay then, I need you to sit on that rock." He pointed. "And open your legs."

"Just like that?" She wasn't sure why she said that to him. No, that wasn't true. She knew exactly why. He was being too clinical. What had she expected? A kiss? A hug? Sweet endearments? This wasn't about any of that. This was about getting her off enough to get her home. Done!

His eyes softened as soon as her words were out.

"This feels weird," she quickly added before he could

say anything. "It feels… wrong." She was sweating and panting. In a world of pain. "Are you sure I can't do this myself?"

"I'm sure." He sounded gruff.

"I think I'll come in all of five seconds. I just need privacy."

He walked to the far ledge and turned his back on her. "Have at it." Now he sounded angry.

Even his back was beautiful. His ass meaty. "You're angry," she whispered.

"I'm not angry. I know what I'm talking about, that's all. I used to hang out with… a female who—"

She rolled her eyes. "With Crystal? You can say her name."

He sighed, turning. "Yes, with Crystal. It wasn't anything. We just—"

"You rutted for a while. I don't care!" she lied. "You can say it." He was seeing Crystal around the time she joined the team. They broke up soon after. Crystal moved onto the next hopeful schmuck. Or maybe Ice broke it off with her… Nah, not likely! It didn't matter… right then, nothing mattered. Oh, by all that was winged and scaled, she hurt so badly.

His eyes narrowed, and he folded his arms across his impressive chest. "Now *you* look angry."

"I'm not angry. I'm so aroused that my stomach is cramping. I'm in pain, you asshole!" She wasn't being fair. "I'm sorry! I'm being a bitch." She gritted her teeth and groaned, squeezing her eyes shut.

"Easing yourself won't work." From his voice, she could tell that Ice was close to her… right in front of her.

Azure opened her eyes. He was right there. She didn't

think her nipples could get any tighter, but they did. Her breath hitched. His scent was all male.

Oh hell!

Ice cupped her jaw. "Stop being so damned irritating and let me ease you." His voice was a soft rumble. "Let me do this one thing for you. People sometimes do things for other people without expecting anything in return."

"Do they... now?" she ground out.

"Always such a hardass." He gave her a grin. It was pinched. His eyes were stormy.

It had her insides doing weird things. Azure nodded, walking the few steps to the wide, flat rock he had pointed at. She sat on the edge, trying hard not to pant too hard.

"Put your legs over my shoulders," he said as he knelt in front of her, his eyes on hers.

When she didn't do as he said, Ice lowered his gaze and sighed before looking back up at her. "What happens on this rock stays on this rock. No judgment. It's you and me."

She did as he asked and slid her legs over his shoulders.

His eyes got this glint. "Make all the noise you need to. Go to fucking town. Don't hold back... okay?"

She nodded. "If I beg you to rut me, you need to ignore me. We can't!"

His lip twitched. "It might end up being me doing all the begging. Fuck, Azure, you have one pretty pussy." Then he eased forward, his eyes between her legs. Ice leaned in and latched his mouth on her clit. No hesitation. No testing the water. He went in straight for the jugular. Or, in this case, straight for her throbbing bundle of nerves.

Azure gripped at the rock beneath her with both her hands and yelled as a bolt of pleasure rushed through her. On the next suckle, she was coming apart with a deep groan.

Her eyes were wide. Her mouth too. Azure had never come so quickly in her whole life.

"Fucking delicious," he whispered against her, before thrusting his tongue deep inside her. This gave new meaning to the term 'eating out.' After tonguing her for a few beats, he moved back to her clit, thrusting two fingers inside her as his hot mouth closed over her sensitive bundle of nerves.

"Oh, by the gods," she groaned. "Ice... oh... Ice." He worked her pussy like a pro. His fingers thrusting in time with his mouth.

She was so wet. She could hear all the noises her body was making. Sucking, wet noises. She could smell herself. The musky, slightly fruity scent of her heat.

Ice groaned. It sounded like he was in agony, which he more than likely was, since it looked like he was more aroused than he'd ever been in his life.

When she looked down, he had his eyes on her... watching. His eyelids were hooded with desire... with desperation. His mouth sucked on her, his tongue laved her. She could see his arm moving back and forth with each quick thrust inside her. His eyes, his fingers... his mouth... all of it. She came apart again, with a cry that sounded far too much like his name for her liking.

Ice was doing her a favor. She shouldn't be screaming his name. She couldn't help it. That coiling sensation was already back at the pit of her stomach. She threaded her fingers through his hair, trying hard not to grip him too tightly. Her hips were rocking against his face. "More... oh... yes... oh... more... I need... I..." She clamped her mouth shut. She couldn't have what she needed most. This would have to do. Right then, the pain was gone. It was working.

Ice kept going... relentless. He groaned... this time in pleasure.

What?

Both of his arms were working. Both? He moaned again... sending a bolt of pleasure right through her. She was rocking against him. Her breasts bouncing lightly. "Oh... yes... right there..." She groaned as his fingers found that spot inside her.

That other arm was working harder and faster. Azure sat up a little, peering down between them. Sure enough, Ice was palming his cock. His hand working his shaft from base to tip in quick jerks.

It was one of the most erotic things she had ever seen. Azure cried out as a third powerful orgasm moved through her, causing her back to bow.

Just as she was coming down, Ice groaned, low and deep. He pulled away. Thick white spurts of seed erupted from his tip. His hand moved quickly over his cock. He was crunched over his middle... looking down. There was another smaller spurt. Ice grunted. Even that sounded sexy. A few seconds later and he stilled. He was panting harder than she was at this point. "I'm sorry," he growled, looking up at her. "I shouldn't have. I'm such a prick I—"

"Don't be silly. You have to shift as well. You were

also pretty wound up. What happens on the rock stays on the rock, right?" She lifted her brows.

He nodded, finally looking up. Aside from a frown, he looked unsure.

"I mean it. You're a strong male but there's only so much a person can take."

"You're right. We'd better get going. This slight reprieve is not going to last." Ice stood, holding his hand out to her. *Shit!* She was still sitting there with her legs wide open. Not that it mattered. Not after what had just happened.

"Let's get out of here," he said.

"Thank you."

"Anytime." He cocked his head and chuckled. "Okay, maybe not any time. Let me just go with 'no problem'!" He nodded a few times. "That works better."

That was his way of drawing a line in the sand. Of telling her that this was a one-time thing. She knew that. He didn't have to spell it out for her.

Before she could say anything else, Ice shifted. She followed suit. Then they were headed back to their lair as fast as their wings would take them.

CHAPTER 11

"ANY CHANCE YOU could open a window, Sire? Perhaps the door?" Ice asked Thunder, breathing through his mouth. Sweat dripped down his forehead. Breathing through his mouth only served to remind him of how decadent Azure had tasted. All he could think about while buried between her legs was how good she would feel on the end of his cock. Of being buried deep inside her. He bit back a groan. Ice knew it would sound a little desperate and a whole lot horny.

Ice put a pillow over his erection, since their light cotton pants did nothing to help keep him together. This was a shit show.

"I used tons of that soap," Azure choked out. Her face was tight with both arousal and pain. She had a hand clasped tightly to her stomach, bunching the fabric of her dress in her hand.

"This is insane," he growled, standing. "Where is the healer?" He kept the pillow firmly in place. Neither Thunder nor Storm would be affected by Azure's heat because they were mated males. They obviously didn't give a shit about how Azure must be feeling right then, either.

"I don't need a healer. I just need... ah... I... need to be... left alone," Azure pushed out.

"Sit!" Thunder pointed at the chair behind Ice. "The healer will be here as soon as she has finished mixing your tincture," he told Azure, who nodded. This tincture was supposed to help ease her heat pains. Where was the female? It felt like they had returned to the lair hours ago when, in reality, they had been back less than an hour and only ten minutes in Thunder's office. "If we make this meeting quick, it won't be necessary," the king went on. "Let me conclude everything you have told us, Azure." He paused. It looked like he was regrouping. "The Earth dragon tried to force you to breed," he spoke to Azure, who nodded once. "You ran and hid in one of the pools. Then these strange creatures abducted the male, pulling him deeper into the caves?" He shook his head, looking deep in thought. "What do you make of this, Storm?" The king turned to his brother and second-in-command.

"It sounds crazy. Are you sure you didn't knock your head?"

Azure looked pale; that, and shell-shocked. She didn't need to have her story torn apart. It irritated Ice.

"Azure didn't knock her head," Ice snarled. "I can vouch that Skarn... or whatever that fucker's name is, didn't leave the cave. I would have seen him. I could scent blood when I entered, and yet Azure wasn't injured.

Azure was shivering and wet from hiding in the pools. She was frantic with worry. I assure you that she knows what she saw. She's one of my best hunters, which takes patience and keen observation skills."

Storm made a noise like he was thinking things through.

"Yes, but—" Thunder started to say.

There was a knock, and a female entered carrying a vial of brown liquid. Her hair was sprinkled with gray. There were fine lines around her eyes. "Here you are," the female said, looking at Azure. "You poor dear." Her eyes went to the king and his brother. "Sire." She curtseyed. "My Prince." She inclined her head at Storm. "May I?"

"Certainly." Thunder waved a hand, motioning for her to enter. "Let's continue," he said to them. "You mentioned that this creature you saw was large, with an elongated jaw. It may have initially been in human form, but you're not sure. The creatures hissed and spoke in a different language. It could see in the dark and more than likely had scales. Is that correct?"

"I know what I saw," Azure said, her voice strong and true. "Thank you," she muttered when the healer handed her the vial.

"It won't taste very nice, but it will help you with the cramps," the healer said.

Azure drank the liquid and grimaced. "There were more than one of them. They overpowered Skarn, a dragon male in his prime. They took him. They have him now." She handed the vial back to the healer.

"Why would these things take Skarn in the first place?" Storm asked.

"Did this happen in the heat cave?" the healer asked Azure. She narrowed her eyes in thought.

"Yes." Azure nodded.

"I heard stories as a child." The older woman lifted her eyes for a moment. "Hmmm… I didn't think they were true, but perhaps I was wrong." She rubbed her chin. "It sounds like the fifth tribe."

"Fifth tribe? What stories?" Thunder asked, his voice animated. "Sit… please." He gestured to one of the chairs.

The older woman sat on the sofa across from them; she was still lost in thought. She licked her lips and cocked her head. "My mother used to tell me these stories when I was a whelp. She is still alive, but her memory is not what it used to be. I will try to remember all I can." She paused again, then continued. "There used to be a fifth dragon tribe. Not just Fire, Air, Earth, and Water."

"A fifth tribe?" Thunder frowned.

The healer nodded.

"What kind of tribe?" Storm leaned forward.

"I can't recall." She shook her head. "The fifth tribe had a falling out with the others. There was war."

"Why was there a falling out?" Thunder's eyes narrowed on the healer.

"Something about a female… but it could have been over power."

"Probably both," Storm said. "Nothing like a female to make males lose their minds."

Especially if she was in heat, Ice thought to himself, risking a look at Azure. There was a touch more color in her cheeks. She wasn't shivering so much anymore. It looked like that tincture might be working.

"Whatever the fight was about, the fifth tribe lost the war," the healer went on. "They fled for their lives. The other four tribes hunted them relentlessly, killing all they could find. Our species were far more… brutal than we are now." The healer scratched her head. "With numbers of the fifth tribe dwindling, they ended up going underground. Deep underground. That's where the stories take different directions. Some spoke of the fifth tribe dying out, never to be seen again. Others said that they adapted to living in the dark. That they thrived down there. There were stories told of an underground lair so big and beautiful it would boggle the mind. As a young female, I remember wanting to be taken by a cave dragon. Taken to a new world." Her eyes twinkled. "It was all nonsense… or at least, I thought it was nonsense. Perhaps, after all this time, cave dragons do exist. It sounds like they took the Earth male."

"Why, though? What would they want with him?" Storm asked.

"Who knows," the healer said.

"They didn't look like… dragons. They definitely didn't sound like dragons, but perhaps I was wrong. It was so dark." Azure sounded much better.

Come to think of it, he felt a little less edgy. His dick was still hard as nails, but his balls were no longer in his throat. The liquid in the vial was definitely doing its job. Then again, perhaps it was news of these cave dragons that took his mind off Azure's scent. Probably a bit of both. He was glad she was coping better. Hopefully, the healer had more where that came from.

"We need to assemble the elders and see what information we can glean on these creatures. I will inform Granite of what has happened. We will need to decide how to proceed." Thunder sounded pissed off.

"I'll get the ball rolling," Storm said.

"Please excuse me, Sire," Azure said, standing. "I'm going back to my chamber. I think it would be best if a couple of mated guards could be placed at—"

"There is no need for guards." Thunder shook his head. "You are still at the height of your heat. You need to pick again, although a cave might not be the best place to spend your heat."

"No." Azure stood taller. "I wasn't happy picking before, and I hate the idea now. It's not what I want."

Thunder sighed and pressed two of his fingers into his closed eyes. "I explained this already." He dropped his hand. "I need you to do this for your tribe. We need female dragons."

"I can't!" Her voice was slightly shrill. "Not after what happened. It was this close." She held two of her fingers a fraction of an inch apart. "Those creatures were terrifying. I'm not sure what would have happened if they had found me. Aside from all of that, it's wrong."

"It was probably your scent that drew them," Ice said, more to himself. "I'm glad they didn't find you." Their eyes locked.

"I've been through too much," she said, her eyes still on him for a moment before they moved to Thunder. "I can't... I won't... I—"

"You must!" Thunder pushed. "You must dig deep. It's what your body wants. What your body needs right now."

"Didn't you hear a word I just said? After nearly being forced and nearly kidnapped, it's not what I want at all! What I need is to be left alone."

"You left with a male you don't even know. It would be better with—"

"Skarn was a mistake," she said.

"Exactly," Thunder spoke gently. "You need to choose a male you know and trust. What about you Ice?"

Holy fuck!

Ice put his hands up, palms forward. "It's not up to me." It was a pussy answer. It wasn't even an answer. He'd dodged the question entirely, and yet he stood behind what he had just said. "If Azure doesn't want to spend her heat with a male, if she doesn't want a whelp right now, she shouldn't have to choose anyone."

"Blaze will be angry if Azure doesn't try to get with whelp," Storm said to Thunder.

"It's one hell of a fuck-up. I think we have bigger fish to fry right now," Thunder told Storm. He looked at Azure. "We need female whelps being born. Females such as you are the most important individuals in this tribe right now. I can't force you. I can ask that you reconsider. That you give it some thought. You may never have this opportunity again. Don't you want to be a mother?"

"I've never given it any thought. I didn't think it was in the cards for me. It's a big decision. One I can't make right now."

"You might never have this chance again," Storm snapped.

She shrugged, looking small and sad. So unlike herself, it was alarming. "It's a risk I'm willing to take."

"Blaze might decide to take action against you. He was ultimately the one who invoked Kikalla," Thunder said. "I would stand up for you, but if he decided to—"

"No!" Ice growled. He pulled in a deep breath and lowered his gaze. "Forgive me, Sire, but that's not fair. I would stand against a decision such as that." He bristled. "You should pick this male," Thunder told Azure. "He cares for you." Before they could say anything else, he added, "You're all dismissed. Azure will need more of your tincture," he told the healer. "Although I am still hopeful that she will do the right thing."

Azure's eyes blazed. Her jaw clenched tight. She'd never been more beautiful, and he didn't think it was her heat talking. Or his dick, for that matter. For just a second, he had wanted her to pick him and to agree. Just a second. It was over before he could analyze it.

CHAPTER 12

Two days later…

AZURE FELT THE earth between her toes. The sun was warm on her back. A soft breeze had the trees around them rustling.

What shocked her was that even though so much had happened, nothing had changed. Not really. She glanced back at her team, who was sitting a little way off having their lunch. Sun and Fog were arguing about something or other. Nothing worth noting. Avalanche took a big bite of his turkey leg, groaning around his food. Ice sat away from the group. Although he had his food in his hand, he had yet to start eating.

Yep, everything was the same, alright. They knew where a herd of elk was grazing. They'd found them a little while ago. Once they finished recharging their batteries, they were going to bag a couple of bulls and then head back to the lair.

All. The. Same. She looked up at the sky. It was the same blue. The sun shone brightly. The earth beneath her feet looked and smelled the same. It was all the damned same. Why did it feel different?

It was her.

Of course, she knew deep down that she had changed. Something had changed inside her. What exactly that thing was, she couldn't say.

"Are you okay?" Ice asked her.

She was shocked to see him standing right there next to her. Azure hadn't heard him come over. She'd been too lost in her own thoughts. "Um… yes, I'm fine."

"You're not eating."

"I'm not hungry."

"You?" Ice snorted, a half-smile on his handsome face. He quickly turned serious.

Crap with scales! That was another thing; their relationship had changed, too. What happened on that rock had opened up a can of worms about a mile wide. All she could think about was his mouth on her. His hands— By the gods, she needed to think about something else, and quick.

His nostrils flared. "Is the last of your heat still troubling you?"

"Must be." She cleared her throat. It wasn't her heat. It was him! It was all a big mess.

"I told you to take all the time you needed. You didn't have to come back so soon."

"I had to. Sitting at home was making me stir crazy."

"I can still smell your heat on you." He lowered his voice a whole lot.

It was more like arousal. Her cheeks flushed.

"It should be over by now." Ice went on, "Are you sure you're okay?"

"Yes." She folded her arms over her chest. "I'm fine. It's just… everything that happened. It's still up here." She touched her temple. "Is there any news?"

"On Skarn?" he snarled the male's name, even though he was still talking under his breath.

"Not Skarn; I know he's still missing." Azure wanted to feel nothing, but she couldn't. She felt bad for the male. She wanted him back in one piece so that there could be recourse. "Did anything come of those meetings Thunder said he was going to have with the elders; with the kings collectively?" There had apparently been meetings. As a team leader, Ice might have heard something. Maybe they had more information on those creatures.

"Not that I know of."

"I'm going to see Storm when we get back. After I'm done with my duties, of course. I want to know what the hell is going on."

"I'll go with you," Ice said.

"Are you going to eat your turkey?" Avalanche shouted at her, throwing a bone at his feet.

"No." She shook her head.

"Can I have yours?" the male asked, his eyes lighting up.

"No!" Ice growled. "Azure needs to keep her strength up."

Avalanche made a noise of acknowledgment.

"I'm plenty strong enough." She gave Ice a hard stare.

"Not if you don't eat," Ice insisted. "You've lost weight." He gave her the once-over, looking disapproving of what he saw.

"Just on my breasts." She palmed her boobs, quickly realizing what she was doing, and stopped. "Um… they were bigger during my heat." *Why was she still talking?* "A side-effect," she muttered.

Ice gave a one-shouldered shrug. "They're still plenty big enough. Look good to me." His eyes flared. "I mean, no different. You need to look after yourself, Azure."

No different.

He would say that. He hadn't seemed to notice before her heat, so he probably couldn't really say either way. He only noticed during her heat because… she was in heat. The thought irked her. Only because she sure as hell noticed him. She had before, and she still did now. More so now than ever before.

"You're right. I need to eat," Azure mumbled as she walked back to the others and grabbed a piece of meat, she took a bite. Everyone was looking at her. "What?" She frowned.

"Nothing," Fog said.

"Nothing at all," Sun added.

"I'm still hungry," Avalanche added.

Some things didn't change, which was a relief. "I'm only going to have this one." She held up the rest of her food.

"Great!" Avalanche grabbed the other piece and took a big bite out of it.

"I still can't believe you didn't come with us on our stag run," Fog muttered to Ice as he sat down.

"Drop it already," Ice answered, picking up his own food.

"Hello! Human females… and you're eligible to mate one of them. Yet you didn't come with us? I don't get it," Sun added.

Something clenched inside her. She continued to chew on her next bite.

"We had a great time. Even Avalanche enjoyed himself," Sun said, stuffing the last of his sandwich in his mouth.

"I went to an all-you-can-eat buffet," Avalanche said around his food, his voice deep.

"An all-you-can-eat buffet of females?" she asked, brows raised.

Avalanche grinned. "An all-you-can-eat buffet of food."

They all laughed.

Avalanche swallowed. "Then I found myself a sweet female and—"

"We don't want to hear about it," Ice muttered. He sounded put out.

"Only because you're jealous. Some of us got our rocks off while you… poor old you got nothing." Fog grinned.

"Not nothing." Sun grinned as well.

Ice gave a tiny shake of the head when she looked his way. It was like he was trying to warn her to keep quiet. The only people who knew that Ice had rescued Azure, aside from the two of them, were the kings, Storm, and the healer. Ice had recommended that they keep it that way.

"Stop being a dick!" Ice muttered.

"You got your hand, Ice. Not much fun in that." Sun laughed.

Ice shrugged. "I don't know… While you were at the stag run, my hand did just fine. No complaints here."

Was he referring to her?

To them?

To what happened between them?

No complaints. Did that mean he'd liked it? He was probably just being nice.

This conversation had raised an interesting question. Why hadn't he gone on the stag run? Why hadn't she asked him sooner? After what had gone down in that cave, with her and Ice and her heat… she'd been in such a state. It hadn't crossed her mind. Not until right then. Until it had been pointed out. Now she couldn't stop trying to come up with answers. Why had Ice gone to the cave? He should never have been there. Azure had picked Skarn. As far as Ice knew, they were in that cave for the sole purpose of breeding.

"Azure." Fog waved his hand in front of her face.

"What? Sorry, I was thinking about… um… something." She sounded like an idiot. Everyone was looking at her.

"I said to finish up because we're hunting in five," Ice told her.

"Oh… of course." She took a big bite, not tasting anything.

CHAPTER 13

Azure made a noise of irritation as soon as she shifted. "I still can't believe it." She was mad at herself. Frustration rode her hard.

Best she get to work. She grabbed the nearest elk carcass and hung it on the closest hook. Then she walked over to the basin and chose one of the knives. She needed to get a move on, since she had four of these things to get through.

"Everyone guts their own kills today," Ice commanded.

"I didn't kill anything," Azure ground out, carving her elk from the throat in a straight vertical line. "That means I clean and skin."

"Yeah, Azure didn't kill anything," Sun said, pointing his thumb in her direction.

Fog gave the male a smack upside the head.

Sun got into Fog's face. "You do that one more time, and I'm—"

"Enough," Ice said. "I said to skin your own kills."

"Yes, you asshole," Fog told Sun. "Azure had a rough weekend," he snarled.

"I didn't kill anything," Azure insisted. "I'm fine. I can do it."

"You could have been killed," Fog said. "You need to take it easy. You saw the male you chose to spend your heat with abducted. Is that what really happened? Some of the males are saying that it was a two-headed beast. That isn't true, is it?"

At the start of the day, Ice had told the team not to ask questions.

"Leave it alone," Ice said, his eyes blazing.

"It's fine," she told Ice. "Long story short, the male was taken. We don't know what took him. I got a glimpse of one of them, but the lighting was bad. I didn't see much. I managed to get away. I'm shook up, but okay."

"That poor male." Fog shook his head, frowning.

"Yeah, that's rough," Sun agreed.

"Do you think he's dead?" Avalanche asked. "You could be with whelp by a male who—"

Ice growled low and deep. "That's enough," he snarled. "I don't want to hear one more word from any of you. It's not any of your business what happened. The three of you are finishing up here." He looked at the elk hanging on the hooks.

Azure gave Ice a tight smile. He was only trying to help. "For the record, I'm not with whelp. We… didn't… I wasn't… It didn't happen," she mumbled, praying they didn't ask her to elaborate as to why it hadn't happened.

She didn't want everyone to know what Skarn had done. She felt ashamed, even though she had nothing to feel ashamed about.

"Get to work," Ice snapped at the males. "Azure and I have a meeting we need to attend," he added, looking at her when he said it.

"Thanks," Azure told the males. "I owe you one."

Fog nodded. "And don't you forget it." He grinned at her.

They washed up and dressed quickly. She could feel the tension coming off Ice as they walked away. "They were trying to be nice," Azure said as soon as they were inside.

"They were being nosy as fuck."

"I suppose they were a little bit nosy, but mostly they were just curious because we've all become friends. We spend a lot of time together. I'd like to think they care about me."

Ice grunted. "I guess."

"Okay, so, we're going to see Storm." It wasn't a question, it was a statement.

Ice nodded. "Yes."

"Do you know if he's in or if he'll even see us?" she asked.

"He'll see us." They arrived at a door just down the hallway from Thunder's office. "Ready?" he asked.

"Yep."

Ice knocked. It took a few long seconds before they heard Storm tell them to enter.

"Oh, good," he said as he saw them. "I was going to call the two of you in for a meeting. Come in. Please, sit." He gestured to the chairs across from him.

The prince's brows lifted once they were seated. "Before you even ask, there is no news on Skarn. He's still missing."

"We don't care about the male," Ice pushed out.

"I was hoping to hear if there was any more news on those creatures?" Azure asked. There had been a part of her that was wondering about Skarn, though. Anger filled her when she thought of him. She wanted him back so that he could face up to what he did. She wanted to look him in the eyes.

"I'm sorry." Storm shook his head. "There is no news on that front. We heard back from the elders, who all told similar stories about a fifth tribe. Several elders from all four tribes swore that the stories were true. The oldest member of the Fire tribe elaborated by saying that the fight was between the Fire King and the king of the fifth tribe. It was over a female. They wanted the same she-dragon. The Fire King won. All was well until the king of the fifth tribe stole the female on the night of their mating ceremony. He took her against her will and forced her to mate with him instead. That is why the Fire King was so furious. That is why he retaliated so heavily. He got his female back, but she was never the same. That's it. You know the rest."

"How sad," she half-whispered. "For the Fire King's female, that is. It sounds like he loved her very much," she added when she was met with a blank stare from the prince.

"I'm not sure if I believe these stories," Storm said.

"There must be some truth to them. Skarn was taken by something," Ice pushed.

"We may never have those answers. It's too much speculation based on fairytales."

"And also, on what Azure saw," Ice insisted.

Storm nodded, looking irritated. He scratched the back of his head and shifted in his chair. "Azure didn't see much of anything," he finally said. "It was too dark."

"She saw enough," Ice pressed on.

Storm sighed.

"Oh… um… we've taken up too much of your time. Thank you for the feedback," Azure said.

"I will let you know if we hear any more," Storm said.

"Are you planning on sending a rescue team into the cave?" Ice asked.

"We discussed this at length, and the decision that was taken was not taken lightly." Storm paused for a few seconds, lacing his fingers together on the desk. "The kings collectively decided that there would be no search party sent. Not for one male. Not after what happened." Storm glanced at her. "We have no idea what kind of tunnel systems they have under the ground, or of the creatures we would have to face… on their terms, and in their environment. It would be too much of a risk."

"What next?" Ice pushed.

"Nothing at this stage. It sounds like these creatures have been there for many years. This is the first sighting we've had of them. For now, the heat caves are out of bounds. We will be extra vigilant. The head guards are aware of the situation. You both know to be careful."

"That's it?" Ice shrugged.

"For now, yes. We have no reason to believe that anything will change. One male was taken. For all we know, they may have been helping Azure. We don't know if they are the enemy. We don't know anything at this stage. It could be the last we see of them."

"Or they could attack our lair." Ice folded his arms.

"We would be ready."

"Would we?" Ice countered. "You mentioned yourself that we have no idea what we would be up against."

"Yes, but at least out here, it would be on our terms and on our playing field. We *are* ready. Our males train daily for such a possibility. Thunder will address our tribe this evening. Rumors are making the rounds. Please don't spread suspicion and fear among our people. Until we know more, we are not telling everyone that this was a fifth tribe. All we have is speculation… bedtime stories. The kings won't incite all of the tribes based on that."

"I'm not spreading anything, my Lord. I'm merely asking questions that others will be asking as well. Our people deserve to know the truth."

"Fair enough," Storm said. "You raise some good points. I will mention them to Thunder. I know the kings are meeting again soon. This will remain a point of discussion. Until you are told otherwise, please keep all information surrounding a fifth tribe a secret. All our people need to know is that Skarn was taken by an unknown foe, but that there is nothing to fear."

"One last question, my Lord, if you don't mind?" Azure asked when it looked like Ice wanted to argue further. Storm was pretty clear about the kings' decisions.

Storm nodded. "Certainly."

"Did our king inform the Earth king of what Skarn planned to do to me?"

"Of course," Storm growled. "It was unacceptable behavior. If he is returned, he will be dealt with, I assure you."

"If he returns, I want to see him. I need five minutes, that's all," she said.

"If he returns, we will discuss it. I'm sure that Granite wouldn't be opposed to you seeing the male. He is greatly angered and disappointed by Skarn's behavior. He wishes to extend his apologies. I had planned on setting up a meeting to inform you of all of this but you saved me the effort by coming."

"Thank you," Azure said.

"Now, if you'll both excuse me, I have a lot of work to do. There are problems at one of the platinum mines."

"Thank you for your time," she told the prince, who was already looking down at his computer.

Ice didn't say anything. They left, and he closed the door behind them. "Why would you even want to see that male?" he growled. "After what he did to you?"

"Keep your voice down," she whispered. "I just do. He did what he did to me. I want to look him in the eyes. I want an apology. I want to be there when his punishment is meted out."

Ice snorted. "An apology would mean nothing. If you ask me, they plan on slapping Skarn on the wrist. He should be put to death."

"That's a bit harsh."

"Harsh!" Ice's eyes were bright and glowing. "Harsh would be several days of torture first. What if those creatures hadn't taken that prick?"

"I would've taken care of myself. I like to think that he would have come to his senses." Although from the look she remembered seeing in Skarn's eyes, she doubted that would have been the case.

"Come to his senses? You don't mean that?"

"I would've handled him." She didn't put much into her counter because she didn't quite believe it herself.

"If any female can stand against a male in his prime, it is you, Azure, but there is a good chance he would have caught you and overpowered you. What then?"

"You would have been there to save me." She reached out and took his hand, squeezing it once before letting go. Her eyes suddenly stung. She swallowed down the lump that had formed in her throat. "You came," she added.

"I might not have made it there in time," Ice said softly. "What if I hadn't gone at all? There are too many what-ifs, which I don't like. If that male ever sees the light of day, he could do it again to another female."

"Let's leave it, for now. We may never see him again."

Ice's jaw was tight. "We can only hope."

Azure felt something inside her soften. "Why did you go to the cave in the first place? What made you skip the stag run? You males live for human females." A stone settled in her gut as she said the last.

"I saw you, Azure. I saw the two of you arguing. We were on the next balcony assembling to leave for the run. It was too far away to hear what you were saying, especially with the wind direction. It was blowing towards the two of you." His eyes flared. "Not that I would have tried to eavesdrop. I could see that you weren't happy. I know you, Azure. I didn't like how upset you looked. I wanted to make sure you were alright. That was all." He pushed out a breath through his nose. "I had this gut feeling. I've learned to listen to those over the years. Turns out I was right." He kept his eyes on her. "You're part of my team. I care what happens to you. If it had been any of the others, I would have done the same for them."

Again, she felt him push her away. A firm reminder that what happened between them had nothing to do with feelings, or real attraction, at least on his part. She needed to get her head on straight.

CHAPTER 14

That evening…

AZURE KNOCKED ON the door and waited. She practically held her breath. When there was no answer, she knocked again.

"Summer," she called through the door. "I know you're not working. Your boss told me that you worked the day shift," she added. "Please, Summer. I need to see you… to explain a few things."

Her friend had been decidedly cold to her since her heat. Answering her texts late and with one-word answers. Summer also kept insisting that she was too busy to see Azure.

Just as she was getting ready to walk away, she heard footfalls on the other side of the door. Summer answered. Instead of the wide smile that normally greeted her, she got a somber look.

"Hi, Azure." Her friend stood there in the hallway, still clutching the door, which was only half-open.

'What's going on?" Azure asked, frowning. "Are you okay?"

"I'm fine. I'm sorry I've been a little... just not..." She shrugged, sighing. "I'm upset with you, Azure. I'm so upset. I can't let it go. I think I might need some time to work through it."

Some time.

Upset.

What?

"I needed to see you, Summer. There's so much you don't know." Azure needed to talk to someone she trusted about what had happened. She needed her best friend. Once Summer had all the facts, she would understand.

"You were in heat." Summer's eyes filled with tears. "You were given a gift, and you wasted it. I would give anything... anything... all of the infertile females would. You had a chance at a family, and you squandered your opportunity. I know it might be hard for you to understand, but I'm angry with you. I can't let go of it at the moment. I need some time."

Summer started to close the door. Azure put her hand on the wood and pressed lightly. "Summer, please... don't. Let me explain. Please, I..." She could've pressed harder, put her foot in the way, but Azure didn't want to force her friend to let her in, to hear her out, so instead, she let the door close in her face.

Her eyes stung, and she had to sniff a few times. Azure sucked in a couple of deep breaths. She leaned her head against the door for a moment, letting the coolness from the wood seep into her. It was going to be okay. Azure wasn't angry; she felt sad and very alone. She had never felt so alone in all of her life.

"Hey, Azure." She heard a familiar, high-pitched voice.

No!

Not now!

She forced a smile. "Hi, Melina… Freeze, good to see you both." She tried to pretend all was well. Like she didn't have a care in the world. Like she wasn't about to bawl her eyes out in front of Summer's door.

"Hi there," Freeze said, looking uncomfortable. He had his arm slung over Melina's shoulders.

"Babe, can you give us a few minutes? I'll see you in a little while," Melina told the male. "I'm going to have a chat with Azure. Maybe head to her place for a coffee or wine or something?"

"Um… you don't have to change your plans or anything." Azure found that the idea of spending some time with the human didn't grate on her nerves like it normally would. Melina was genuinely a nice person.

"I want to. We missed our girl's night on Saturday. You go, baby… I won't be long," she told Freeze. *Baby?* It was such a strange term of endearment. Azure didn't understand humans much.

"Okay, but don't take too long." Freeze kissed Melina firmly on the mouth. His hand cupped her ass as he did.

Melina giggled, pushing him away. "Go already."

"I'll miss you," Freeze said as he walked away. "See you around," he told Azure, giving them a wave.

"You look like you had plans," Azure told the other woman. "Don't change them for me."

"You sound like you could use a friend and that something is weighing heavily on your mind," Melina said, her eyes filled with sincerity. "Let's go and have something to drink. You don't have to tell me what's going on. We could just talk about this and that. If you feel like you want to tell me, know that you can trust me." The other woman gave her a warm smile. "I'm really hoping you have some wine."

Azure laughed. "I do, actually. I was given a bottle for my birthday. I haven't had any occasion to drink it. Today is as good a day as any." She found that she already felt a little better. It was all due to the little human. Someone she hadn't given the time of day to. Someone she'd avoided. Azure felt guilty for being such a bitch. "Let's go."

"I've decided to open a salon here at the lair. I'm going to do hair, nails… I might even bring in a clothing range."

"That sounds great. I think the humans living here would love that." There were more and more every day.

"Humans… huh. It wouldn't just be for the humans. I mean, look at you… you're gorgeous. You have a body I would kill for, and yet—"

"You think I have a good body?" Azure wasn't sure if the human was trying to blow smoke up her ass or if she really meant it.

"Are you freaking kidding me?" Melina stopped walking and gave her the once-over. "Long, toned legs… legs that go on for damned miles, and then you have a narrow waist. I know that somewhere underneath that sack of a dress is an ass that could crack nuts."

"Nuts? Why would I want to crack nuts with my ass?"

They started walking again. Melina laughed. "Not literally… it's a saying. You have a tight ass, that's what it means. Then your boobs… they're perfect. Like the perfect size. Your hair is great too. It's thick and shiny, but…" Melina reached up and ran her fingers through Azure's strands, "it could do with a cut. It's too long. It's pulling down… not doing you any favors. I'd put in some layers. Take at least five inches off the bottom. I'd put you in a dress… one that actually accentuates your assets, because trust me, girl, you've got it going on."

They arrived at Azure's chamber and went inside. She gestured for Melina to take a seat while she fished out the bottle of wine, holding it up. "I hope this is okay?"

"Ooh, a red… yum. That looks perfect."

Azure found the opener and then went hunting for wine glasses, finding some at the back of one of the cupboards. They needed to be rinsed. By the time she made it back to Melina, the female had opened the bottle. The other woman poured, insisting that they touch glasses. It was a human thing. Azure wasn't sure what it meant, but she did it anyway.

Melina took a sip, groaning. "That's so good."

Azure followed suit. It burned a little down her throat, tasting pungent. She must have grimaced or made a face because Melina laughed. "You don't look like you agree."

"I've heard that alcohol is an acquired taste."

"Exactly, you need to drink more to develop a taste." The human held her glass up for a second and then took another sip. "So, that guy you were with got abducted? You must have been so afraid?"

She knew that Melina was giving her an opening. She knew that the female wouldn't push her to say anything she didn't want to. More than anything, she felt she could trust Melina. That perhaps they could be friends. She'd been wrong to judge the female just because she was a human. She saw that now. Azure nodded. "I was terrified." A tear tracked down her cheek. By scale, she hadn't meant to cry. Azure rubbed her hand over her face.

"Oh, honey. You poor thing. I can't imagine how awful it must have been."

"Skarn's abduction isn't the half of it," Azure said, starting from the beginning. "I didn't want to choose any of our males." She told Melina what happened. All of it.

"That pig! He deserved to be taken. Here I was, feeling so sorry for him. He tried to rape you." She took a big gulp of her wine. "Oh my gosh, Azure." She reached out and touched Azure's wrist for a second. "It's terrible. I'm so sorry that happened."

Azure took a big sip of her wine. This time, the burn felt good. "Yep." She pulled in a deep breath. "It didn't end there."

"There's more?" Melina's brows rose comically high.

Shit! Azure hadn't meant to say anything about this part. She probably shouldn't.

Instead of pushing her, Melina waited, and again she got the impression that she wouldn't have to say anything if she didn't feel like it. Azure pushed out a breath. She told the other woman about what happened with Ice. All of it.

"Thank god he pitched up to help you." She giggled. "I've seen him; he's really good-looking." She added, "I don't think I've ever seen eyes quite that blue."

"That's just it. I noticed him before. I mean, I'd have

to be blind not to have, but," Azure shrugged, "he's essentially my boss. I can't be attracted to my boss. Plus, we've become friends over the last few months. He invited me to join the guys on the stag run before all of this happened. He treats me like one of the guys, which I wanted. I worked so hard to be seen as one of the team. Now I'm regretting it. I don't want to be one of the males anymore."

"I assure you that he doesn't see you as one of the guys. Maybe he was going to make his move on the stag run." Melina took a sip of her wine. "Have you ever thought of it like that?"

"No!" Azure snorted.

"Don't be so sure. He didn't go on the stag run. He followed you, instead."

"He was worried about me."

"Because he cares." She bobbed her brows. "A little too much, maybe?"

"No." Azure shook her head. "It's not like that… at least, not for him. He's made it very clear about where we stand. Clear that there's nothing there. That it didn't mean anything. He was helping me out. It was a necessity, not something he wanted."

Melina leveled her with a pointed stare. "He's a man. I'm pretty sure he enjoyed himself a whole heck of a lot, too."

Azure felt her cheeks heat when she recalled Ice easing himself. The sounds he made. The little jerks of his hips as he was coming.

Melina made this little noise, which turned into a laugh. "Oh, yes… I can tell. Ice enjoyed himself plenty."

"I was in heat. A female's heat tends to make a male a

little crazy. I can't trust anything that happened while he was seduced by my scent."

"Fair enough." She could see that Melina wasn't buying it.

"I don't think he feels the same way. Ice told me that the reason he came after me was that he had a gut feeling something was wrong. That he would have done it for any of the guys on the team. Ice has said similar things since it happened. I think you're wrong. I think I might have feelings for a male who doesn't feel the same about me. A male who is eligible to mate a human female. He'll be expected to attend a stag run soon since he missed the last one." She chewed on her lower lip. "This is such a mess. I need to get Ice out of my head and—"

"You might be surprised," Melina pressed. "If he keeps pointing out that it didn't mean anything, it probably meant more than he's willing to admit."

Azure shrugged. "Maybe." She wasn't convinced. "I have so many confusing feelings right now. I'm disappointed I didn't spend my heat with someone. I'm relieved I didn't spend my heat with someone. I'm not sure I want to be a mother, and... I want to be with someone who loves me. Someone I love back. I want a family. I don't want to raise a child between two homes. After all that, I'm sad I will probably never have a heat again and yet very relieved. I'm a mess!"

"My parents divorced when I was still a baby," Melina told her. "It's not fun being carted between two homes. I was with my dad on weekends and every other holiday. I spent the rest of the time with my mom. They both remarried. My dad and stepmom had kids of their own. It wasn't that she was ever nasty to me or anything, but I always felt like I was second best to my half-brother and sister. Divorce isn't easy on the kids. Sure, it's better than being in an unhappy household... blah... blah but if it can be avoided, it should be." Melina looked downtrodden for a moment. She stared at the table before leveling her gaze with Azure's. "You made the right decision. It wasn't just a decision for yourself, but for the child you would have brought into this world."

"Exactly!" Azure sucked in a breath. "You hit the nail on the head. It's not that I don't want a baby." She hesitated for a few moments. "I just didn't want one on those terms. It's all been so confusing to me. All these warring emotions. Even when it comes to the Earth dragon. I feel bad that Skarn was taken by those creatures, and yet I want the male to pay for what he did to me. After all that happened, I shouldn't have feelings for anyone, and yet... here I am. My feelings for Ice have grown. I went from finding him attractive and liking him as a person to... something that could be real. It's confusing, that's all." She sighed.

"That's the way life works, I'm afraid. You can't switch your feelings on and off. You can want something and be terrified of it all at once. Life is complex and beautiful. It's also quite simple. If you want Ice, you should go after him."

"No way!" Azure shook her head. "He'll turn me down. I know he will, and rightly so. He's my superior. Besides, I wouldn't know the first thing about seducing a male."

"What do you normally do? Surely, you've..." she widened her eyes, "you know... you've...?"

Azure laughed. "Rutted?" Humans could be so strange.

They were talking frankly about relationships and sex, and yet the female couldn't bring herself to say the word.

"Yes, surely you've been with a guy?"

Azure nodded. "Of course. Mostly males will approach me, and I will decide if I am interested in having sex with them. On occasion, I will approach a male. I just ask straight out if he wants to rut." She shrugged. "I can't do that with Ice." It felt all wrong going about it that way.

Melina frowned. "Are you telling me that you haven't been on a date before?"

Azure gave the human a look that hopefully conveyed her feelings. Namely, that she thought she was crazy. "Dragon males don't want to date me. They want to rut me and that's all. I am not relationship material. I have sex from time to time... Come to think of it, it's been a while since I had any interest in a male. I digress, no... no dating. Not ever."

"What? Why not?" the human spluttered.

"Up until recently, I was infertile. I more than likely won't have another heat. I'm useless to our males."

"Do *not* say that!" Melina practically yelled at her. "I don't ever want to hear you put yourself down like that again. You are *not* useless. You are more than just a womb and freaking ovaries, do you hear me?"

"Um... I guess."

"I guess?" Melina was animated. Her eyes blazed. "What is this '*I guess*' bullshit? The answer should be a resounding 'yes' because it's true. You're a beautiful, intelligent woman. You're a sweet person. You're kickass at your job... I've heard the guys talking. Don't put yourself down. Don't settle for less." She smiled suddenly. "You ultimately know that. It's the reason why you chose Skarn and then promptly changed your mind about spending your heat with him. It's the reason you stuck to your guns when Thunder tried to bully you into choosing again. You know it deep down inside. You need to believe it up there." Melina glanced at Azure's forehead before taking a sip of her wine. "As to your earlier comment about Ice not wanting to settle down, a man will settle down with the right woman." She chuckled. "You need to learn how to seduce him."

"I don't want to seduce Ice." She shook her head. "I'd make a fool of myself."

"You won't! What you need to know is that we're women, Azure. We can be subtle if need be." Melina winked at her. "I'm not saying you should blurt it out to him or wait in his bed for him."

Azure choked out a laugh. It surprised her how much better she felt now that her feelings were out in the open. "No, I won't do that." It was because this was about more than just sex to her.

"Let's start with a haircut." She took a few strands of Azure's hair between her fingers.

Azure frowned. "Shorter hair isn't going to get Ice to notice me."

"It won't be just your hair."

"I can't suddenly start wearing makeup either. It's not me."

"It could be you, but that's not what I'm suggesting. You're pretty enough without makeup… I'd kill for your eyelashes. You need to get him to notice you, if he hasn't already. If you ask me, he's noticed you plenty. More than you think."

"How do I get him to notice me?" Azure asked.

"I'm going to give you a few tips. Little things you can try. The most important thing of all is that you pay attention to his reactions. And that you do so with an open mind."

"What do you mean by pay attention?"

"Watch for subtle hints that he might feel the same as you do. How does he look at you when he thinks you're not watching? Perhaps he makes a point of not looking at all."

Azure shook her head. "That makes no sense."

"Guys who are into girls more than they want to let on, tend to ignore them… they intentionally don't look, because if they did, they would give themselves away. Does that make sense?"

Azure nodded, even though it didn't. Not completely.

Melina laughed. "I can tell that you're not convinced. That's okay. Try to follow my tips and then pay attention to his reaction. I'll come by tomorrow evening, and you can tell me all about it. I'm sure you'll have him eating out of your hand in no time."

"You think so?" Azure heard hope in her voice. This was crazy, but she had to at least give it a shot. If she was subtle enough, maybe Ice would never know she was trying to seduce him. If she found him to be totally closed to her advances, she'd have to move on.

Melina nodded, her blonde curls bouncing. "I absolutely think this will work. Now, tell me, when do you see Ice, aside from work?"

"That's just it. I mainly see him at work. We sometimes get together afterward, but then mostly it's the whole team… not just him and me."

"Okay, so, it needs to be seriously subtle since you'll more than likely be at work. You're not going to suddenly be overtly sexual or flirt."

Azure felt her cheeks heat. "No way. That wouldn't work at all."

"Firstly, you're going to be yourself, but with a difference."

"What difference?"

"I'll tell you in a minute. Secondly, you're going to think laterally… use your environment or the situation to your advantage."

"Think laterally," Azure whispered. This was making no sense. Hopefully, once Melina finished, she'd have a better idea. She took a big swig of her wine, putting the glass down with a clink.

"Yes. Come by my place about an hour before your shift tomorrow. I'm going to cut your hair. Now, onto the tips. Listen carefully."

Azure was all ears. Human females were incredibly sensual. They exuded sex appeal. Melina was no different. It was one of the reasons she had been so jealous of them… of her. One of the main reasons she hadn't wanted to befriend this female. Her thinking had been all wrong. She felt ashamed for how she had treated Melina and other human females as well. Not that she'd been a bitch, she just hadn't been welcoming… or very nice, for that matter. Things were going to change. Azure made a decision to help Melina, just as the human was helping her. She knew exactly how she could do it.

CHAPTER 15

The next day...

AZURE SHOT PAST him. Ice felt the air around him displace from her wings. For a split second, the female was close. Close enough to wing-clip her. For a moment, he was tempted, but he hesitated and lost his chance. Right then, she wasn't too far ahead, close enough that he could pick up her scent. Berries... maybe cherry. Sweet, with a little note of tartness, a hint of spice, and the smoky scent of her dragon.

And because he was so far up his own damned ass, Azure got ahead. Fog too. The herd of moose scattered like leaves in the wind. Ice locked onto a target, realizing just before he was about to make the kill that the animal he had chosen was a female, and pregnant, at that. He could scent it on her. He pulled up. Too late to lock onto another.

Fog snarled, his claws still deep in his kill. Azure shifted, grinning. She was covered in blood. Holy shit, but she looked good, even spattered in all that gore. Red was a good color on her.

"Too slow, Ice." She chuckled. It was low and throaty.

Ice shifted, eyes still on the female.

"Yeah," Sun said as soon as he shifted. "It's not like you to miss a kill. Azure had a decent excuse yesterday. You? Not so much." Sun and Avalanche had bagged their own kills earlier. Avalanche brought down a boar, which made for good eating. He held back a sigh as Sun's words sank in. The male was right.

It was Azure. She had him off his game. There was something different about her since her heat, but he couldn't put his finger on it. The fact that he knew what her pussy tasted like didn't help things. When he caught the lingering scent of her heat yesterday, his cock had stirred. The bastard had started to take on a life of its own. He'd been forced to think of his grandmother. His dear, sweet grandmother. How fucking rude was that?

He'd been so sure that it was her heat on the weekend making him crazy. Ice could blame her lingering heat yesterday. He had no excuses for still checking her out today. Yet here he was, unable to peel his eyes off her.

What.

The.

Actual.

Fuck?

"Is it just me, or is it extra muggy today?" Azure lifted her hair off her shoulders and groaned. "I'm hot!"

She sure was. All the males' jaws dropped when she tilted her head back a moment before dropping her hair.

"I'm covered in blood." She proceeded to wipe the red on her belly, dragging her hand up and over her chest.

Fuuuuuuck!

Ice looked away. He would have to visit his grandmother later. His sweet, dear granny. He pictured her face. Her eyes. He thought about the cookies she baked him. His mom also baked a mean cookie. He thought about both females. Anything to stop what was going on between his legs.

"Mind if I wash off in the lake?" Azure asked.

"Um…" He cleared his throat. "Sure thing." He nodded. Better that she was in the water. Neck-deep would be good.

"Thanks." She smiled at him. Azure had a great smile. It lit up her whole face. Especially her eyes. He wanted to tell her that, but it would be inappropriate on all levels. He needed to get over his shit when it came to her. Perhaps it wasn't such a bad thing that his name was back down for the stag run this weekend. He was eligible to take a mate, and since he hadn't gone last weekend, he was back on the list for the upcoming one. His name would come up more often than before. It was how it worked.

"A swim sounds good." Fog jogged after Azure, his feet squelching in the mud as he hit the water's edge.

Ice's eyes narrowed when Sun followed. "I'm pretty hot myself." The male chuckled. And if he wasn't mistaken, there was this edge to his voice that Ice didn't like. He really needed to have a talk with them again about flirting with Azure. It wasn't allowed. This had nothing to do with jealousy and everything to do with work ethic.

Avalanche sat down with a groan. "I'm hungry," the male announced.

"You already ate everything we brought with us," Ice told him. "You killed a pheasant and ate the thing in one-minute flat, feathers and all. And don't even ask me if you can have a moose leg. The answer is no." He watched Azure jog into the lake. She dove in as soon as the water was just above her knees.

"We should be permitted to stay in our dragon forms and eat our kills every now and then," Avalanche grumbled.

Ice didn't respond. He was too busy watching what was going on in the water. The three of them were splashing each other. The she-dragon laughed, diving back into the water. Sun went after her. They came up; the male had his hands on her hips. They were both laughing hard. Sun dunked Azure.

Ice grit his teeth so hard he was sure he might crack a molar if he wasn't careful. He even growled.

"What is it?" Avalanche asked.

"We need to get back." He looked up at the sky. "It's getting late. We still have work to do back at the lair." He glanced at the felled animals. Ice put two fingers to his lips and whistled loudly.

They instantly stopped their roughhousing. Fog was just about to throw Azure into deeper water.

"That's enough. We're leaving!" There was a hard edge to his voice.

"Okay." Fog put the female down. The two males ran out of the water. Azure followed more slowly.

Yep… it was like a scene from one of those low-grade human movies. He'd watched quite a few on his computer. The plan was to get to know humans as much as possible if he was going to mate one. That meant watching their programs and movies. Oh yes, this ticked all the boxes when it came to the sexy scenes.

Water dripped down her body, tracing every curve. Her nipples were tight. The water must be cold. She shook her hair. Water went flying around her.

Gorgeous.

Fucking insanely beautiful.

No! That wasn't it. Azure had always been pretty. There was something else. Something new. Something he couldn't quite put his finger on. He looked to his right, and all the males were staring, even Avalanche. Fog's mouth had dropped right open. The male had a semi. He had a fucking semi. Sun too.

No way!

Just no!

This pissed him the fuck off. When he looked back, Azure had her hair twisted in one hand; she squeezed. More water dripped down the front of her body. She was still standing in the water. What the fuck was she doing? She was completely oblivious to the effect she was having on all of them.

"We need to leave, Azure," he growled. "Now! We're not on a break."

"Oh… um…" She started jogging. Her tits bounced with every graceful footfall. "I'm coming." Her arms pumped.

Fuuuuuck!

Those words shot straight to his cock. *I'm coming.* Right down into his balls, which clenched tight. "It's not fucking acceptable," he growled even louder at her. "No fucking around during work," he snarled at her, even though she hadn't been alone. "Let's go!" he bit out, already in mid-shift. His cock was hard. He didn't want anyone seeing. The shift hurt like a bitch, but he deserved it. He was taking his attraction for Azure out on her. Not right! He was pissed off at his lack of control. Even more pissed off at how he felt when he looked at her shocked face. It morphed into confusion, and then... something else he didn't like. Hurt! He'd hurt her.

She was going to be hard on herself after his outburst. It wasn't even her fault that he was an asshole. This needed to stop. He was just desperate for a female. Once that particular problem was rectified on the weekend, all would be well.

CHAPTER 16

"OH, NO." MELINA'S face fell as soon as Azure opened the door. "You look depressed. What happened?" She walked into Azure's chamber. "You need to tell me everything."

"It was a disaster." Azure smiled, despite what she had just said. "I think I did it all wrong. That's not entirely true; it did work, only not on Ice." Azure shook her head.

"I brought wine." Melina held up a bottle. "It's a lovely oaky chardonnay."

"Sounds good." That was the thing about wine; it always sounded better than it actually tasted. Anyway, she'd drink it. Melina had been kind enough to give up more of her own time to be there, and she'd brought the wine. Azure noted that she carried a bag with her as well. It was casually slung over her shoulder.

Melina put it down in the living room and followed

Azure into the kitchen. Placing two wine glasses on the counter, she handed Melina a bottle opener.

Melina got to work opening the wine. "What happened? Tell me all of it."

"At first, I thought it might be working. Not that I had done anything much to begin with, mind you." She shrugged. "Ice seemed off his game the whole day. Not himself. It might have been something else. I definitely can't assume it was because of me. It more than likely was something else bugging him. He just seemed distracted."

"Was he looking at you a whole lot, or not at all?" Melina asked, pulling the cork. She started pouring.

"Not that I noticed. I decided to try to step it up after I made a kill; we were about to head back to the lair, and it felt like a good time. I shifted back into my human form and I noticed him looking, so I did that move you showed me."

"Which one?" Melina asked animatedly, her eyes wide.

"The one where I hold my hair up, close my eyes, and tilt my head up. I groaned as well and mentioned how muggy it was."

Melina laughed, sounding excited. "That's great."

"You made me practice it twenty times last night, so I had it down," Azure said. She wanted to laugh about the whole thing, but she couldn't, not after what had happened. "Don't get too excited yet. I haven't told you everything. At this point, he was looking at me… he was looking plenty. In fact, I was so sure I could see desire written in his eyes. They were narrowed on me and smoldering. His jaw was tight."

"Did he look angry?" Melina's eyes were wide.

Azure gave a nod. "He did." Melina had told her that a look of desire and anger were easy to confuse. Just because a male looked angry in certain circumstances didn't mean that he was. She had seen the look that Melina spoke of. Ice had it. He did! She might not know how to seduce a male, but she knew desire when she saw it. Maybe she was just being a hopeful fool. She couldn't trust herself where he was concerned.

Melina took a sip of her wine. "Go on. What happened next?"

Azure took a sip of her own wine. It was actually pretty good. "I had blood all over me from killing a moose bull."

"Ewwww." The human made a face. "That's disgusting."

"I hunt and kill game for our tribe to eat. That's what I do. It means that there's blood sometimes... in fact, most times." Azure shrugged. Humans could be so weird. They ate meat but couldn't handle the thought of an animal dying, or blood. How did they think that meat got on their plate? She didn't say any of that. "We make a quick, clean kill. The animals don't suffer. The moose I killed today was dead before he knew what had happened to him."

Melina took a big sip of her wine. She flapped her hand. "I didn't mean to be rude. On to the good stuff... what happened next?"

"Seeing him looking at me like that made me bold. I first complained about the muggy heat, and then I complained about being dirty by rubbing my hand over my belly and between my breasts. You said to do something to draw his gaze to erogenous zones, right?"

"Definitely." Melina nodded. "You did exactly the right thing."

"Sun and Fog were ogling me so hard I thought their eyes might fall out of their skulls. It was pretty funny."

"And Ice?"

"He was looking too. Not like them." She shrugged. "There was a big, beautiful lake right there."

"You didn't!" Melina leaned forward.

"I did."

Melina squealed so hard it hurt her ears. "You are the best student I have ever had." She looked up at the ceiling for a second. "Not that I've ever taught someone how to seduce a man, but still. You picked it all up so quickly. Please tell me that you suggested a swim?"

"That's exactly what I did. I had hoped that Ice would join, but he didn't. It was Sun and Fog instead."

Melina giggled and clapped her hands. "Tell me why that is still good?" Melina lifted her brows.

Azure explained like a dutiful student, "Having other guys looking at me and showing interest in me will hopefully make him jealous. I don't know how comfortable I am with that part."

"Tell me what happened next, because so far, it all sounds perfect. We'll chat about your concerns after I have the bigger picture."

"We were fooling around in the water. Splashing each other. Dunking one another. The males were picking me up and tossing me into the deeper part of the lake, and then Ice whistled and told us it was time to go."

"Okay." Melina sipped more wine and nodded for her to go on.

"I took my time getting out of the water."

"So that the drops could cascade down your naked body," Melina said dramatically.

"I guess." It wasn't like that. She'd been a little winded. The water felt good. Normally Ice was relaxed and easygoing. "I squeezed the water out of my hair while I walked, and Ice shouted at me to hurry up. He looked seriously pissed off. So I started jogging over to them... doing what he asked in the first place. And then he lost it. I've never seen him so mad. He started shouting about fucking around during work and how it's unacceptable. He shouted at *me*. His anger was aimed at *me*. Then he shifted and flew away. We had to scramble to try to catch up."

Azure was shocked to see Melina grinning broadly. "What about when you got back to the lair?"

Azure shrugged. "Ice was gone when we got back. He's never done that before. He just took off. All three males were the biggest pains after we returned. They tried to help me with everything. They were like flies buzzing around me. I was unsuccessful when it came to Ice. All I managed to do was piss him off royally. It worked on the others, which I didn't want. I've worked hard enough in this team for my place. To be treated like everyone else."

"Except you aren't like everyone else, Azure. You're a gorgeous woman. That doesn't mean you can't do a good job."

"I don't want them to flirt with me. I don't want to be treated like a hot piece of ass. I have to work with these males."

"Like it or not, you *are* a hot piece of ass." Melina lifted a brow. "If you don't think they noticed before, you're crazy. You're embracing your feminine side. Your sexual side, and there's nothing wrong with that. In fact, it gives you power."

"I don't know if I like that kind of power, especially when it doesn't work on the one person I want it to work on."

"Oh, it worked alright." Melina gave her a sly smile.

"No." Azure frowned. "No way! You're wrong there. He shouted at me."

"I am not wrong. I know men." Melina swirled the wine in her glass. "Ice was upset because he *was* reacting to you. He didn't want to. Sometimes people fight their attraction. Especially in your case, where it's not exactly above-board for him to date you."

"Maybe." Was Melina right?

"Not maybe, definitely. This is great."

Azure took a sip of her wine because she didn't know what to say. She wasn't quite sure she agreed.

"You have to trust me. Carry on with the whole thing. It's working."

"Okay, but it's going to have to be even more subtle… just for him. I can't do any of those moves you taught me in front of the whole team. I just can't. I know you say I should use it, but… it doesn't feel right."

"Okay… cool. Be subtle. Aim all of that sexual energy at Ice. Make him crazy. He won't be able to keep ignoring his feelings. I promise you." She used her finger to make a cross over her heart.

"Okay." Azure sighed. "I hated him being so pissed off at me."

"You need to get him angry like that more often. It will mean it's working."

"It might get me fired."

"It might get you Ice. Think about that." Melina looked at her pointedly. "Trust me on this, please."

"Okay." Azure nodded once. "I will stick with it."

"I brought a couple of things with me."

Here we go. "You did?"

"I most definitely did."

"Like what?" She could guess.

"Clothes and makeup." She looked at Azure pointedly.

"I'm not so sure—"

"Hang on a second." Melina widened her eyes. "Before you go all negative on me, try one or two things on. That's all I ask."

"I'm not wearing them outside of this chamber." Azure shook her head.

"You don't have to. Try them on for me." Melina winked at her. "It'll be fun. I'd like to put a touch of makeup on you as well."

Azure narrowed her eyes and gave Melina a pointed look. "I'm definitely not wearing makeup."

"I'm talking about a little mascara… perhaps some lip gloss. We'll take it off afterward, I swear."

Azure sighed. "Okay… okay, that sounds acceptable. When are you opening your salon?"

"In a couple of weeks." Melina jumped up from her chair. "I'm going to practice on you right now. Let's get started."

Azure was afraid. She was very afraid.

CHAPTER 17

The next day…

T HE AIR WAS crisp. The day was young and full of possibilities. It was normally Ice's favorite time of day. He loved his job. Enjoyed heading out with his team for an adventure. Not today. He felt apprehensive and tense. Ice couldn't seem to shake it. What had happened yesterday… and a few days ago… was over, behind him. It was done with. It *should* be done with, and yet here he was, still stressing about it. About her. Azure. He pulled a hand through his hair, trying to calm the fuck down.

"Why are you pacing like that?" Fog asked. "Is there something I should know about?"

Crap! Ice hadn't even realized he was walking up and down the balcony.

"What's going on?" Fog frowned when he turned to face the male.

"I'm eager to get going. That's all. I'm away this weekend. We need to get our quota of game in before then." It sounded plausible.

"About that." Fog looked serious... too serious. "We'll be two people short on Saturday, since I'm going on the stag run with you. I only found out this morning."

Ice frowned hard. "You? Why? You went last weekend."

Fog rubbed his hands together. "I just made the list. I made the list, bro," he repeated, a grin splitting his face. "I can take a mate. I'm so excited. There are so many amazing females to choose from. I can only hope that I find the right one. Someone who blows my mind. Although," Fog rubbed his chin, "I'm thinking of staying."

Ice frowned. "Why would you stay?"

"There is someone here who I feel I might be developing feelings for."

"Oh?" Ice didn't like this one bit. "Who?"

"I'd rather not say, at this stage. I'm greatly attracted to this female. I... want to explore it. If we are compatible, then—" He shrugged, looking excited.

"Not Azure!" Ice practically growled, managing to somehow keep his voice lowered. *What the fuck?* He was going to give himself away. "She's on our team. Don't get any ideas. You would need to find another position if you were—"

"What?" Fog folded his arms. "Why not Azure?" he whispered back, looking up and down the balcony, checking to see if they were still alone.

He knew it. Ice fucking knew it. The way he had looked at her yesterday. The way *all* of them had looked at her yesterday. *Fuck!* This was a disaster. "The female works with you. We have to work together." He wasn't making a good argument. "It's against the rules. You can't go after her."

Fog narrowed his eyes. Ice could see him thinking it through. "I think it's against the rules for you to fuck around with one of your subordinates. Me, on the other hand…" He shook his head. "I think I'm okay."

"It's against the rules, Fog. I'm telling you."

"I've flirted and propositioned her on numerous occasions since she joined our team. You never crapped on me before. You never warned me about this rule. Why is it a big deal all of a sudden?"

"Because you never actually meant it before."

"Who says I didn't mean it? I meant it." Fog's eyes blazed. "I meant it one hundred percent."

"You did not!" Ice shot back. "You were fucking around."

"Of course, I meant it." Fog was animated. The male must have seen the look Ice gave him, because he went on. "I really did. I swear. I always thought Azure was sexy as fuck." He stepped closer to Ice, whispering softly. "I might not have gone after her with mating her in mind, but I seriously wanted to rut her. I still do. That part has never changed."

This was a fucking shit show! "Okay, let's say it wasn't against all the rules and you were permitted to test compatibility with Azure…"

The male's eyes lit right up.

"I'm not for one minute saying that it's okay. Don't misunderstand me." He shook his head.

Fog nodded.

"Let's just say for argument's sake that the rules are out the window. Azure has never been interested in you before. Why would she be interested now?"

"There's a very good reason. A great reason," Fog said. Not actually saying why. *Fucker!*

"Yes, asshole, and the reason is…?" Ice prompted.

"I'm interested in mating her. This isn't just about rutting. Azure is one hell of a female. She's sweet and kickass, all in one."

"Yeah, she is." Ice realized that he was nodding and agreeing with the male. Fog would take that as an affirmation that he could proceed.

"Exactly. I can see myself with her. I could see us raising a family together."

Fuck that! "She would more than likely never come into heat again. You know that, right?"

"Of course I know that."

"You would be okay with that?"

"Absolutely!" Fog was quick to say.

"You wouldn't pursue this and then drop her if and when it doesn't happen?" Ice was feeling protective, which was okay since she was in his team and therefore under his care.

"No way! I would never do that to her." Fog was adamant.

"I'm glad you feel that way, but it's still against the rules. You need to leave our team if you want to progress with that particular person. That's final."

"Don't be a dick," Fog said. "Let me test compatibility. Give me that."

"No, and if you call me a dick again, I'll have yours," Ice snapped.

"What's going on?" Azure asked as she walked up to them. "Is everything okay?"

"Great." Ice smiled, sounding far too happy to mean it. It would be clear to anyone with half a brain that something was up.

"All good," Fog muttered. "You look great, by the way. There's something different about you." He looked Azure up and down. Ice was grateful that she still wore a dress. It was stupid, since they'd seen each other naked countless times. It shouldn't matter.

"Nothing," Azure said, sounding very much like there was something.

Ice pretended not to be interested. He looked out at the view instead of at Azure, who looked fucking amazing even in the plain, shapeless garments that she-dragons favored. She always looked incredible.

"Out with it. Tell us already." Fog smiled at her, keeping his eyes on hers. Fog leaned forward just a little, and unwittingly Ice did too. Something had changed. Ice wanted to know what it was.

"Um… I'm not sure. Um… my friend cut my hair a couple of days ago." She touched the ends. "Do you like it?" She glanced at Ice as she said it, her gaze moving back to Fog. Azure ran her hand through her hair. "It's layered to give it more body." She giggled softly; even that was sexy as fuck, since her voice had a smoky edge.

"Your friend was right. It looks great. Really fantastic." Fog was laying it on thick.

"Also, she put some makeup on me last night." Azure shook her head like it was the craziest thing, which it was.

"That human face paint?" Ice blurted before he could stop himself. "I didn't think you'd be into that kind of thing."

"I'm not. Not really." She shook her head. "Melina is so sweet. I didn't want to upset her. She'd gone to so much trouble by bringing the stuff over to my place. Anyway, it wasn't as bad as I thought it would be. She's actually really good at it."

Ice narrowed his eyes, his gaze moving to her shiny lips. "I see she convinced you to try something new."

Azure rubbed her lips together. She had an amazing mouth. Full and lush. Holy shit, he was staring at it.

"Yep. I liked the gloss. It feels nice." She rubbed her lips together again, drawing his eye.

Fuuuuck. He could picture those lips wrapped around his—

No!

"Looks good," Fog said, grinning. "Smells great, too. What is that flavor?" Fog openly smelled the air. "It's so good."

Ice wanted to pop him one in the snout. The prick was flirting with Azure. He'd need to have another talk with him. None of them were dating Azure.

"It does, doesn't it?" Azure's eyes were bright.

"Something fruity," Fog said, still sniffing. The male needed to stop already. It was fucking annoying.

"Strawberry," Ice blurted. "It's strawberry." His voice had an edge.

"You're right." Azure smiled at him.

"Smells so good," Fog repeated himself for the third or fourth time.

"Tastes good too." He watched her lick her lips. Ice fixed on the slow glide of her tongue. "Mmmmmm," she said.

Ice turned. Sun and Avalanche were there. "We're going!" he snapped, turning back to Azure and Fog. "Now! You and I are having a meeting after shift," he told Fog.

If that male thought he could test compatibility with a member of his team, he could think again. *Fuck that!* Not on his watch.

CHAPTER 18

Later that day…

W AS SHE IN the right place? This didn't look like anything. She'd never been to this part of the lair before.

Azure frowned. "Hello?" Azure raised her voice. She could hear breathing and a heartbeat coming from inside the room. This had to be it.

"Helloooooo!" Melina called from inside.

"So this is your salon?" Azure smiled, standing at the entrance to the open space. Her voice echoed a little.

"That's the face I was hoping to see yesterday." Melina smiled back.

Azure grinned broadly.

"Come in, come in," the human said. "What do you think?" She walked a full circle, looking around the large room. "I know it doesn't look like much, but it will be transformed in a couple of weeks, you'll see." Her voice was animated. "This is where I'll do nails. This section is where hair will be washed. I'll cut and style over there." She pointed at a corner section. "That's the bathroom." She gestured to a closed door. "It'll double as the changing rooms. I'll put up racks of clothing along this whole wall. It'll be a one-stop-shop. Who knows, perhaps I'll be able to employ others in the future."

"I'm sure you'll need help soon enough. Our males are mating more and more humans who love this kind of thing."

"I see you're wearing the lip gloss I gave you."

"I am." Azure rubbed her lips together. "I think I like it."

"See, I'm already converting you. This is just as much for you she-dragons as it is for us humans. I want a mix of customers."

"Sounds like a plan. I'll be your first dragon customer and advocate."

"Thanks so much." Melina giggled. She looked excited. "I can't wait." She looked around the room, clearly already seeing everything in place.

Azure looked around the empty space, too, not really sure what to envision herself. It was not like she had ever been to a salon. "Let me know what I can do to help." She owed the female. Even if things didn't work out with Ice, she felt better in her own skin. She felt better in general. More confident. More open to the possibilities of what the future might hold.

"Do you mean that?" Melina raised her brows.

"Of course. I would be happy to help you in any way you need me to. I can fetch, carry… anything. You name it."

"You are so sweet," Melina gushed.

"No, you're sweet, Mel. Thank you for helping me. For being kind when I was… offish to you."

"You were offish?" Melina put her hands on her hips, giving her a look.

Azure laughed. "Yes, I was. I shouldn't have been. It was wrong of me. Thank you for not giving up. I consider you to be a good friend. You're here for me and so I'm definitely here for you."

"I'm glad we're friends." Melina reached out and gave her hand a squeeze. "I want to repaint the space." She looked around them again, her eyes glinting. "White is boring. Maybe you can help me pick something out. A warm tone with an accent wall… We'll figure something out that will be perfect for this space and then you could help me paint?"

"Sure. Although I have no idea what an accent wall is."

They both laughed. Then Melina clapped her hands. "I'm so excited. Freeze will put up shelves. I've ordered stock. Thunder has been amazing. He gave me capital to start up the business. Can you believe it?"

"That's great, and yes, I can believe it. The more humans who join our tribe, the more changes will be required. Human doctors have been hired. They hired a human chef for the kitchens, since many of our dishes need to accommodate humans now. There will be more of such changes." She shrugged. "Change is good." Azure had come to realize that.

"Now, Miss Glossy Lips, I'm sure you thought you could get away with not telling me what happened today. If that's the case, you thought wrong. I want to hear what put that smile on your face. You're looking radiant. Did Ice kiss you?"

Azure snort-laughed. "No, not even close. In fact, I'm not sure why I'm so happy. He was like a bear with a sore head the entire day. He snapped at all of us and more than once. When he wasn't being grumpy as hell, he was sullen and quiet."

"And?"

"And what?"

"I know there's more, even though all of what you have just told me is great, and you know it." Melina smiled broadly.

"There is more. This lip gloss worked. I know it did. Fog was hitting on me. Ice couldn't take his eyes off my lips."

"Did you lick them like I told you to?"

"Yes."

Melina shrieked. "Did you do it while he was looking at them?"

Azure nodded. "He definitely liked what he saw." There was no hiding the fire in his eyes. The hunger in that stare. His Adam's apple had worked. "He knew it was strawberry scented. Fog's flirtatious comments pissed him off."

"Then he was grumpy and sullen the whole day."

"Exactly." Azure chewed on her lower lip.

"You're my best student ever. You get an A-plus."

Azure laughed. "I'm your only student," she pushed out between chuckles. "I'm still not sure about all of this. I'm not into playing games."

"You told me you can't straight-out tell him."

Azure sighed and shook her head. "That wouldn't work."

"Then you have to make it impossible for him to ignore you. You need to make him come to you."

"Still." She licked her lips. "I wish I could just…" Azure shook her head. "You're right. If I'm serious, I have to keep trying. I can keep my efforts really subtle. I'm not in any rush. Even if it takes weeks or months. I'll wear him down until he won't be able to say no. In fact, he'll come to me."

"That's my girl." Melina shoulder-bumped her.

"Enough about me," Azure said. "Tell me more about what your plans are for this place. Do you have any idea on a color?" She frowned. "Oh, and you have to tell me what an accent wall is."

"Do you want to come to my place for a coffee? I can show you some ideas I have on my laptop."

"That sounds amazing."

"Let's go, then." They started walking back to the other side of the lair, where all the single people lived. The chambers only had one bedroom. "Freeze is getting sick of me talking about the salon," Melina said. "He pretends he's not, but I can tell that he is. In his defense, I do talk about it a lot. It'll be nice to chat with someone who's actually interested. Poor guy." She got this starry look in her eyes when she talked about her male.

"I'm surprised you guys aren't mated yet. Normally, shifters act quickly when they are in love. Sorry, if I've overstepped you must tell me."

"Not at all." Melina laughed. "He's asked me three times already, but I keep telling him I'm not ready yet."

"Why? I thought you loved him. It must be driving him insane."

"I *do* love him, but I want to wait a little. Humans don't rush into things like marriage. Besides, it's good for a guy to wait sometimes. Men love the chase. They like to feel like they've achieved something. If they work for it, they appreciate it more." She sniggered. "Between you and me, I am going to cave soon... he's just so adorable." The stars in her eyes were back. "If he thinks we're going to rush down the aisle, he's mistaken. Once I have a ring on my finger, I want to take time to plan an amazing wedding. I don't want to rush that either."

"Sounds like you have everything figured out."

"That's normally when things fall apart." Melina's eyes widened, and she pursed her lips together.

"Nonsense. Freeze is nuts about you. This is all so exciting."

"You never know." Melina got this sly look. "Maybe we can plan a double wedding."

"Please!" Azure laughed. She lowered her voice. "Just because Ice is attracted to me, doesn't mean he's interested in anything other than a good time. Dragon males mostly aren't."

"Excuse me, young lady." Melina wagged a finger at her. "Do I need to lecture you again?"

"No," Azure said. "I am worth it. I am intelligent. I have a lot to offer."

"You keep telling yourself that." Melina nodded once.

That was just it. Azure wasn't convinced. She'd seen too many dragon females sidelined. Too many beautiful, intelligent females just like her. Lust and love were two very different things.

CHAPTER 19

"A LLOW ME," FOG said, leaning down to pick up Azure's newly felled elk. "You made two kills today. The least I can do is help you with one of them. Great work, by the way." He winked at her.

The female put her foot on the elk, preventing him from picking it up. The fucker slowly pulled himself upright, letting his eyes drift over her body as he did.

Azure folded her arms across her chest. "You made a kill of your own. I've got this."

"Not necessary. I will carry two elk." The male was thick-skinned. He grinned at her. "I don't mind."

"I will help Fog," Sun chipped in, walking over to the two of them. "Fog can carry the carcass halfway, and I will carry it the rest of the way." He grinned at Azure so hard it was sickening. Both of them had been flirting like this non-fucking-stop. It was downright annoying.

"I'll skin it for you. That was a great kill," Avalanche gushed, looking more like a love-sick puppy than a huge shifter male. This was new. Avalanche, too, now? This was fucking insane. It was pissing him the hell off.

"That's okay. Thanks for the kind offers, but I'll manage just fine." She smiled at the three males.

At least Azure wasn't accepting any of their bullshit... because it *was* bullshit. She turned away from the males, toward him. "Ready when you are, Ice." He knew she was talking about shifting and leaving, but there was this undertone. Maybe it was just him, but it seemed like she was flirting. It was happening in a way that wasn't direct, which was confusing. It was more than likely his overactive, overeager imagination.

"Let's get going." His voice was a rough rasp. "Azure is perfectly capable of carrying her own kills. No one gets special privileges on this team. Understood?"

The males nodded begrudgingly.

Azure gave him a half-smile and mouthed, "Thank you."

He wanted to smile back and congratulate her on her second successful hunt for the day, but he held back. She'd received enough compliments from the others to last a lifetime. "Let's go." He shifted, watching as the others followed suit.

It took them an hour to get back. The game they hunted moved freely over their vast dragon lands.

Ice and the rest of the males landed ahead of Azure. He could see her flying slowly towards the lair. It gave him a few minutes with the males. "Azure is off-limits."

"What?" Sun spat. "Why? Fog mentioned something along those lines, but I didn't believe him. I thought he was bullshitting."

Avalanche grunted.

"Fog wasn't bullshitting." Ice glanced at Azure, who was getting closer. "Azure is off-limits. It is not permitted to fuck around with someone on your team. Someone you work with closely."

"I think you might have that wrong," Sun muttered. "I have a friend who works—"

"I don't give a shit about other teams within this tribe. I'm the leader, and I'm putting my foot down. I've been watching you flirt with Azure for days. She doesn't like it. I think it's disrespectful as fuck," he snarled.

"It isn't meant to be," Fog said.

"Not at all," Sun said. "I really like Azure."

Holy shit!

Avalanche grunted again. Thankfully, one of them kept his mouth shut.

"This isn't up for debate; it's how it is. If we get a full quota of kills tomorrow, we get Saturday off," he told the males just as Azure landed. She dropped her kills and shifted, immediately hoisting up one of the elk, taking it to the outdoor kitchen area, where she hung it on the hook.

"Let's get to work," he growled at the males, who were still busy watching Azure. Hadn't they heard a single thing he had just said?

Azure fetched her second elk and took that through to the cleaning area, hanging the carcass on a hook as well.

Azure was just picking up her hunting knife when he entered the area. "You did good today," he said, getting a knife of his own. Ice had been hard on her all week. Azure didn't deserve it. He felt bad.

"Thanks." She glanced his way, a shy smile toying with her lips.

"You're cleaning both of those." He smiled at her, trying hard to get back to that place where they were comfortable with each other. Where they were friends.

"Oh, I know." She laughed, looking down. Azure had a look at her nails, inspecting them. Her nails? Then she gave a little giggle. "It worked."

"What worked?" he asked. By now, the others had joined them. They were already hard at work gutting their elks.

"Oh… nothing." She held up her hand. Her fingernails were colored with a soft white color. They had an iridescent finish, reminding him of a shell. "My friend Melina gave me a manicure."

"A what?"

"She did my nails. I didn't think the varnish would make it through me shifting into my dragon form and back, but it's held up. Go figure!" She chuckled. It was throaty and sexy as sin. At that moment, Ice was unsure if there was even a possibility of going back to how things had been. He was doubting it more and more by the day… by the second. Then he thought about what she had just said.

Her hair.

Her nails.

Makeup.

What the fuck?

"Can I have a quick word with you?" he asked.

She frowned. "Did I do something wrong?" She licked her lips.

"No, but I need to discuss a couple of things with you."

Her eyes widened. "Is there word on Skarn?"

"No," he shook his head, "nothing like that."

Her eyes narrowed into his. "What then?" Ice could see the others eavesdropping on their conversation.

"Walk with me?" he asked. "It won't take long."

She looked apprehensive, but she didn't push him further. Instead, she put down the knife and followed him outside.

Ice pushed out a breath. He needed to word this delicately, but it was a conversation that needed to happen.

What was this about?

She got this sinking feeling in the pit of her stomach. This wasn't going to be good. Not a chance. She could see it in the rigid way he held himself. Even in the way he had asked her.

After walking for a few minutes, Ice stopped. He pulled in a deep breath. She watched his chest expand. He exhaled slowly, deliberately. *Oh, no!*

"Is everything okay with you?" he finally asked, turning to face her.

"Yes, I'm doing well." She was. Well, she had been up until five minutes ago. Maybe she was overthinking this. Maybe he really wanted to know how she was. "Thanks for asking," she quickly added.

"How are things with Summer?"

That was a strange question. "I haven't really seen her since my heat."

"Oh." He frowned. "I thought you would've talked with her. I'm sure... I... Okay." He still looked confused. Like he was trying to find a reason for her and Summer not talking.

"I tried to go to see her, but she's mad I didn't spend my heat with someone… that I didn't at least try to become pregnant. She thinks that my heat was wasted." Tears pricked in her eyes for a moment.

A look of concern bled into his features. "That's rough. You did tell her what happened, right?"

Azure shook her head. "She didn't give me much of a chance. She's not talking to me right now. She said she needs some space."

"Space?" Ice muttered. "I'm sure if she knew what you had been through—all of it—she'd feel differently."

Azure shrugged.

"I know you've been hanging out with one of the humans. I'm hoping you've been talking to someone about your ordeal. Is this human a good friend?" He still looked genuinely concerned, and it warmed her.

"I've become quite good friends with Melina. That's Freeze's girlfriend," she told him. "She's easy to talk to. I had to talk to someone." Maybe he'd be mad at her for telling Melina all that had happened. Even the stuff that had been between them.

"I've seen her with the male." Ice nodded. "I'm glad to hear it. I take it she's the one who is helping you with… other things."

"Other things?" She frowned, not sure where he was going with this.

"Your hair, nails… the face paint?" It was like he had a list in his head.

The sinking feeling hit her again. "Um… yes… lip gloss is hardly face paint, though."

Ice made this face and took a step back before roughing his hair up a little. "I need to talk to you for a minute as your superior, Azure."

"Okay." *Crap!*

"You work in a team of males…" He paused.

"Yes," she prompted, folding her arms. "I'm aware." Azure was sure to keep her eyes locked with his.

"I'm not sure that it's appropriate."

"What exactly isn't appropriate?" He wasn't going there. No way! If he was going to go there, he was going to damn well spell it out for her, all of it, and to her face.

"The beauty stuff. Lip gloss and nail paint… Come on, Azure. You work with males. They're following you around like a bunch of horny teenagers. Humans don't understand us. I'm sure your friend means well, but you should know better."

"So, what you're saying is the others hitting on me is *my* fault?" She narrowed her eyes. "How is that my fault, exactly?"

"Well, like I said, the nails, the…" He exhaled audibly, his hand finding its way back in his hair.

"You think the color on my nails is turning them into horny teenagers?"

"Well, when you put it like that… I guess it's not the nails. It's… I don't know, you're different. You're…" He looked like he was at a loss for words. He shrugged.

"Has my behavior changed?"

"Yes… no… yes, it has. You're… different." He sounded frustrated.

"But you can't say how, exactly. Am I more feminine?"

"Yes!" he pushed out. "Definitely. It's like you were almost one of the males last week, and this week…" He shrugged. "I don't know, but whatever has changed, I need you to change it back. It's not working like this. I can't have the males acting like they have been. It's disruptive and seriously fucking annoying." His voice got gruff.

"Let me get this straight; I'm more feminine and I need to stop it immediately?" *Hell no!*

"Yes, that just about sums it up." He took to looking smug.

The audacity of this male. "You want me to be more like a male? Should I wear a strap-on cock? Apparently, you can buy them."

He leveled her with a stare. "That's not what I expect at all. When you put it like that, it sounds stupid."

"That's because it *is* stupid. I'm a female, Ice. I can't change that. I don't want to. I don't want to hide who I am either, just because I work with a bunch of horny males. I shouldn't have to. This shouldn't be on me at all."

"You're right! You can't change who you are, but you can tone it down, please? Try for me." He was not playing that particular card. No damned way!

She shook her head. "I'm not toning anything down. How should I tone down being a female? Next, you'll tell me I need to wear those human coverings when we're in human form."

"I was considering bringing in a uniform policy. That we are dressed at all times, unless in our dragon form." He looked deadly serious. His eyes clouded when she choked out a laugh.

"That's crazy. It won't work. We're shifters." *Was he jealous?* This looked like jealousy. It pissed her off, but it also made her happy. It meant that Ice might have feelings for her. "What's going on with you?"

"My team is a mess. I've never seen so much drooling and flirting in all my life. Avalanche has started now, too." He sounded angry. His eyes blazed.

"Speak to them. *They're* the problem, *not* me."

"I did speak to them, multiple times, and it's not working. It needs to stop, Azure. Please stop with the strawberry glossy lip shit, as well. I'm going to have to start beating them soon."

"What's really going on here, Ice? It can't be Fog and Sun hitting on me, because they both asked me to rut with them just last week, and you didn't bat an eye. They flirt with me plenty. They have for months."

"Not like this. They're like lovesick puppies. All three of them. Fog told me the other day that he wants to check compatibility with you since he's permitted to mate now."

"Oh, good for him." Azure was pleased for the male. "Thing is, Fog could've pursued mating me last week or last month. The list refers to finding a human. He didn't. I'm sure you've got it wrong."

"I didn't get it wrong. He told me very clearly that he wants to approach you as a potential mate."

"Oh?" She'd have to let him know that she wasn't interested.

His eyes turned stormy, and he clenched his jaw. "Don't tell me you're actually considering Fog as a mate?" Holy shit, he was jealous. He had to be. "One of you would have to leave this team before I would allow it. No fucking around with a fellow teammate… period. I won't have it." He shook his head vehemently.

Shit!

Was this jealousy?

If it was, he'd just excluded himself. It couldn't be jealousy. Or was she misreading this whole thing?

"Stop with all the bullshit, already. You're leading them on." He sounded exasperated.

"I am not leading them on! Do you really think that hair and nails are causing all this?"

"I do," he deadpanned, folding his arms across his impressive chest. *Not noticing!*

"There is nothing in any of the rule books that tells me I can't cut my hair or paint my nails. That's absurd."

"You are the first female hunter, so of course there aren't any rules. Besides, dragon females don't do all that stuff. Why are you doing it all of a sudden? You don't need it."

For a second, she was too thrilled with hearing him say that, but she shook it off. "Well, maybe dragon females *should* do that stuff." Her voice was animated.

"Not during work hours. Don't force me to add a whole bunch of new rules. Rules pertaining specifically to you. I will if I have to."

"Don't be a dick, Ice."

His throat worked. "Don't speak to me like that." He kept his voice even.

"If the shoe fits."

His lip twitched, but he quickly schooled all of his emotions. "We're naked; there are no shoes. Bottom line," he exhaled through his nose, "I make the rules. I'm your superior. I can throw a whole lot of rules at *all* of you if need be. I can make life unpleasant for the whole team."

"Thank you for not singling me out… this once." Her voice was raised. He was being a huge dick.

"All the bullshit needs to stop. That's all! No special treatment because you're female. No—"

"I don't expect or accept special treatment, and you know it," she threw at him, everything inside her bristling. Her scales rubbed. "It's unfair to even say that to me. Talk to the others. They're the ones who—"

"I have." He sounded defeated. "I'm going to have to take a hard stance on this soon, and it's not what I want."

"I recently had my first and, more than likely, only heat." She swallowed hard. A late heat was rare; a female who went into heat again, after a late start, was even rarer still. She had no false expectations. "The whole thing is fresh in everyone's memory." His jaw clenched, like maybe he was thinking about what went down between the two of them. Her cheeks heated a little because she was thinking about it big time. "It'll blow over, Ice. Give it time. You'll see. They'll forget, lose interest, and move on. Especially when it doesn't happen again. Don't make a big deal out of it."

"You're right." He nodded, looking more relaxed. "You're absolutely right. In the meanwhile, I'll kick their asses when they step out of line." He shook his head. "I *was* being a dick. I apologize. You're right; I'm making something out of nothing."

Disappointment hit. She had to work to keep the smile on her face. Perhaps this really was about work. Perhaps it had nothing to do with them. It was all wishful thinking on her part. There was still a part of her that knew what she had seen. Desire. She'd seen it in his eyes, in the way he'd looked at her. Azure would hold on to that and keep chipping away.

"There's something else I need to mention. I already informed the others."

She nodded once.

"Fog and I are going on the stag run this weekend."

Act cool! Stay calm. Breathe.

Inside, she was reeling. She prayed it didn't show. "Oh… okay." She rubbed her lips together. "That's unexpected."

"I am on the list to pick a mate. I missed the last one, and so…" He lifted his brows. "Fog will be joining me now that he is on the list as well. If we don't make quota, I will need you, Sun, and Avalanche to hunt on Saturday."

"No problem." Her voice was tight. Her whole body felt tightly wound. All she wanted was to get away. To lose herself in her work. To hide in her chamber.

"I want you to lead the team in our absence."

"Me?" She touched a hand to her chest, frowning. She was the newest member. This was a big deal. A huge deal.

"Yes, you." Ice smiled. "Don't underestimate yourself, Azure. You're a fantastic hunter, even with colored nails and lips that smell edible."

She cleared her throat. "Good to know." Her heart was still sinking like a gigantic rock. She'd been completely off base. Ice wouldn't be going on a stag run if he was even remotely interested. It would hurt her if he was going for sex, but that wasn't it, either. Ice was going to find himself a future mate. A human mate. Something she could never be, no matter how hard she tried. He was right; she'd been an idiot. No more!

CHAPTER 20

Her phone buzzed for the fifth or sixth time. There was more knocking on her door. "I know you're in there," Melina said. "It can't be that bad!" she shouted, even though shouting wasn't necessary. "Let me in so that we can talk about it." She didn't just knock on the door this time, she banged on it.

Humans!

Her friend was making a scene. Others would hear. Also, Melina had helped her out so much that she owed the female an explanation. She sighed, since a conversation was the last thing she felt like right now. Azure was too upset, too raw. She took deep breaths as she marched to the door. *Melina was trying to help. She was being a good friend.* The fact that dragon males were assholes didn't have anything to do with human females. "I'm done with all the beauty nonsense," Azure said as she threw the door open.

Melina took a step back and gave her a measured look. "Did you chip a nail or something?" She was completely serious.

Azure rolled her eyes and bust out a laugh. "No, my nails are perfect." She held up both hands.

"Oh, good. So, it's something else that's got you all riled up then." Melina walked inside.

Azure closed the door. "I guess. You'd better come in." She gestured to her living room. "Do you want something to drink?"

Melina shook her head. "I need to know what happened. You look upset." Her eyes were filled with concern.

"He's going on the stag run this weekend." She had to work not to get emotional, which was tough since she was on the verge of tears. Azure chewed on her bottom lip.

"That's great!" Melina yelled. She was doing it again, acting all irrational.

Azure groaned and covered her face with her hand for a moment. "How do you figure? He's on the mating list. He's going into human territory to find a mate."

"No, he's going to run away from you. He's going to sleep with another woman in the hopes that he'll forget you."

"Even if that were true, how is that a good thing?"

"It's good because you're not going to give him the chance to run away, or to sleep with another woman." She shook her head.

"How will I do that? Should I tie him to his bed? Injure him so that he can't fly? Beg him not to go? Because none of those are going to work for me."

Melina giggled. "No, silly. Although, tying him to the bed might work…" She winked at Azure, pretending to give it some real thought.

"I'm not tying him to any bed. We discussed this previously."

"In that case, I think the only course of action will be to go on the stag run as well," she deadpanned, like that was the easiest thing in the world for her to do.

Azure's mouth fell open. "You want me to do what?"

"You mentioned that he invited you to go on a run before. You're going to accept that invitation… that's all." She gave a sassy smile.

"I was invited previously when the whole team was going. He won't want me on this one. Especially if he's running away from me."

Melina shrugged. "Semantics. You're going to go, anyway."

"I can't." She shook her head. "I'm in charge on Saturday if we don't make our quota of game tomorrow."

"That means you'll have to make your quota, because you're going."

"It doesn't work that way. We might not find any game." She sounded exasperated.

"How often does that happen? You're dragon shifters; you're built to kill."

"We mostly do because we're efficient hunters."

"I'd say!" Melina snorted.

"We don't kill indiscriminately, though. We give the animals a fair chance at escape. That way, the stronger, faster animals will have a chance to reproduce. There are plenty of rules surrounding what we can take out, and what we can't. As well as the way in which we approach things, including how we choose our targets. It changes with the seasons."

"I love you, hon,' but I don't want to talk about hunting." Melina wrinkled her nose.

Azure sighed. "I can't just go. It doesn't work like that."

"The men go regularly. Why can't the women go as well? That's bullcrap!"

"I suppose it is. I never thought of it that way." The things Melina told her made sense.

"Stand up for your rights. You're going on the stag run," Melina insisted. "Get your quota tomorrow and then get your name on the list. Make it happen for yourself, especially if you want Ice."

Azure's shoulders slumped. "I *do* want Ice, but I don't know if I should do it. There are so many things that could go wrong."

"You'd better not be backing down because something could go wrong." Melina wagged her finger at Azure. "I know you're stronger than that. Of course you should go for it. Do you want Ice to sleep with another woman? Do you want him to possibly find a mate? It could happen, you know!"

"I know, and that's the thing; what if I go and he leaves with a human, anyway?" Her gut churned. There was only one thing worse than knowing Ice was going to pick a female to rut; it would be witnessing him do it first hand.

Melina narrowed her eyes. "He won't leave with someone else if you're there. Ice won't leave you in a pickup joint all by yourself. It will never happen."

"Are you sure?" Melina had never steered her wrong before. She trusted the other female... her friend.

"One hundred percent sure. He'll be jealous when all the guys hit on you." She bobbed her brows.

"I don't want a whole lot of males to hit on me. It's irritating."

"Enjoy it. Most guys are really nice."

"I don't want them. I don't want to play games." She sighed. "But I can't just tell Ice how I feel. I know he would turn me down."

"Exactly. Go, have a little fun and watch Ice come to you. It's what you've wanted all along."

"I'm still so scared he doesn't respond the way you think he will," Azure insisted.

"He will!" Melina looked sure. "Dragon men are possessive. He'll growl and get angry and then maybe you can tell him how you feel. Don't worry too much about it, just go with the flow."

"What if no one hits on me?"

Melina laughed. "Holy shit, lady, you really have no idea how gorgeous you are. Even after I've told you plenty of times. The guys at the pickup joint won't be able to resist, since I'm going to help you out in the wardrobe department. I'll also teach you how to put on a touch of makeup like we did the other day. The guys will go nuts. Trust me on this."

"Okay." Fear churned in her belly. If it weren't for Melina, she definitely wouldn't have the courage to do something like this. Her friend was right, as always. If she really wanted Ice, she needed to go after him.

CHAPTER 21

THERE WAS ALREADY a small group of males assembled on the balcony. Ice was one of them. By all that was scaled, she was nervous. There was no backing out now. Azure was no coward. She was doing this. By the end of this weekend, she needed to know one way or the other if there was a future for her and Ice. No more games! This was it!

She walked over to the male in question, and he did a double-take when he saw her. "What are you doing here?" he asked as she dropped her overnight bag at her feet. He was frowning heavily.

"I decided that I want to go on a stag run." She kept her voice even, like it was no biggie.

"You can't!" he pushed out.

"Why not?" She narrowed her eyes at him. "You invited me last time; what's changed?"

"The whole team was going last time. I thought we could… It was stupid of me." He shook his head. "I shouldn't have invited you. The stag run is no place for a female."

"Why is that?" She folded her arms.

"We're going to rut. And some of us are going to find mates."

"That's okay," she lied through her teeth. It wasn't okay. Not at all. That was why she was there in the first place. "Because I'm going for exactly the same reason as you are." That part was true, only, not with some random male. Fingers crossed.

"What?" he blurted, sounding completely out of sorts. *Asshole!* Why were all those things okay for them and not for her? She pulled in a deep breath. Reminding herself of all the things Melina had told her about Ice's motivations. Namely, he was running away. Of course he wasn't happy to see her.

"Before you say one more word, Ice, I need to point out that we're not at work right now," she quickly added. "Furthermore, it's normal for a female in her prime to want to go out and to have some fun."

His eyes widened dramatically. "It's not normal for a dragon female to go on a stag run, though, Azure. What's gotten into you?" He looked completely off-kilter. "Don't do this. It isn't right."

"Good thing I'm not your run-of-the-mill dragon female, then." The more he spoke, the more he pissed her the hell off.

His eyes flared with annoyance. "You're not on the list."

"Actually, I am. I went to see Storm, and he thinks it's a great idea. Infertile dragon females are overlooked all the time. Perhaps there's a human I'll click with." She shrugged.

His jaw tightened. "You said they all have small dicks. All of a sudden, you want to rut one?"

"According to my friend, Melina, it's not about size, it's how a male uses what he's got. I think I agree with her. Now, if you'll excuse me." She pulled her dress over her head and shifted, putting an end to their conversation just as Fog sauntered up.

"Hi, Azure. Are you coming with us?" He sounded happy. "Is she coming with us?" she heard him ask Ice, who grunted.

All of this anger and animosity was because Ice was interested in her. Azure had to believe it. This was going to work out. It had to.

That evening…

Azure tugged at the waist of her skinny jeans. How did humans wear these tight garments? She walked to the other side of the strange room and then back again. It was nice so far. Not that she'd seen much more than the inside of the chamber at the bed-and-breakfast. Although, they called it a garden suite, not a chamber which was fitting since it was in the garden. Azure looked down at her feet; her high heels were just as uncomfortable as the clothes. They squeezed her feet to the point of pain, and she hadn't even left yet. How was she supposed to go anywhere for the next couple of hours and actually enjoy herself? Her admiration for humans was growing. Particularly human females. If it weren't for the fact that she was a shifter, with superhuman balance and agility, she would have broken her neck falling by now.

Azure stepped out of the shoes, slipping her feet into flat sandals instead. Thankfully, Melina had insisted she take a couple of outfits and shoe options. The sandals were much more comfortable. Without the heels, it felt bearable. Azure took a last look in the mirror. She wore a silver top with a slightly plunging neckline and no bra. There was no way she was putting herself through that. It looked good. Made her breasts look bigger somehow, but without showing them off too much. What had Melina called it? "Whispering sexy and screaming sophistication." She wasn't sold on the sophistication part, especially since she was wearing flats, but it didn't matter to her. All that mattered was finding a way to convince Ice to let down his walls and to take a chance on her. And it wasn't ultimately about how someone looked; it was about how they made you feel.

Azure moved closer to the mirror to check out her face. She'd taken forever to do her own makeup. The first attempt had left her looking like a raccoon. This was good. The very basics with a tinted lip gloss, cherry flavor this time. Her hair was down. She looked good. She had this.

The males had left fifteen minutes earlier. She'd told them that she wasn't quite ready yet, that they should go ahead of her. Melina had insisted she do this so that she could make an entrance. It all felt like too much. Regardless, she'd followed her friend's advice. It was now time for her to go and have some fun. Pity her palms felt sweaty and her mouth dry. It didn't matter that she'd drunk a whole bottle of water. Nothing helped. She'd never been more nervous than she was right now.

Grabbing a small purse, she slung it over her shoulder and left her room, clicking the door behind her. Azure grabbed her chest and gasped when someone walked up to her. "Fog," she pushed out. "You gave me a fright."

He smiled at her. "Sorry, I didn't mean to scare you."

"You didn't. I just wasn't expecting any of you to still be here." She glanced around them, even though she knew they were alone. "Where are the others? Were you running late as well?"

"Nah, I thought I would wait for you. This is your first time in human territory." He pushed his hands into his jeans. "You look absolutely amazing." He looked her up and down. "Almost better dressed than naked." He got this look in his eyes.

Crap!

This was bad. Fog was hitting on her.

"Thank you."

"I mean it… wow!" He lifted his brows. Why couldn't she have feelings for Fog instead? Why? He was such a nice guy.

She looked down at the floor and then back up at him. "Thanks, and thanks for waiting." She chewed on her lower lip. "You know that we're friends, right? That's how I see you… as a friend." She didn't want to string him along and possibly hurt him.

"You never know, because the night is young. We—"

Azure took his hand and squeezed it once before letting it go. "It's not going to change. I see you as my friend, Fog. Ice mentioned that you were interested in exploring more with me—"

Fog's expression turned stormy. "He warned you off and threatened your place on the team; is that how it went down?"

"No," she shook her head, "that's not it. I don't have

those kinds of feelings for you. Trust me when I tell you, it's got nothing to do with you. I wish I could change how I feel but I can't."

"Ouch!" He grabbed the place just over his heart. "You're already giving the whole 'it's not you, it's me' speech, and we haven't even... done anything."

"Sorry." She made a face. "I feel terrible."

"Don't. It's not your fault. I had to try my luck." He smiled.

"No hard feelings, then?"

"None at all." What an amazing guy. Any woman would be lucky to have him. Why, oh why, couldn't she have feelings for him? Why Ice? Her belly churned at the thought of going out now. Of facing him. This was it.

"Shall we?" He pointed to a waiting black vehicle.

"Is that an... U-ber?"

"Yep." He chuckled. "You'll get used to it. It's crazy different from our lives back at the lair. I enjoy coming here."

"I'll say it's different." She looked to the east, at all the twinkling lights of the city. Their B&B was on the outskirts of town. It was owned by the dragons for them to use during the stag runs. "Is it far? The place we're going to," she asked as they climbed into the vehicle.

"Good evening," the driver said.

"Hi... um... evening," she muttered.

"I see you're headed to The Lonestar Cocktail Bar. It'll be about a fifteen-minute drive," the driver said.

"Thank you," she told him before turning to Fog. "What can I expect when we get there?" The car pulled away.

Fog grinned. "Relax. You're going to have a good time.

It's a fun night away... try to remember that. You look like you'd rather poke your eyes out."

Azure giggled. "You're right!" She nodded like mad, then forced herself to stop. "I guess I'm a little bit nervous."

"I'd say." He chuckled. "I'll stick with you until you feel comfortable."

"Thank you." They picked up speed, the lights drawing closer.

They talked about nothing in particular. Azure was careful not to mention anything about them being shifters. Nothing to do with the lair. She was under strict orders, as were them all, to keep who they were a secret from the humans.

All too soon, they pulled up to The Lonestar. Azure swallowed thickly. "Come on! You look like you're about to walk to your death or something." Fog laughed.

"I'll be okay once we're inside." She prayed that was true. Azure climbed out of the Uber, thanking the driver as she did, closing the door.

"It's not that bad, I promise," Fog told her.

"I know."

"They're just humans," he reassured her lightly.

Only, she wasn't there for the humans. If only that were true. Her life would be a lot less complicated.

"After you." Fog gestured to the door. "You look amazing and smell even better."

Azure just stood there, looking at the door. There were two males, one on either side of the door, and a long line of people queued down the road.

One of the males waved at Fog. "Are you one of the hockey players?" They were big for human males, and both wore black suits and ties.

Fog winked at her. "You've got this! Yes!" he yelled, walking up to the entrance.

"Name?" The male had a clipboard. "I'm Jack Smith, and this is Tiffany Scott. She's also on the list."

The male spent half a minute looking at his list. He then unclipped a rope. "Welcome to the Lonestar, Mr. Smith... Miss Scott." He inclined his head. "I trust you will have a fantastic evening."

"Thank you," Fog said. "We most certainly will. Isn't that right, Tiffany?"

"Um... yes... for sure." Hopefully. Maybe. Was she making a mistake? This was her last chance to back out. Melina would have some choice words for her right then. She'd tell her not to be such a wimp; to go in and have some fun, Ice be damned. And that was exactly what she was going to do. She smiled at Fog. "Let's do this."

"That's more like it."

Shoulders back, head held high, Azure walked into the noisy, smelly environment. Fog put a hand to her back and steered her through the crowd. There was an ocean of people, or at least it felt that way. Bodies gyrated on a dancefloor. "That's the bar," Fog said, pointing at a whole lot more people.

The bar itself was all gleaming steel, forming silver stars. The lights were a little brighter on that side of the establishment. Colored lights flashed above the dancefloor section and the booths on the far side were dimly lit. She could smell food, alcohol, and body odor. Azure sneezed into her hand as a human female walked past. All those scents, as well as plenty of different kinds of perfume. "How do you deal with that?"

Fog laughed. "You get used to it."

"I highly doubt it." She laughed as well.

"Let's hit the bar and get a drink."

"Sounds good." She almost stumbled when she caught sight of *him*.

Ice.

Her breath caught in her chest, and her heart hammered faster. He wore a plain white t-shirt and a pair of jeans. How did he look so darned good? How? He looked her way. His eyes were a vivid blue. His hair was dark and slightly overgrown, yet perfect somehow.

Keep cool!

Relax!

She smiled and waved at him. It's what she normally would have done. Ice inclined his head ever so slightly. If she'd blinked, she would have missed it. He went back to talking to one of the other shifter males. There were females in their group as well. Females who were hanging on their every word. Scantily clad human females. *Suck it up! You've got this.*

"Drink?"

"Make it a double."

Fog smiled. "Coming right up."

"Hey, gorgeous," a human male said to her as she walked past.

Ignoring the male, she kept walking, noticing that many of the males looked at her she walked past. They really looked as if they were interested in her. Azure wasn't going to lead anyone on or do something out of character just to make Ice notice her. She was going to be herself and hopefully that would be enough. It had to be.

CHAPTER 22

*H*OLY FUCKING SHIT!
Ice felt everything in him tighten as he looked up and straight into Azure's eyes. It was like she had called to him like a homing beacon.

Beautiful.

So fucking sexy it made his scales rub.

Her long legs were encased in blue jeans. She wore a shimmery top that drew his eyes first to plump-as-fuck nipples and then to full mounds he wanted to squeeze with both hands. Her face looked almost devoid of makeup. Good, she didn't need it. She was gorgeous without even trying.

Azure gave him a cheesy grin and waved. She looked relaxed, all set to have one hell of a good time. She would have no problem finding one, looking like that. The males around her were eating her up with their eyes. If given half a chance, they'd eat her up with a whole lot more.

Mine!

His dragon pushed just below the surface of his skin. *Fuck!* Any more of this and his eyes would start to glow.

Not yours!

No!

He inclined his head, because ignoring her outright would be rude. It was the last thing he wanted, but until he got some semblance of control, he needed to stay far away from her. As it stood, he was sorely tempted to go over there and… And what?

Kiss her?

Leave with her?

Start beating all the males who were looking at her?

He couldn't do any of those things. *Why the fuck not?* He could barely remember all the reasons against doing just that. Ice wanted to go to her. He wanted it so badly he vibrated with the need. This was Azure. His teammate. His friend. She wasn't just some female. Something had changed after her heat. Something he couldn't quite put his finger on. He didn't like it much. Ice was worried about her. She was acting irrationally… not herself. Azure was an adult. She was in charge of her own life and her own destiny. Who was he to interfere?

She'd made it abundantly clear why she was there. To find a human to rut. That shouldn't infuriate him since he was there for the same reason. It did though; it infuriated him big fucking time.

His gaze drifted back to her. She was at the bar, laughing at something Fog was saying. He could see males itching to move in but holding off. Fog was a big male. They would be intimidated. Good! Or was it? He knew Fog's intentions. This was such a fucking mess. One he was staying out of.

Azure was not his.

He needed to stick to his original plan. Ice needed to get laid. His thoughts immediately went to Azure. *Not her!* Anyone else but her.

Fuck!

"Did you want another beer?" Mist asked, holding up his own empty bottle.

Ice looked down; his beer was still half full. "I'm good." He turned to the female in the little red dress. She wore the highest heels he had ever seen. Her tits were practically touching her chin. She beamed at him as soon as their eyes locked. "Drink?" he asked, just because she was there. This was all so fucking wrong.

"I'll have another one of these." It was an almost empty pink cocktail.

She must have noticed his expression because she added, "It's a Cosmopolitan."

"One of those, bro," he told Mist, pointing at the female's drink. "It's a Cosmopolitan." Maybe this was a bad idea. He should just head back to the B&B alone and be done with it.

No!

He needed a female. He needed to rut all the thoughts of a certain she-dragon right from his mind, once and for all. It had been too long since he was last with someone. Azure was the closest he'd gotten to a female in the longest damn time, and it was fucking with his brain.

"Really?" Mist raised his brows. "A Cosmo?"

"I'll get the next round," Ice promised.

The male nodded. "You owe me. It's a nightmare trying to get through a crowd with one of those." He glanced at the female's drink.

"Yeah, I'll owe you," Ice muttered.

The male smirked. "She is pretty hot, if you're into that sort of thing." He looked at the female's deep cleavage.

"Get the drinks already," Ice pressed, annoyed. Such banter was normal between males; it shouldn't be an issue. It wouldn't be if he wasn't so tightly wound.

Don't look at her!

Don't look!

"I've never seen you here before," the female purred.

"That's because I've never been here before. We're from out of town. Remind me of your name." She'd been introduced earlier, but he'd forgotten.

"It's Lilly."

"Like the flower." It was a stupid thing to say, but he didn't feel much like talking.

She smiled brightly. "That's right, and yours?" She narrowed her eyes. "I think your friend said that it was Ice." She widened her eyes. "Interesting name."

"It's my nickname; everyone calls me Ice."

"You guys are an amateur hockey team, or something? How cool!" That was their ruse. It worked.

"Thanks." It wasn't something he wanted to talk about, since he didn't know all that much about the sport, just some basics they'd had to study up on.

"When are you playing? I'd love to come and watch." She rubbed her bright red lips together.

"We already played earlier today." He half-smiled. "We leave for home tomorrow."

Her whole face fell. "Oh, that's a pity. Where is home?"

"I would much rather hear about you. What do you do? Tell me about yourself." He took another sip of his beer, forcing himself to concentrate on what the human was saying.

"I'm a pre-school teacher. I love little kids. Always have. I'm from a big family. I have three brothers and one sister."

"Oh, wow!"

"It's great, actually. I loved growing up surrounded by people. The house was always busy. Family gatherings are still one of my favorites. We get together regularly."

"Sounds amazing." He nodded. "It must be one huge gathering?" *Holy shit!* He couldn't think of what to say. The whole conversation was stilted.

"Yep, especially since most of my siblings are married with kids of their own. What about you?"

"Only child, I'm afraid. I always wanted a brother or a sister, but it wasn't on the cards for our family." He shrugged, shaking his head.

"I can't imagine being a single child. I mean, I'm sure there are good aspects to being an only child, like new clothing. If I got anything new, I treasured it." She laughed, finishing her drink and putting it down on a nearby table.

Lilly was sweet. He liked her. Why did he still want to look over at the bar, then? Why? It was pissing him off. He took another sip of his beer. Lilly kept talking about her family. How much she enjoyed being an aunt. He nodded and smiled and made all the right sounds to let her know that he was listening, which he was. It was a struggle, but he managed. He kept his eyes glued on the female. She had big blue eyes and blonde hair that had a light curl to it. Ice was sure that under all that makeup were a couple of freckles. He wasn't sure why she tried so hard; she was beautiful. If only his body would respond to her like it should. He got nothing. Yet, when it came to Azure, it would happen at the drop of a hat, and at the most inopportune moments. It was all shades of fucked up.

Lilly laughed, pulling him out of his musings. "That's when Tommy jumped out of the closet, and—"

"Here's your drink," Mist said, holding the cocktail out to the female.

"Thanks so much," she said, taking the glass, which was relatively full, considering the treacherous walk.

"Thanks, bro," he said to Mist.

The male smirked. "Did you see Azure?" he asked. "She's here, at the bar with Fog."

"Oh?" He looked over to where Mist was pointing. Fog was talking to a human female, and some male was grinning at Azure, who appeared to be in a conversation with him.

Fuck!

"I'm glad to see she got here okay," Ice mumbled. He had been about to stay to make sure she got to the bar safely when Fog had put up his hand. Since Ice was trying to stay away from the female, he'd grit his teeth and left it alone.

"Wow, she looks freaking hot," Mist said, eyes wide. She had about ten males all lined up to offer her a drink. "That silver top she's wearing… Fuck me," he growled. "I'm considering elbowing my way to the front that of that queue."

"She's not here for one of us." Ice's voice had an edge. Azure was here for a human.

He glanced her way. She was laughing at something the male was saying. She shook her head, and the asshole walked away. He pushed out a breath, but his relief was short-lived when another prick stepped up, saying something to Azure that made her smile.

"How long have you been playing hockey?" Lilly asked, not liking that his attention had been diverted.

He noticed that Mist was talking to some other female.

"Oh… um…" He couldn't remember what Lilly had asked him.

She frowned. "Hockey? How long have you been playing?"

"Oh… sorry." He shook his head. "My mind was elsewhere for a second. I'm all yours now."

Lilly gave him a huge smile, biting down on her lower lip. It made him feel like the biggest prick alive, but he was going to find a female—if Lilly wasn't game for a hookup—and move the fuck on.

CHAPTER 23

F OG NUDGED HER. "Azure," he said.

"Yes?" she asked, turning around on her barstool and looking his way. He was just putting his cellphone into his pocket. The female Fog had been talking to looked put out. She even gave Azure a dirty look, pursing her lips. Azure wanted to tell the human that she had nothing to worry about, but didn't. She didn't seem all that friendly.

"You do know that you're actually supposed to accept a drink from a male, or at least talk to one." He looked at the male who was walking away. "That's the fifth or sixth male you've turned down."

"I suppose you're right." She shrugged. "None of them have been that interesting."

"They'll be too afraid to approach you soon."

"I don't mind." She glanced back at where she'd seen

Ice standing, talking to that same female. The one in the red dress with the serious curves.

What? Where was he? Where were they?

The spot where they had been standing was empty.

Fog chuckled. "If you're looking for Ice, he left."

"Um… what? Ahhhhh… um… no… I—" Shit! *What did she say to that?* Left? Ice left? Her heart plummeted. Any hope she had been holding out faded. "I wasn't… looking for him," she practically whispered.

Fog all out laughed. "Please! You can stop there. Don't even try to deny it. I've watched the two of you trying not to look at each other for the last two hours and failing dismally."

"What?" She made a face. "No, you have it wrong." She shook her head, feeling worse and worse. Ice had left.

"I finally understand why the two of you have been acting weird all week. I understand what that energy I've been feeling was. Sexual tension." He chuckled.

She frowned. "What are you talking about?"

"And why you won't give me the time of day. Because let's face it, I'm a handsome male, with a whole lot to offer." He flexed his bicep.

She smiled, unable to laugh, even though she wanted to… because where was the female in the red dress? Where? Had Ice left with her? She looked around the place, not seeing the human anywhere. Maybe they didn't leave together. Maybe she was—

"The two of you are… I don't know exactly what you are, but there's something there. That much is apparent."

"No." She shook her head, her eyes stinging. Her mind racing. "No… not at all. You're wrong." Her lip wobbled, so she bit down on it, looking towards the bathrooms. Maybe the female was in there.

"I'm not wrong." He touched the side of her arm, drawing back her attention to him. He sighed. "He left with her."

"I know."

"He doesn't want her."

"Funny way of showing it, since he left with her." Azure was having to work not to cry. *She. Would. Not!*

"Ice wants *you*."

"You're wrong!" she almost growled, her dragon right there beneath the surface. "He's such an asshole," she pushed out. "I don't know what I see in him."

"I don't either, but here we are," Fog said, eyebrows raised. "Actually, when he's not stuck up his own ass, he's a good male and the two of you would be good together." He rolled his eyes. "I still think I'm the better male for you, but what can you do?" He shrugged.

Azure choked out a laugh, still trying not to cry. She sniffed a few times. "He left with someone else, so this conversation isn't even worth having."

"You dressed up and came all this way. I think you should finish it."

She narrowed her eyes. "Finish it how?"

"Go and tell him how you feel."

"What? Now?" she choked out. "You've lost your mind."

"I already called you an Uber. It's waiting outside. Ice is in room number eleven."

"Are you really suggesting I barge in on them?"

"If you hurry, you will make it before anything happens."

"How do you know that?" She shook her head. "They left—"

"A couple of minutes ago. Not long at all. I called the B&B and had them lock his room; he'll have to go to the reception to get a key. He wouldn't have taken one with him."

"He might have."

"He didn't. I know Ice. That's why I'm shocked it took me this long to figure it out. He can't see straight for wanting you so much. He doesn't want that female. If you are serious, go now, tell him how you feel. He's too stubborn to go to you. Too hard-assed to break a rule, even though it's a bullshit rule. It's just the way he is."

If she left right then…

"Just go already." Fog grinned. "I can keep a secret. I think it's—"

Azure didn't wait to hear the rest of what he said. She grabbed her purse and ran. Then she slid into the seat in the Uber and yelled, "Please hurry."

This was crazy.

This was stupid.

She'd never had to work so hard for a male in her life. Then again, it had never counted before. It did now. It counted big time.

CHAPTER 24

T HE UBER PULLED into the parking lot in front of the B&B. Her heart was going nuts. She could hear the beat in her head. Her mouth was completely dry. Then she was on the sidewalk. She couldn't remember getting out of the vehicle, let alone saying goodbye to the driver, who was pulling away from the curb. She just stood there for a few moments, looking at the units. They were built in a U-shape, with a garden in the center. Most of the suites were bathed in darkness. The reception was to the right, lights blazing in contrast. Were they in there now, getting a key, or in his room?

Now that she was there, fear took hold of her. What was she doing? This was crazy. Was she really going to barge into his room? What if they were already…?

She swallowed thickly.

If they were already rutting, she would claim she had

made a mistake and run away. The sight would surely put her off Ice for life, which was a good thing. A great thing! If she managed to intercept them, she'd give him a piece of her mind and leave. If what Fog was saying was true, then why... why had he left with the human? She didn't get it. There was no way Azure was going to beg or plead for him to be with her. She was worth more than that. If he didn't see it, he could go to hell. One way or another, this would be over soon. These stupid games were done with, as far as she was concerned.

Azure marched up to room eleven. By all that was scaled and winged, the lights were off. She paced in front of his suite, not sure what to do. She couldn't hear anything or anyone inside. There were noises of rutting, but not from in there.

Only one way to know for sure; she lifted her hand to grab the handle of the door. Her excuse would only work if she barged in. "Here goes nothing," she whispered to herself and tried the door.

It was locked.

"Azure." She looked to the right and straight into glacial blue eyes... eyes that were narrowed. "What are you doing? That's my room." Ice walked towards her, key in hand.

"Oh... um... is it?" No, this was not how she was playing it. The time had come for honesty. She pulled in a deep breath, squaring her shoulders. "I know it's your room."

"Why were you about to go into my room?" He lifted his brows. "Without even knocking first."

"I— Wait a minute, where's your human?" Shit, that came out sounding catty.

"My human? Lilly isn't *my* anything." He folded his arms across his chest. "Her house was on the way here. I dropped her off before…" His eyes flared with understanding. "You thought I brought her back here with me." He scrubbed a hand over his face. "Why would you barge in if you thought that I was with her?"

"To tell you what a jerk you are. To tell you that I wasted my time coming here. You don't get it. You don't get any of it. You're an asshole. There, I said it. I'm going to bed now. Have a nice night." She turned, wanting to run, wanting to hide. Instead, she started walking through the garden that led to her suite. She could hear footfalls behind her and so she picked up her pace.

"Azure, wait." Ice gripped her arm lightly, letting go as soon as she stopped walking. "Why did you come with us on this weekend?" His voice was soft.

"Forget it." She shook her head, not wanting to turn around. "I've made a big enough fool of myself."

"Azure." There was so much longing thrown into that one word. She turned to look into his eyes, which were hooded and yet blazing. "Why did you come?"

"You know why." There was anger laced in her voice.

"To rut with a human." His jaw tightened, as if maybe he didn't like the idea much. "That's what you told me. If that's true, why were you sending them all away one after the other?"

"You were watching me?" Maybe Fog was right. Maybe. "Why didn't you come back with the female?" She turned all the way around, facing him head-on.

It looked like he might be putting his tongue on the roof of his mouth. "I didn't want her… not even close. I tried to convince myself otherwise, but I was being an idiot."

"At least we agree on something. Why didn't you want her? She's beautiful. Lovely blonde hair and abundant curves like I've heard you males talk so much about."

"I don't know. Perhaps I'm more partial to hair the color of a moonless night and eyes like amethysts. This is a bad idea, Azure." He shook his head. "*We* are a bad idea." He cupped her jaw. "*This* is definitely a bad idea." He dragged his thumb across her lower lip.

Azure wanted to lean into him. To moan as he touched her, but she refrained. "You're right. It's a terrible idea." She started to back away.

"I can't stop thinking about you." He framed her face with both his hands, stopping her in her tracks.

She swallowed thickly.

"I can't stop thinking about us." He leaned in and brushed his mouth across hers ever so gently. "About kissing you... and so much more."

Her chest heaved. It was like she couldn't get enough air into her lungs... to her brain, which was short-circuiting. Ice *did* notice her. He *did* want her. He may have left with the human, but he didn't bring her back here. Ice wanted her. Not any of the humans. *Her!*

"Say yes... please. One night," he pleaded, his eyes on hers.

She nodded once. How could she refuse? One night, though? Just the one. Would it be enough?

It would have to be.

Ice picked her up and began to walk, taking long strides. Azure put her legs around his waist, rubbing herself against him shamelessly. His arms banded tightly around her. His chest was wide and hard. She slid her arms around his shoulders and kissed his neck. By now, she was panting a little. He tasted the same as he scented. Delicious! His body was hard, his shoulders broad. She wove her hands into his hair. Something she'd wanted to do so many times before. It was so soft and silky.

Still walking, Ice kissed her gently. He put her back to the door, fumbling. The key finally slid into the lock, the bolt slid free. Breaking the kiss, he opened the door, walking into the room. Ice kicked the door closed as he nipped at her earlobe. He gave an almost inaudible growl, and she felt it low in her belly, which tightened with need. Then his mouth was on hers again.

This time, their coming together was a violent clash as their mouths meshed. The need that unfurled inside scared her. She shoved her hands back into his hair as he pulled away. She tightened her grip, afraid he was going to stop.

Ice sucked in air through his nostrils. "Fuck, but you smell so good. I want you so badly." His breath was hot against her lips.

"I want… you… too." He put her down on the bed.

"I'm going to feast on that pretty pussy of yours," he growled.

Her clit throbbed. Azure knew what Ice could do with his mouth, his tongue, his hands.

Ice's nostrils flared. "I can't fucking wait to taste you again." He touched the hem of her top. "You're overdressed." His eyes were bright, almost glowing.

Azure pulled her top over her head while Ice unbuttoned her jeans. He leaned forward and sucked on one of her nipples. She felt a zing of need in her core. Her clit throbbed even harder. Azure let her head fall back and groaned.

"Been wanting to do that," Ice murmured, cupping both her breasts in his big, warm hands. "Been craving you," he muttered.

He had?

What?

Ice looked up. His eyes were filled with a hunger like she'd never seen before. She was pretty sure they matched her own.

Ice went onto his knees, and the bed dipped. He gripped her jeans in her hands and helped her take them off. When he put her legs down, he planted her feet on either side of him, so that she was wide open for him. Then he peeled off his shirt. Her mouth went dry in an instant. She'd seen him naked countless times, but this was something else. He still wore his jeans. His skin was bronzed. His chest, his broad shoulders, his biceps, all of it made her drink him in. She wanted him so damned badly.

For a few moments, he just looked at her and from the expression on his face, she could tell that he liked what he saw. Ice bit down on his lower lip, his teeth denting his flesh. He made this noise in the back of his throat as his eyes tracked over her.

His hot breath hit her clit a moment before his tongue laved her. Her back came off the bed and her eyes rolled. It felt better than when she was in heat, and that was saying something. His hot mouth closed over her sensitive nub and she all-out mewled, loving the suction action. Then his tongue laved her in steady, insistent strokes.

"Oh… oh gods." Her voice was so high-pitched that she didn't recognize it. Her back bowed, but his body kept her ass pinned in place. "That's good," she choked out. "So good." The sensation was all the more pronounced because she was unable to move away. Not that she wanted to. *Hells!*

His mouth closed over her clit for a second time as two fingers breached her opening. They hit the right spot from the word go, and the coiling sensation became a tight pull as everything seemed to stop for a split second. She was sure that her heart missed a beat. That everything in her paused just before the rush of her orgasm hit. She moaned, low and deep. His hand continued to pump, his mouth to suck.

He eventually slowed his movements, softened his touch, until he finally stopped. Her head fell back. Her hands released the sheets, which were bunched in her fingers.

"You're good at that," she finally managed to push out between ragged pants.

"I'm good at a lot of things." He gave her a cocky grin.

"You're especially good at being a hardass."

Instead of answering, Ice placed soft kisses on her belly, making his way back to her breasts. He worshipped both of them, going from one to the other. She moaned.

"You're plenty curvy. Your breasts are like soft, ripe peaches. Your nipples remind me of cherries. Firm and sweet." Ice looked up; his eyes had this feral look to them. His body tensed and a muscle in his jaw ticced. Ice looked angry. It definitely wasn't anger, though; it was desire… for her.

All for her.

Ice flipped her over onto her belly. "Is this okay?" he asked, his voice almost hesitant. "You tell me what you want. If you're not comfortable—"

"Of course this is okay… better than okay."

"You have one hell of an ass and I need to give both sides of you equal attention." His voice was gruff.

Her pussy was the perfect shade of pink. Her ass was tight. Who was he kidding? Everything about this female was amazing.

Using one hand to hold his cock, he clasped her hip with the other and positioned himself at her entrance. "Speak to me. I'm happy to stop at any time." He had to be careful after what happened with that fuckhead male, Skarn. The last thing he wanted was to scare her, or remind her in any way of what had gone down during her heat.

Azure turned, looking back over her shoulder. "I feel safe with you." *Thank fuck!*

He felt his Adam's apple work. Ice nodded once. "I'm glad." He pushed ever so gently against her opening and waited a few seconds. He needed to take it slow to begin with. The urge to protect this female rode him hard. Even if protecting her meant protecting her from himself.

Azure made a whimpering noise and pushed back against him. His balls pulled tighter. Her back bowed and her ass lifted higher.

Taking a deep breath, he pushed into her slowly. Her greedy sheath clutched him tightly. Her pussy sucked on him, so he pushed in another inch. *Fucking heaven!*

"Oh, by the gods," she choked out, her hands clutching at the sheets. She whimpered and panted. It sounded like she was enjoying it, but he needed to be sure.

"You good?" he managed to growl.

"Yes... great... I'm great. I want more." She was panting, and to his amazement, continued to push back at him, even rocking a little. Trying to take him deeper.

"I got you." He pushed in another inch before sliding back out. She whimpered as he thrust back in, deeper this time.

Slow and steady!

Slow and...

He groaned... *Fuck.* Her wet, velvet walls created the tightest friction he had ever experienced. His balls were already in his throat. Sweat dripped off of him as he tried to keep himself from coming. It had been a while for him. It was also her. This particular female.

Ice pushed in deeper, finally feeling his hips hit her tight as fuck ass. He paused, his breath was ragged but not from exertion.

"Yes!" Azure cried. "More!" Her hips rocked back.

Damn. He wasn't going to fucking last. Licking his fingers, Ice leaned over her, quickly finding the bundle of nerves nestled between her folds. He zoned in, using tight circles with the tip of his finger. Her pussy clenched around him and he moaned. *Holy fucking shit!*

Azure moaned as well. When he finally had it together enough, he began to thrust into her in deep, slow strokes. Her pussy spasmed around him almost immediately, and he had to grit his teeth. When her sheath clenched tight, he clamped his jaw even more. He felt how his neck muscles corded. Keeping his touch soft, he continued to fuck her hard.

Azure was making these noises that shot right to his cock. Her body made noises, too. Wet noises. Music to his ears... all of it.

Hold on!

Hold... on!

He strummed her clit faster, working to keep his touch gentle. He worked his cock in and out of her tight heat. Finally, he felt her pussy flutter and then tighten around him. Azure groaned deep. She rocked backward using jerky movements. As much as he wanted to make her come again, he didn't have the strength to hold back for much longer.

Her pussy walls stopped undulating so hard and her sheath tightened right up like a glove.

He could hardly move, she was so tight. Could hardly breathe as the first spasm of his orgasm hit. Within a second or two, pleasure was rushing through him, making him growl. Instinct took over as he clamped his mouth on her shoulder and bit down. Holding her in place. His hands closed on her hips.

Mine.

Blinding pleasure continued to course through him. He pinned her down, fucking her hard. Azure squirmed beneath him, screaming a cuss as her pussy released and clenched in time with another orgasm. Just when he thought he was done, another spurt of come left him. He growled fiercely as a final wave of pleasure rolled through him. He was shaking by the time he spent his last. He let her go... reeling.

What the fuck?

"What the...!" he mumbled. "Shit! Azure. Fuck!" He pulled out. She was flat on her stomach, panting hard.

He could see the mark his teeth had left. Ice had bitten her almost hard enough to draw blood. "I just... I... I got carried away."

"It's okay." Her voice was slightly slurred, her breath still coming in hard pants. "Don't worry. I know you didn't mean it like that."

"No. Not like that. Shit! I'm sorry." Biting was mating behavior. What the fuck had he been thinking? He hadn't been thinking at all. His blasted dragon. The fucker was pleased with itself.

Mine!

"I didn't hurt you or make you panic, or…?"

"Do I look panicked?" She turned onto her side. "I'm trying to bask in the afterglow and you're ruining it. Stop freaking out, already. It's okay… by all things scaled." She leveled him with a stare. "You've ruined it now."

Maybe it was better not to think about things so much. It looked like she was considering leaving, like she was looking for her clothes. He didn't like that so much. His dragon hated the idea. "Stay right where you are," he said. "I ruined the moment. I'll get you back there again."

She smiled, and something tightened inside him. "I doubt you'd be able to recreate that."

"Want to bet?"

"Oh, and what happened to no hands?"

Ice laughed. "It's been a while. I couldn't hold out. Looks like I have something to prove." Everything in him tightened. "Stay? Please."

Azure nodded once.

Ice grinned. *No overthinking.* He didn't want to ruin this. If he was honest with himself, he'd wanted this for a long time. Longer than he realized.

CHAPTER 25

"**W**HAT DID I tell you?" Fog smirked as soon as he caught a snoutful of her. "I was right!"

"Yes, you were right." She smiled, feeling warm all over. Last night was amazing. She couldn't get it out of her head. Couldn't get this smile off her face.

Fog did a double-take. "Wait a minute." He sniggered. "Is that what I think it is?" He pointed at her.

"Shhhhh." She looked around them.

"Oh, my god. It totally is, isn't it?" He narrowed his eyes on her neck before chuckling harder.

"Stop," Azure said under her breath.

He laughed. "Seriously?" He lifted his brows. "Are you telling me that—?"

"Don't!" she hissed as more and more of the males joined them. It was nearly time for them to leave. They were heading to the waiting SUVs to drive to a location where shifting and flying back would be less of a risk. "I should be saying the same to you, only for the opposite reason." She gave him a look. "What happened? I thought you liked that female you were talking to when I left." She could scent that he hadn't spent the night with anyone.

He shrugged. "She had a couple of nasty things to say about you after you left. I won't have some female diss one of my friends."

Azure smiled. "That's sweet. Thanks. You could've picked someone else."

"It was late. I was tired. I came back alone." He shrugged. "And you?" He lowered his voice. "*Is* that what I think it is?"

She widened her eyes and gave a shake of her head. "No, it's not."

"Sure looks like it to me."

"Drop it!" she hissed. Ice had just arrived. He stayed at the other end of the group, talking to Mist. The two of them hadn't discussed it, but she knew he wouldn't want word to get out that they'd spent the night together.

"What the hell happened to your neck, Azure?" one of the other males asked her, eyes narrowed. "That looks like..." He laughed. "Holy shit, I didn't realize that human males enjoyed biting." He laughed harder. "Does this mean you're mated to one?"

Azure gave him a dirty look. "No, it does not mean that at all. I wouldn't talk if I was you." She looked at the remnants of the hickey still on his neck.

The male continued to chuckle. "I guess you're right." He rubbed the spot on his skin. "Definitely not mated... no way! I'm still too young."

Ice had bitten her again… harder this time, leaving a definite mark that was still there this morning. He'd apologized again but didn't elaborate. Last night had been surreal. It had been amazing. What now, though? Was that it? Was it a one-time thing, as Ice had alluded to?

Maybe she shouldn't have left in the early hours of the morning. Azure hadn't wanted anyone seeing her leave his room. What if it had been a mistake to sneak out? They probably should have talked about the next step—or if there even was one—before jumping into bed together.

Azure snuck a glance his way, but Ice was still in conversation with Mist. Then they were piling into the vehicles and on their way. Ice was in one of the other vehicles. It was several hours before they arrived back at the lair. Ice kept his distance.

They eventually landed on the long, wide balcony, one by one shifting back into their human form.

Sun was there, waiting for them. He ran over to her before she could even pull her dress over her head. "He's here… Skarn is here. He arrived this morning."

"He's here?" Ice growled, stepping in next to her. "Where is he?" His eyes blazed.

"The male is with the healers."

"Healers? Why?" she asked.

"Skarn was in a bad way when one of the patrols found him. He walked most of the way here," Sun said, talking quickly.

"Walked?" Ice was frowning heavily. "Why would he have walked? That doesn't make sense. Couldn't he shift?"

"I heard he was battered and bleeding. There are guards posted outside his door. The Earth dragons are here, Granite included."

Her heart was beating fast. "I want to see him," Azure said.

"I'll go with you," Ice said, pulling a pair of pants on.

Azure nodded once before slipping her dress over her head. She smoothed her hair.

"I wonder what happened to him," Fog mused. "He's been missing for a week. That's a long time. I'll come too. I'd like to—"

"No!" both she and Ice said at once. They looked at one another, then Ice looked at Fog. "Stay out of it. We won't be able to gather any information if a whole crowd of us arrive there."

"The three of us are hardly a crowd, but," Fog nodded a couple of times, "that's okay. I'll leave it to the two of you."

"Find out all about it and give the rest of us the lowdown at work tomorrow." Sun's eyes were wide.

"This isn't something to gossip about at work." Ice kept his voice low. "Are the two of you middle-aged housewives or something?" Ice looked from Sun to Fog. Azure wasn't familiar with the term, but she could guess what it meant.

"No." Sun shook his head. "We're interested… that's all."

"Thanks for letting us know. The two of you should head home. I'll look after Azure," Ice said.

"Okay… fine with me." Sun put his hands up, stepping backward. "I know when I'm being dismissed." He grinned to show that he didn't mind.

Fog got this shit-eating grin. "I'm sure you will look after Azure," he said, before quickly adding, "Since you're her superior and all." If they'd been sitting at a table, she would've kicked Fog in the shins for those comments.

"Exactly," Ice growled, either oblivious to the undertones or choosing to ignore them.

The males left, leaving the balcony mostly empty. Ice's whole demeanor softened as he turned to her. "Are you okay?"

She nodded. "I'm fine." She forced a smile, her gut churning.

"Are you sure you want to see him?" Azure noticed how he bristled. His eyes narrowed and his jaw tightened.

"Yes."

Ice nodded once, his eyes locking with hers. "You shouldn't have left like that," he said under his breath, taking a small step towards her, closing most of the space between them.

"Are you saying I should've stayed?" She cocked her head. "Left after the sun came up?" She raised a brow. This was unexpected. She didn't want to get too hopeful, though. Didn't want to read into this too much.

"You shouldn't have snuck out." He shook his head. "You could've said goodbye."

"You were sleeping... snoring, actually."

He choked out a laugh. "I don't snore. I wouldn't have minded if you'd woken me up."

"You hadn't been sleeping for very long. I didn't want to disturb you."

"*You* disturb *me?* Not possible."

Her heart fluttered. By all that was scaled, this was headed in a direction she hadn't expected. Was he flirting with her? He was being kind... so incredibly sweet. He pulled in a breath. "Are you sure you don't want to wait until tomorrow to face this asshole?" His whole stance changed. His jaw tightened, and he seemed to grow taller.

"No. I want to get it over with."

"Okay, then." He nodded once. "I'm coming with you, Azure. Don't try to—"

"I could do with the company." She started reaching out to take his hand but stopped herself.

They began walking in the general direction of the healer's wing. "Why do you think he walked?" she asked.

"He probably couldn't shift."

"He must have been injured badly," she said.

"One can only hope." There was a growl in Ice's voice.

"I wonder what happened to him. Why they kept him so long?"

"I'm hoping torture was involved." Another growl.

"I have to say, there was a part of me that hoped he wouldn't come back. It makes me feel bad, and then feeling bad makes me feel like an idiot."

"You're not an idiot, you're a good person. I'm sorry he's back. The only reason I can find it in myself to be glad is so that he can be punished."

"I'm with you there," she said.

They arrived at the entrance to the healer's wing. There were two guards posted at the start of the wing. Azure could see more next to a door down the hallway. Whether it was to keep others out or Skarn in was unknown.

"Sorry." Both guards moved to block the entrance. From their markings, she could tell that they were Earth dragons. "No one is permitted to enter."

"We just—"

"No! I have my instructions," the male said.

"Who gave the instruction?"

"It came directly from our king... Granite. And until we're told otherwise, you may not enter this wing of the lair."

"That's ridiculous!" Ice pushed out.

"They have their orders." Azure touched the side of his arm.

"It's bullshit. They have no say since this isn't even their lair."

"Even if they let you through," a voice broke in as one of the males from down the hallway walked towards them. He was an Air dragon. "I wouldn't be permitted to let you into the room. Orders from Thunder. No one goes in, and no one comes out." He started back towards the door.

"What happened to him?" Ice asked the Air male.

"I'm not at liberty to say," he said, taking up his place at the door.

Ice looked back at the Earth male. "I don't know," the male said. "Even if I did, I wouldn't be permitted to discuss it."

Ice cussed softly as they walked away. "We're going to see the king, or Storm... anyone in the know. This is bull. You deserve to know what the hell is going on. You're a part of this. You were there when he was taken. That male must answer to you. He must answer for what he did."

She was shocked at the venom in his voice. It warmed her how angry he was on her behalf. They needed to talk, but the timing was all wrong. Azure didn't want to get her hopes up that there was now something between them. At the same time, it was at the forefront of her mind. She was anxious to ask him, but not right then. Perhaps later.

There was a multitude of guards when they arrived at the royal offices. Both Earth and Air guards lined the hall.

Just as before, two males stepped in front of them. "You may not enter," an Earth guard said.

"We need to see the king," Ice said.

"Nope. That's not going to happen. He and the Earth King are in the middle of a meeting."

"What about Storm?" Ice asked.

"He's in there too. I'm not sure how long they will be. Could go on all day." The male shrugged.

"Would I be able to leave a message for the prince? Azure was with the Earth male when he was taken. We want an update on the situation," Ice asked the guard.

"Who are you to this female?"

"Her name is Azure." There was a menacing edge to Ice's voice. "I am her direct superior. And as such, I'm responsible for her wellbeing."

Direct superior. *Ouch!* He could've said he was her friend.

"We'll come back later... or tomorrow morning," Azure said. "It's not like anyone is going anywhere. It can wait."

Ice finally nodded once, and they turned to leave. "I'll walk you to your chamber," he muttered.

They walked in silence. Azure wanted to bring up their relationship, but something held her back. Something told her that if she pushed, she might lose what little they had before it was anything. Besides, she'd decided to stop chasing

Ice. It was up to him now. If he wanted her, he could make his intentions clear, and if not, then that was his loss.

Her phone started ringing. She fished it out of the side pocket of her overnight bag. The caller ID told her it was Melina. "Hey." Azure smiled.

"Hi! Where are you? I'm outside your door. There's lots to talk about."

"We got delayed," Azure said. "We had to make a detour after arriving back."

"We?" Melina drew out the word, clearly intrigued.

"Ice and me. He was… helping me with something."

"Helping? Sounds interesting…" Melina paused, and Azure prayed she wouldn't say anything since Ice would be able to hear. "I see. No problem. I wanted to see how you were after your trip, but if you're busy—"

They rounded the corner to her section of the lair, and there was Melina, standing outside Azure's door. Mel grinned and waved at them. She put her phone away, and Azure did the same. Azure found herself grinning right back. It was nice to see the human.

They closed the distance. "I'm so sorry. I'm intruding. I'll just…" Melina started backtracking. "I thought I would… I can go if—"

"Don't go on account of me," Ice said. "I'm headed for home." He gestured down the hallway. "I wanted to walk Azure to her chamber. Are you going to be okay?" he asked Azure, their eyes locking.

"Of course."

He narrowed his eyes on hers. "You won't be afraid or…"

"No. They're guarding Skarn. He's not going anywhere," Azure said, looking at Melina. "That's where we just came from, but they wouldn't let us see him," she told the other female. "The kings are in some sort of meeting, so they wouldn't see us. We heard Skarn had to walk here. That he was pretty beat up." She shrugged.

"That ties into with what Freeze heard from a buddy of his. His friend was one of the guards on patrol who found Skarn," Melina said, looking up and down the hallway.

"What did he say?" Ice asked.

"This stays between us," Melina spoke under her breath. "This buddy of Freeze's was given instructions not to say anything to anyone. He broke a direct order by telling Freeze."

"Of course we won't say anything," Azure said.

Melina's eyes widened. "They're saying that his wings had been cut off."

"What?" Azure asked, her eyes wide. "He didn't have wings?"

"No wings." Mel shook her head. "That's why he had to walk. His back was a torn-up mess, even in his human form. His feet were blistered and bleeding, so it all points to it."

"Holy shit!" Ice muttered. "Who the fuck would do such a thing? Cut a dragon's wings off... He did deserve it," he muttered the last.

"Did Skarn say anything after they found him?" Azure asked.

"The guy was too out of it to talk. They spotted him collapsed in a ravine nearby. He didn't regain consciousness. That's if the rumors are to be believed. Freeze says that his friend can be trusted."

"It makes sense," Ice rasped, still deep in thought. "Hopefully, we'll find out more tomorrow. Let me know if you need anything," he told Azure. "I mean it."

She nodded. "I'll be fine. Thanks."

"I'll see you tomorrow?"

Azure nodded again. "I had a good time. Thanks."

His mouth went up at the corners but didn't quite form a smile. "Me too." He looked at Melina. "Good to see you. I'm glad that Azure has such a good friend."

"That she does," Melina said.

They said their goodbyes and watched as he walked away. Melina widened her eyes but thankfully didn't say anything until they were inside. "You guys totally did it," she blurted as soon as the door clicked shut. "Don't even try to deny it. You did the deed."

Azure bit down on her lip for a second. "We did."

Melina gave a soft shriek, jumping up and down a few times. "I knew it. I could see it from a mile away. There was so much chemistry between the two of you."

"Oh, no! Is it that obvious?" Azure made a face.

"To me, it is." Melina nodded.

"Don't get too excited." Azure held up a hand. "I think it might have been a one-time thing."

"It wasn't." The other female shook her head. "He was alluding to wanting to stay with you tonight."

"No, he wasn't." Azure shook her head.

"He so was. *Are you sure you're going to be okay? You won't be frightened all on your own in this big lair?*" Melina put on a fake voice. "*I'll walk you to your chamber so that you can invite me in for lots of hardcore sex.*" Melina laughed. "That's what he was hoping for. You didn't get those huge hints?"

"No… just no. That's not it at all." Azure tucked some hair behind her ear.

"Of course, it is! You're really not good at any of this.

He's totally into you. He was hoping you would invite him in. Or that maybe you'll call him and invite him after I go. He left a door open for you with all of that 'are you sure you'll be okay' nonsense."

"Do you think so? Maybe he was genuinely checking if I was alright. He might not have had ulterior motives."

Melina sniggered. "Oh, that man had some serious ulterior motives. If I hadn't been here, he would've made his intentions far clearer."

Could it be? Had Ice hoped to spend more time with her?

"How was it, by the way? The sex," Melina whispered the last. "Was it everything you thought it would be?"

"Yes," Azure said the word softly. She nodded. "It was amazing." She closed her eyes for a few seconds. "Everything I thought it would be and more."

"Oh, thank god!" Mel held her chest dramatically. "Sometimes, when we build something up in our minds, it can be a huge letdown. That wasn't the case with you guys." She was grinning, almost more excited than Azure herself.

"It wasn't a letdown at all, not even close. The opposite is true. We also talked. It was so easy to be with him. The only problem is that I'm falling for him even harder than before, and…" She shrugged. "I have no idea how he feels about me. I know he's attracted to me. I don't know if he sees me as more, though. This might be a fun weekend for him and nothing more. That's what I'm used to from dragon males."

"I think he does see it as more. He wouldn't have gone with you to find out about Skarn. He seems to genuinely care."

"He told the guards he was there in his capacity as my superior."

Melina snorted. "Don't listen to what he tells the guards. It's how he looks at you. How he talks to you."

"You're right. I need to relax and see how things unfold." Azure pulled in a deep breath.

"Exactly. Try not to get too inside your own head. Just go with it. Have some fun. You can start by messaging Ice to tell him you're feeling nervous all on your own."

Azure rolled her eyes. "I'm not doing that. I promised myself I wasn't going to run after him. I'm sticking to it."

"You wouldn't be running after him after he left you all of those hints. Give him a hint right back. I'm willing to bet my salon and this ring that he'll come running." She held up her hand and a radiant ring sparkled.

"Maybe. I'll give it some— Wait just a minute." Azure grabbed Mel's hand. "You accepted Freeze's proposal?"

Melina was smiling broadly. She nodded once, her eyes glinting. "I did indeed."

It was Azure's turn to shriek and jump up and down. "I'm so happy for you. For both of you." She hugged the human. "I'm sure Freeze was thrilled."

"He was so thrilled he nipped me when we had celebration sex," Melina confided. "Oh my god, it was the best freaking orgasm I've ever had."

"Oh, so he's never bitten you before?" she blurted, feeling a little shocked.

"No, that's reserved for mates. You know that." Melina shook her head. "Apparently, when he really bites me—I'm talking hard enough to leave a mark—it's going to be next level. I can't imagine it being better than it was last night. I couldn't talk for several minutes afterward."

Azure nodded. "So I've heard," she mumbled. *Heard!*

Azure hadn't just heard, she'd experienced it first-hand. Ice had been adamant that he hadn't meant it in that way. He'd looked so shell-shocked she'd believed him. Although she knew it was reserved for mates. They both did. Every dragon knew. Casual rutting never involved biting. It wasn't done. Freeze and Mel were living together. They were serious about each other, and yet he'd only nipped her for the first time last night. Azure shouldn't be so shocked. She knew all of this, but still…

"I'm going to get out of your hair," Melina said. "I wanted to fill you in about Skarn and check to see how your weekend went."

"Thanks. I appreciate it." Azure still hadn't heard anything from Summer. Not a word. It amazed her how the world worked sometimes. How those you thought were your friends don't end up being friends at all, and people you never thought you'd get along with end up being intrinsically woven into the fabric of your life.

"You should call that hunk of a man. Tell him how afraid you are and that you're not sure you can spend the night alone."

Azure choked out a laugh, giving Melina a fake dirty look. "I'm not doing it!"

"You should," Mel said as she walked to the front door.

"No! You taught me that males enjoy the hunt… the chase."

Melina laughed. "I did say that. Like I said, you're my best student. You're probably right."

Azure snort-laughed. "I'm your only student, and I'm definitely right."

CHAPTER 26

I CE COULD NOT get Azure off his mind.

Despite flying for hours earlier that day, he was still buzzing with energy. He tried working out to release some of it, taking a long shower afterward. Then he sharpened his hunting knives. Short of going back out for another long, hard flight, he was at a loose end. He paced outside on his balcony, not sure of what to do.

Last night had gone by so quickly. He'd told himself it would just be that once. One night and then back to work as usual on Monday, but he'd been kidding himself.

When he'd woken up to find her gone, he'd been strangely disappointed. It was the wrong emotion to have. He should have felt relieved that one of them was thinking straight. Neither of them wanted their relationship to get out at this point.

Relationship?

Holy fucking shit!
Is that what this was?

Ice jumped up. *Fuck!* He raked a hand through his hair. His dragon wanted him to go to her. He felt unsettled... off-kilter. He wondered if she was feeling it, too.

Ice grabbed his cellphone and texted Azure.

Ice: Can I come over? I think we need to talk.

Ice checked his phone a hundred fucking times over the next half hour. Nothing! Not a thing. Maybe she was with her human friend. What if she was ignoring him? He'd bitten her... twice. He'd left a temporary mark. Maybe he'd scared her off. He'd sure as shit scared himself a whole lot.

Like an asshole, he checked his phone again. Still nothing. Patience had never been one of his strong suits. They needed to talk. He didn't want to wait until tomorrow, but he also didn't want to intrude on her personal space.

Fuck it!

With a low growl, he grabbed his phone and left his chamber. It didn't take him more than a few minutes to get to Azure's place.

There was no one in the hallway. It was now or never.

His phone finally beeped with an incoming message. He checked, disappointed when he saw that it was from his mother, asking if he had met anyone on the weekend.

Not now, Mom, he thought to himself, making a mental note to call her in the morning.

Decision made, Ice turned his phone off and knocked on Azure's door. He was just about to knock a second time a few moments later when the door opened.

There she was. "Ice?" She looked shocked... that and beautiful. Her hair was piled on top of her head in a messy, slightly lopsided bun. She had a towel wrapped around her, with soapsuds on her shoulders and a small sud on her chin. Cute as fuck. "I thought you were ignoring me."

"Ignoring you...?" She frowned. "I wouldn't ignore you."

"Good to know. Are you going to invite me in?"

Her mouth twitched. "Yeah... sure. I was just taking a bath." She moved to the side so that he could walk into her chamber. Her eyes dipped to his cock as he walked past her. They flared with both shock and excitement as they landed on his crotch. He caught a snoutful of her arousal. Right then, he went from having a semi to balls in his throat and fully erect. His pants were tented.

"A bath sounds good." He closed the distance between them, taking her mouth. Damn, but she tasted sweet.

Azure dug her hands into his hair. She made this little sound at the back of her throat. He felt her towel land at their feet. "Don't let me stop you," he whispered against her lips. "I could wash your back."

"I didn't think it was my back you were hoping to wash."

He laughed. "I want to wash you all over... after I fuck you," he growled.

The scent of her arousal went up a notch. "Sounds like my kind of bath."

He picked her up. Azure wrapped her legs around his waist. He kissed her softly on her gorgeous mouth.

"We're really going to do it in the tub?" She had this sexy smile on her lips. Excitement lit her eyes.

"Oh, yes." He nodded, walking into the bathroom. There were several candles lit, and the lighting was set to dim. "Did you know I was on my way?"

She giggled. "No, smartass, this is how I often take a bath. The foam bath was a gift from Melina. I normally just do candles. I love a good soak. It relaxes me."

"I didn't know that about you." There was a whole lot he didn't know. "I do know something else that is said to relax a female."

"Oh, really now?" She giggled.

He put her down next to the large tub. Ice noted that the water was about two-thirds of the way, with a crap ton of bubbles. He dropped his pants and got in first, holding a hand out to her. Azure took his hand and climbed in. Ice sat back, loving the feel of the warm, soapy water.

Azure didn't waste any time straddling his hips. She groaned as her sex connected with his cock. The way she slipped all over him told him how needy she was.

Ice leaned back further, making more space for her. He kept his hands firmly on her hips.

Azure dragged her pussy along the length of him, making him grunt. "Are you sure this will work?" She looked around them. "This tub isn't all that big."

"It'll work just fine." He narrowed his eyes. "Have you never had sex in the tub before?"

She shook her head.

"We need to fix that, and any other injustices. Rutting underwater feels fucking amazing. I have the added bonus of watching you slide all over my dick while wet and soapy. Doesn't get much better than that." He leaned in, taking one of her nipples in his mouth.

Azure groaned and arched into him. Receptive, beautiful, sweet, kickass. She was everything a male could ask for.

"I think I like it already," Azure groaned.

"You're beautiful," he murmured as he pulled back, looking up at her.

"You're not so bad yourself. Your eyes are the bluest blue." She leaned her forehead against his shoulder and shook with laughter. "That was the lamest compliment ever."

"No, it wasn't," he countered.

"It was." She let her hands glide down to his biceps, still smiling. Her face was pink-tinged. He loved the sincerity of her compliment, fucking loved the way her eyes ate him up, looking hungry and desire-filled.

Ice let his hand sink below the soapy water. He zoned in on her clit using firm, tight strokes that had her moaning hard from the word go. Then he plunged a finger inside her, and she arched against him, trying to rock her hips. She gripped him tightly around his shoulders and panted like a woman possessed.

"You're so perfect," he whispered. She arched her back, rocking against his hand, her mouth slightly open, soap suds dripping down her chest. By the gods, she was magnificent. Her nipples were tight pink nubs.

"You too," she groaned.

"Fuck!" he ground out as her hand circled his cock. He pumped his finger in and out of her, using his thumb to rub on her clit at the same time. Azure moaned. "You ready for me?" he asked, his voice a deep rasp. Any more of this, and he'd come too early.

"Yes." Her voice was husky. Her hand still palming him, she guided his cock into her snug heat.

Ice couldn't help but groan as he breached her very tight opening. Azure felt perfect… so right… so damned incredible. Her wet, velvet sheath devoured him. Leaving him aching to come from the word go. "You feel so fucking good, Azure."

"I'm embarrassed to say that I won't last very long," she groaned as she bounced on his cock, still slow and careful. Not quite… not… almost… he hissed as she pushed herself all the way onto him, right to the hilt. He gripped her hips a little tighter.

They sat like that for the longest time. Panting, Azure finally started moving. It was a beautiful thing to behold. To see the pleasure on her face, in her eyes. He thrust up into her from below, unable to stay still. He fucked her using hard, even strokes. She gave back as good as she got.

Ice snarled as he lifted her slightly, putting her in a better position to rut her from below. Azure threw her head back, taking hold of each side of the tub. Her jaw was slack as he pulled out.

"I thought you wanted me to slip and slide on your cock," she moaned. "I'm supposed to be the one doing the work."

"Rutting is a joint effort." Her breasts bounced with each thrust. So fucking sexy, he felt his sack tighten. Her hair was slowly loosening from the bun; more and more strands fell around her face, which was flushed with pleasure.

"Oh… oh… Ice…" she moaned as her pussy tightened around his dick. He loved hearing his name on her lips. Loved how she watched him. "I'm… I'm… going… to…" She bounced harder, taking him deeper.

"Do it!" he groaned out, barely holding on. It wasn't like him to come this easily. She shouted his name, drawing it out as her channel held him, so damned tight that his eyes actually watered with the intensity of his orgasm.

He wanted to shout her name as well, but he couldn't. He had to grit his teeth and work hard at not losing control. His dragon wanted him to bite her again.

Bite!

Mark.

Mine!

No!

Fuck no!

His orgasm exploded through him. Azure kept bouncing, and he kept thrusting until they were both spent. Then she leaned forward on his chest, panting hard. "We made a mess," she finally said, pulling back. There was a smile on her face. It was almost a mile wide.

"What do you mean? We're in the bath. How could we make a mess?" His dick stayed hard inside her. Throbbing, wanting more.

She giggled, looking over the side of the bath, pulling off of him as she did. Ice followed suit, and sure enough, the floor was covered with soapy water.

"Oh, shit." He grinned.

"There's more water on the floor than in the tub." She laughed.

"It's ridiculous." He laughed as well.

"So much for washing me." She quirked a brow.

"We'll just have to move to the shower."

Azure sucked in a breath; she looked down at him, her eyes hooded.

"Don't tell me you've never had sex in a shower?"

"Never." She shook her head slowly.

"We need to rectify that as a matter of extreme urgency." He stood, taking her with him.

"What about the floor?" she asked as they stepped out of the tub onto the soaked bathmat.

"We'll get to that a little later… On our hands and knees."

She giggled. "I somehow doubt we'll get anything clean that way."

"We'll get it clean, alright." He grinned at her. "Then I'll cook you dinner."

"Sounds amazing."

They needed to talk at some point, but not tonight. Ice had no idea what this was or where it was going, but right now, all he wanted to do was enjoy the moment.

CHAPTER 27

A ZURE SAT UPRIGHT in bed. Her alarm was blaring. She was tired and a little sore.

Sore!

Everything came rushing back to her. The sex, the conversation, more sex… dinner, followed by even more great sex. They finally ended up in her bed, exhausted.

She sucked in a breath as she looked next to her. The bed was empty. That meant that Ice had snuck out at some point… but oh, how sweet! There was a rose on her pillow. A rose made out of paper. Simple but effective. She picked it up. Ice had gone to the trouble to make this for her. Last night didn't feel like a quick rut, either. It felt like something more. This silly little paper rose felt like something more, too. Azure smiled. She'd thought about asking him where they were headed, but their relationship seemed a little fragile right now. Like this rose. Something that could easily go in either direction. Try to put pressure on what they had, and it could be crushed before it had a chance to develop.

Azure checked her phone. She had several messages. One from Mel, one from Storm, and two from Ice.

The first one from Ice was when he was asking if he could come over. She grinned. He'd sent the text before he'd come by yesterday.

Then there was one from Melina, wanting to know if Azure had messaged Ice. If they had spent another night together. Azure chuckled to herself. If only her friend knew.

Then the one from Storm had her sobering right up. He wanted to see her and Ice first thing this morning.

The last one was from Ice wanting to know if she'd gotten the message from Storm.

Shit! Throwing the covers off herself, she jumped out of bed, dashing for the shower. A few minutes later and she was throwing on a dress. Her hair was still wet, but it would have to do. Their meeting was in ten minutes.

There was a knock at the door just as she was grabbing a banana. "Coming!" she yelled.

"Hey," Ice said as she opened the door. "I wasn't sure you'd seen the message from Storm."

"I… um…"

Ice kissed her. A quick brush of the lips. "Sorry, I didn't say good morning," he said as he pulled back.

"Morning." She smiled. His mouth was an inch or two away, and so she kissed him again. *Oh, shit! Shit!* She was falling hard. So darned hard, it was scary and wonderful. "I got the message."

He pulled away. "Are you ready to go?"

She nodded. "I was on my way out when you knocked."

They walked out into the hallway. "At least we'll get some answers," Ice said.

"I hope so. I just want to see him and then never think of his sorry ass again," she said.

"I want to punch him in the face a couple of times, maybe break a rib or two... hell, I'd like to skin that bastard alive. Gut him while I'm at it. Then, yeah, we wouldn't have to think of that bastard again."

"Hang him on a hook and finish the job those creatures started," she added. "I'll take an apology over all of that stuff. After that, the Earth dragons can decide what to do with him." She shrugged.

"I hope it involves bleeding and screaming," Ice muttered.

"Thanks for coming with me. I'm glad I don't have to be alone."

"Anytime." He took her hand and squeezed it for a second before letting go. "I have to attend as your superior."

"Oh... of course." She nodded a couple of times, feeling like an idiot.

"I'm not just here as your superior, though. You know that, right?"

"Yes... thanks." She smiled. Her mouth felt a little dry. Nerves made her stomach feel like she'd swallowed a rock. She could see Storm's office up ahead. They were right on time. She wondered if Skarn was in there now. Azure hoped so; the sooner she faced the male, the sooner she could put the whole incident behind her.

"Ready?" Ice put a hand to her back.

"Yes." She was as ready as she'd ever be. Azure squared her shoulders.

"Let's do this." He knocked on Storm's door.

The prince called for them to enter. Storm was sitting behind his desk. As usual, he wore a suit and tie. He stood for a moment, gesturing to some chairs. "Please sit."

Azure noted that Skarn wasn't there. They did as the male asked.

"I'm sure you will have heard that Skarn was picked up by one of our patrols yesterday morning."

"We heard," Ice said.

Azure nodded once.

"The male was unconscious and bleeding. He had been walking for over thirty hours. He was dehydrated, his feet were blistered and bleeding…" Storm pushed his fingers into the corners of his eyes. "Worst of all, his wings had been hacked from his body."

"Where is he?" Ice asked.

"We're getting to that," Storm said.

"Who took him in the first place?" she asked.

"Blaze, Granite, and Thunder met late yesterday afternoon," Storm went on without answering her question.

"We're aware," Ice said. "We tried to meet with you but were turned away. We'd heard that Skarn was back."

"My guards informed me that you tried to meet with the Earth male in the infirmary. Skarn was able to tell us some of what he went through. He was able to give information on the beings that took him. The kings have decided that most of the information is need-to-know at this stage."

Ice narrowed his eyes. "What does that mean exactly?"

"Some of the information will not be shared with the tribe. In fact, most of the information will be kept a secret. Information on these creatures. Information on what transpired in those caves. It is important that you know that Skarn suffered greatly during his incarceration."

"Good," Ice growled.

"His wings were removed on the day they captured him." Storm picked up a gold pen, rolling it between his fingers.

Azure frowned. "That doesn't make sense. Did they use silver? His wings would have grown back after a day or two, yet he was found wingless a week later." She spoke almost to herself. Thinking out loud.

"His wings did grow back," Storm said. "The creatures didn't use silver. They hacked Skarn's wings off. They threw him in a pitch-black room in the bowels of the earth. He was questioned relentlessly for hours at a time, over several days. We believe that they had indeed scented your heat. That is what drew them to the heat cave. What drew them to you," Storm told her. "Once they were convinced that you had left, they decided to take Skarn for questioning."

"You don't plan on telling anyone about what happened? Why it happened? Who the perpetrators were?" Ice's voice was animated.

"The Water King will be informed, of course."

"These creatures could be planning a war against us," Ice continued.

"We don't believe that it is the case. We don't want to cause unnecessary fear among the tribes. The royals and second in commands will be informed. Only those who need to know. It's *not* something you should concern yourselves with, I assure you," Storm told Ice, still playing with the pen.

Ice's jaw was tight. "With all due respect, let us be the judge of that."

"It's out of my hands. I have been given my orders." Storm shrugged.

Ice's eyes were blazing. "What about a suitable punishment for the male? At the very least, he needs to apologize to Azure for what he tried to do to her."

"Skarn is an Earth dragon. It was up to Granite to decide. The Earth King feels that Skarn suffered enough. That—"

"What?" Ice snarled.

"He had his wings cut from his body twice. Do you have any idea how painful that is?"

"Not painful enough," Ice growled.

"I want to see him," Azure said.

Storm looked at the big, gold watch on his wrist. "The Earth dragons left twenty minutes ago. They took Skarn with them."

Ice jumped to his feet; the chair he had been sitting on clattered to the floor behind him. "That's unacceptable!" he growled. His eyes were narrowed and glowing. His hands tightly fisted.

"Watch your tone and sit down," Storm growled.

"Azure wanted to talk to the male," Ice said. "It was her one request."

"Granite felt that—" Storm started to say.

"What about Azure's feelings? Does she have no say

in any of this? That asshole tried to force himself on her. If she wasn't the strong, resourceful female that she is, he would have raped her. Do you comprehend that reality?"

"Don't speak to me like I'm a child. I know what Skarn did. I'm fully aware of what happened."

"Yes, but can you comprehend what it is that he did? I'm not talking about the facts here," she said, her voice shaking. "Have you ever felt weak and afraid? Like your voice or your opinion didn't count? Small, powerless, defenseless. Have you ever felt voiceless?" She knew full well that the male had never felt any of those things. Not for one minute. None of the other kings had either, for that matter.

Storm squirmed in his seat. She could see him trying to come up with something to say and failing.

"I didn't think so. What if it had been one of your sisters? What if Skarn had tried to force himself on one of them?"

Storm growled low in his throat, dropping the pen on the table with a clatter.

"Exactly," Ice said.

She put her hand on Ice's arm to calm him down. "At the very least, I wanted an apology from the male."

"The Earth dragons chose to take him back."

"You didn't fight hard enough for one of your own." Ice was struggling to keep his decorum. "Thunder should have. You should have."

"I'm so disappointed." Azure's voice hitched as she spoke. She felt a lump rise in her throat. She wasn't sure why this was so important. No, that wasn't true. She needed the male to know that what he had done wasn't right. She needed him to understand that. Somehow, she didn't think he did, which meant that he might hurt someone else in the future. That was her fear.

"That's it then?" Ice's voice was deep and hard. "There will be no more mention of this, and that prick will get away with it?"

"I'm sorry." Storm really did look apologetic. Azure almost felt sorry for him.

"Not good enough!" Ice snarled.

Azure took Ice's arm. "Leave it," she told him. He was going to get himself in big trouble. "Let's go. We need to get to work." She pulled on his arm.

By now, Storm was standing, and he and Ice were having a stare-down. She could feel Ice shaking with rage.

Azure sighed with relief when she managed to finally pull Ice away. The door was slightly ajar. She kept tugging at him until they were finally outside in the hallway. Azure shut the door. "It's fucking unacceptable," Ice growled as soon as they were outside.

Two guards were standing there. "Hi, Azure," one of the males said.

"Oh, hi, Cirrus." She recognized him because he and Summer hung out together on and off.

"How are you?" Cirrus asked, frowning.

"Doing okay," she mumbled, not really wanting to engage in conversation. "How is Summer?" It was something she had been wondering since she hadn't heard from the other female since the day Summer closed the door in Azure's face. It felt like a long time ago, even though it wasn't.

"Fine. I'm seeing her tomorrow evening, actually. I will tell her I saw you."

Azure nodded once. They said quick goodbyes.

The other male inclined his head as she and Ice walked past. They walked in silence for a minute or two.

"The information is going to be kept from us on a 'need-to-know' basis?" Ice growled, still clearly pissed off.

"What was that all about?" she asked. It wasn't adding up. Why not just tell the tribes exactly what was going on? Why all the need for secrecy?

"I don't know. I don't like it. I don't like any of it." He turned to face her, taking both her hands. "Are you okay?" His whole demeanor softened.

She nodded.

"Are you sure, Azure? You're not just saying that. I don't mind if you take the day off. Heck, take a couple of days. I'm going to put a formal complaint in about this. If those—"

"Don't." She shook her head. "Thank you for everything—for caring so much. But I don't want to drag this out. I want to put the whole thing behind me. I want to look to the future. I want to be happy, and I won't be able to do that if I'm looking back."

"You're right." Ice gave her the sexiest half-smile. He let her hands go. "Sexy, resourceful, *and* highly intelligent."

"How did you get so lucky?" she blurted, wanting to bite her tongue the instant the words were out.

Ice choked out a laugh. For a second, he looked like he was going to say something, but thought better of it. He finally said, "We'd better get going. The others will be waiting."

It wasn't exactly the reaction she'd been hoping for.

CHAPTER 28

The next day…

WINGS AND THINGS was pretty busy for a weeknight, Azure thought to herself as she looked around the restaurant/bar. It was situated in a large part of the lair overlooking the ocean. "I'll buy the next round," Fog shouted. "Is everyone having the same as before?"

Avalanche grunted. "Don't forget the umbrella."

They all laughed.

"I can't believe you're drinking a piña colada, dude," Sun said between chuckles.

"I like them," Avalanche announced. "Coconutty pineapple goodness." He licked his lips and pushed an empty cocktail glass away.

"Actually, I think I'll try one, too," Azure said, still smiling.

"You too, now?" Fog rolled his eyes, shaking his head. "I'll have another beer, since you offered," Ice said.

"Me, too," Sun added, putting his empty bottle down with a bang as Fog walked away. "Thanks, bro," he shouted after him. They continued to talk about work for a few minutes.

Then Sun piped up, "You haven't told us anything about how the stag run went, Ice. You're being quiet about it."

"I'm always quiet about things that are my personal business," Ice said. They sat around a large table in the bar section of the restaurant. There were empty plates to the side, since they'd just finished eating. The team sometimes had dinner together. This was nothing unusual.

"Don't be like that," Sun pushed. "I know you spent the night with someone. Just like I know Fog was a pussy and wasted a perfectly good stag run by sleeping alone. Such a fucking waste."

"Again," Ice's voice dropped by a few octaves, "none of your fucking business. How is your mom doing?"

Sun's shoulders dipped. "Much better. It's been nearly eight months since my dad passed away. It seems to be getting easier for her. I must go and visit her again soon."

"I need to visit my mom, as well," Ice muttered.

"Did somebody say piña colada?" Fog laughed as he deposited a tray on the table. "I organized two umbrellas for you, Avalanche."

"Thanks, bro." The male grabbed his drink and started slurping.

"Hey, Ice, I thought I heard your voice." *Crap with scales!* It was Crystal. The she-dragon pulled up a chair and sat down next to Ice without asking if she could join them. *Damned rude,* Azure thought. Crystal didn't even greet the rest of them. "How have you been?" the female asked, eyes firmly on Ice. She wore a tight blue dress. It wasn't their usual garb, but something she must have ordered from a catalog, like Melina did. The dress suited the she-dragon. Her fiery red hair cascaded around her shoulders. No wonder she was so popular with the males. Aside from being fertile, she was gorgeous.

"I'm good." Ice glanced her way before looking back at Crystal.

"I've been missing you lately," the she-dragon sighed. "You stopped calling a couple of months ago."

"Yeah, well—" Ice started to say.

"How's your drink?" Fog asked Azure, pulling her attention to him instead of the conversation going on across from her.

"Um…" She hadn't even tried it yet.

"Ignore them," he said under his breath. "Try it!" he urged her, pushing her cocktail closer. Azure took a sip, not tasting much of anything. Crystal had pulled her chair up right next to Ice.

"How is work?" the redhead asked, leaning in so close that she might as well get on his lap.

Argh! It was annoying.

"Your eyes are glowing," Fog said. "Are you two still…?" He widened his eyes.

She nodded.

"Interesting. He's not into her," Fog whispered. "Not even a little bit. Keeps giving her one-word answers. He's not biting." He winked at her. "I wouldn't worry."

Crystal put her hand on Ice's leg.

Fog laughed. "Chill," he warned. "You just growled."

"Do you blame me?" she whispered back. "I'm feeling…" She shook her head.

"Possessive?"

"That wasn't the first word that came to mind, but…" She nodded.

"Jealous?" Fog lifted a brow.

"Both," she muttered, feeling irritated with herself. Ice didn't owe her anything. He hadn't made any promises. She needed to do what Fog had suggested and chill. Easier said than done when a gorgeous and very fertile she-dragon was all over Ice. Not to mention that the two of them had a history.

"So, it's serious, then?" Fog asked. "It looks like it is for you."

Azure didn't say anything. She didn't have to.

Across the table, Ice was shaking his head at Crystal. "Why would we want to leave? We're having a good time right here," Azure heard him say.

By all that was scaled, the female was trying to get Ice to leave with her. Azure's scales rubbed so hard she was sure she could hear them under her skin. Her teeth felt sharper, too. She wanted to rip out the other female's gorgeous locks. Maybe gouge out her eyes while she was at it.

"We'll stay. I'll order a drink," Crystal purred. "I see you're hanging out with your work friends." The female exaggerated the word 'friends.'

Azure's phone vibrated on the table. She noticed that Ice had his phone in his hand, that he was watching her.

She checked her messages.

Ice: Want to get out of here?

She bit back a smile.

Azure: I'd love to, but we just got our drinks.

He typed back, ignoring something Crystal was saying.

Ice: Forget the drinks. It's suddenly become a little crowded at our table.

Azure: That so?

Ice: Most definitely. I'm not sure what I ever saw in her.

Azure bit back the biggest grin as her phone vibrated again straight away.

Ice: You leave first. Give me two minutes, and I'll be right behind you.

Azure: If we both leave before we finish our drinks, they'll know.

"Who are you messaging?" Crystal whined, looking put out. The female was pouting.

"No one you know," Ice muttered.

It was true; even though they were sitting at the same table, Crystal didn't know who Azure was at all.

Azure: I'm game! They'll totally know, but I don't care.

She hesitated and then pushed "send" anyway.

Ice's mouth twitched. He picked up his beer and downed half of it in one go, making her want to laugh.

Azure took a sip of her drink. She made a face. "I'm not sure I like this piña whatever it's called."

"What?" Avalanche looked at her like she'd lost her ever-loving mind. "You can't be serious!"

"Maybe they made mine wrong?" she suggested.

"Let me try it." Avalanche grabbed her glass and took a sip. "It's delicious." Now he was looking at her like she'd suddenly sprouted a second nose.

"You keep it," she told him. "It's too sweet and far too creamy."

His eyes lit up. "Don't mind if I do." He slid her glass next to his half-empty one.

Crystal continued to talk to Ice, oblivious to the fact that he wasn't really listening. The female sat so close to him that their thighs had to be touching under the table. There was nowhere for Ice to go. He'd moved his chair as far away from her as he could.

Azure: Let's do this.

"Can I get you something else?" Fog asked her, looking concerned.

"No, thanks." She smiled at him. "I really appreciate the offer, but I'm tired. I think I'm going to head on home." She touched the side of his arm, feeling bad.

"No." Fog was looking at her like she'd just broken his heart. "Stay a little longer. One more drink."

"I can't. I'll see you all tomorrow. Have a lovely evening," she said, noting that Crystal didn't even look at her. "Enjoy the drink," she told Avalanche, who showed her two thumbs up.

They all said their goodbyes, and Azure left. It couldn't have been more than a minute later, and someone put their hand to her back. "I was trying to think of an excuse to leave when Crystal showed up."

"She's really pretty. Love her red hair."

"Pretty is an accurate description of Crystal. She's pretty shallow and pretty self-centered. Pretty annoying would be on the top of my list." Ice looked irritated.

"You seemed like you were quite close at one stage. I must say, I was surprised when you stopped seeing each other."

"Crystal isn't my type. My mother introduced us. I was taken by her looks for a while, but," he shrugged, "there's not much to her. Not much substance."

"She's a little rude."

"She considers most people to be beneath her." Ice shook his head.

"She should watch her step," Azure said. "I know that she is very fertile, and that she gets heats often, but with this Kikalla crap, they might force her to start popping out whelps."

Ice laughed. "She'd hate that. Enough talk about Crystal." He gripped her arm to stop her from walking. His eyes glinted with humor.

"What?" she asked, narrowing her eyes.

Ice smiled, and his three sexy dimples came to the fore. "Have you ever had sex in a public place?" He had this look in his eyes. It was downright naughty.

Azure choked out a laugh. "No, and you're not serious." She looked up and down the hallway, frowning. "What kind of public place? Not right here?" Her eyes widened.

Ice laughed. "No, not here in the hallway. Somewhere a little more discreet." He bit down on his full lower lip.

His teeth denting the flesh. "It's been torture sitting across from you for hours." He stepped in close, his face just shy of being buried in her hair. "You look amazing." He moved in a little closer and sniffed. "You smell fucking incredible, too."

"You're not so bad yourself." Her heart was racing a little faster. "Now, how do you suggest we have discreet sex in public?"

Ice moved back a step and started talking about work. She could hear someone approaching. A few minutes later, they were alone again. "Does that mean you're interested in trying it? Because you haven't lived unless you've had hard, sweaty sex in a public place."

She giggled. "How public are we talking? I know you said discreet, but—" She made a face.

He grabbed her hand and led her a few feet to a door. Ice bobbed his eyebrows. He opened the door and pulled her inside. She spotted brooms, buckets, a dustpan... it was a closet for cleaning supplies. "You do know that my chamber is just up the hallway?" She giggled.

"Live a little," he said, reaching for the top button of her jeans.

"Anyone could come in." Her voice was a touch husky. She realized that the thought turned her on.

"They won't." He positioned her ass against the door. "They might try. Besides, that's half the thrill of doing it in a public place. Potentially getting caught."

"Holy shit! This is happening." She felt heat suffuse her cheeks. Her belly clenched tight with... longing. "Someone could hear us," she whispered.

"We need to be really quiet. Can you be really quiet, Azure?" He pulled down her zipper.

"I can try," she whispered, her heart racing.

Ice dropped to his knees in front of her; he looked up at her and smiled. It was wicked and sexy. By all that was scaled, they were really doing this. She gripped his shoulders, then lifted each leg so that he could take her jeans off. Ice picked up one of her feet, hooking her leg over his broad shoulder. His eyes were glued to her pussy. She felt his breath against her sex. It both tickled and ignited a need inside her. He made a groan of pleasure as he sniffed at her. Then his tongue was on her clit, and she was fighting to keep quiet from the word go. His tongue was big and hot, making her groan softly as he used it on her in easy strokes. One hand was flat on the door behind her, and the other clutched at his soft hair. It felt amazing. He felt amazing.

His tongue zoned in on her clit and laved over it a good couple of times. *By the gods!* She was rocking her hips, but couldn't stop. Azure gripped his hair tighter. He sucked on her bundle of nerves, making her rock against him. Then he opened his mouth and sucked. Not too hard, not too soft. She moaned again, this time the sound coming from somewhere deep inside her. It was low and raw, and it hurt her throat because she had to swallow it back. *Quiet!*

Then he pushed a finger inside her, her mouth fell open. She gritted her teeth to stop from crying out when he crooked that finger, pushing it in and out.

"Tight," he mumbled, his lips against her clit.

By now, she was panting, making soft moaning noises each time his finger slid back into her. There was a coiling sensation in the pit of her stomach. Her skin felt tight. Her eyes wide. Her—

Ice stopped. She tried to hold him there, between her legs, but he pulled away. A feral grin on his sexy mouth. He rose, his hands pulling down his cotton pants as he licked his lips. "Love how you taste," he murmured. "You need to be quiet, Azure." His cock sprang free.

"You need to be quiet, Ice," she whispered right back.

His pants had slipped to halfway down his thighs. His cock was long and thick. His chest was bare. Ice was incredibly sexy. She was shaking with need. That thick, heavy feeling was still there in the pit of her stomach. Her clit throbbed as he gripped her thighs, his eyes on hers. He lifted her easily. "Put your legs around my waist." She hooked her ankles at his back, his cock flush up against her sex. "That's it." He flashed a grin. It was wild. "I can't wait to make you come in silence." He held her up off the floor like it was nothing. Hunting was physical work, and he was strong. His biceps bulged. Her back was up against the door.

"I could live inside your snug pussy." His gaze dropped there, to the junction of her thighs. Her throat closed hearing him talk like that.

Azure licked her lips. She was so needy and achy. So ready.

"So pretty," he whispered, rubbing the tip of his thumb over her clit. "Your nub is swollen. We're going to do this with no hands." He winked at her, making her want to giggle. She was too turned on for that.

The tip of his cock was suddenly at her opening. Nudging its way in. "Oh god... oh..." she whispered.

Ice looked down between them at where they were joined. "I love how my cock stretches your cunt."

He talked dirty. It just made her want more. It made her

drenched. "Tight and wet. You squeeze me almost to the point of pain." He was frowning, a sheen of sweat on his brow. "I fucking love it. Love it all." He pulled out and then pushed back in. Within a few seconds, he was flush against her. He was breathing deeply. His huge chest expanding and contracting against her, brushing up against her breasts. Her nipples were so tight that they hurt.

He kissed her neck, nipped at her ear, and she groaned.

"You feel good," he spoke against her lobe. "Fucking good," a low growl.

"You do too." She was appalled at how strangled her words were. Breathless and strangled.

"We need to be quick. Shhhhhh!" It was all the warning he gave as his grip tightened on her thighs. Azure clutched at his shoulders. His face became a mask of what could easily be misconstrued as fury as he pulled out of her. When all of those thick inches jackknifed back in, it had her mouth falling open and her back bowing.

So good.

Soooo freaking good.

Holy shit!

Holy dragon wings!

There was no other way to describe it but rough and primal. Ice held her firmly as he plowed into her from below. His knees were slightly bent, his jaw clenched tightly. His eyes glowed. They were intense. So beautiful. There was a dull thud as her ass hit the door with each hard thrust. *Shit!*

Ice grinned, and he anchored her more securely against the wooden surface. Her breasts jerked between them, since she wasn't wearing a bra under her shirt.

None of it mattered because she was about to come. It was right there. Her orgasm. Pulling, kneading, coiling, growing. Azure had to bite back her cries. It made her feel everything so much more acutely. He was relentless and strong and—

Then she was coming apart. The orgasm that tore through her had her clenching her eyes tight. It had her bucking against him. It felt like a tornado of pleasure ripping right through her. Like it might just tear her apart if she wasn't careful. It consumed all of her, not just one part, all of her. Every nerve, every cell, every single one, and all at once. Azure was going to scream. She could feel it building inside her. There was no stopping it. No… way… to stop it. Unless! Out of pure desperation, she bit down on his shoulder, her teeth sinking into the bare flesh.

Ice tensed. He stopped moving for a second, and then he growled long and low. His hips pistoned. His cock seemed to grow inside her. She could feel the spurts as he let go. Pleasure continued to rush through her like a wildfire on a windy day. Ice's movements were jerky and rough.

It was only when he slowed down that she was able to let him go. Moving less and less until he finally stopped altogether.

Azure slumped against him; she felt boneless. They were both breathing heavily. She was shaking a little. Or was it him? Maybe both of them. Yep, definitely both. It took a few minutes before she could talk. "I'm sorry. I just… I… I was going to scream. I didn't… I…"

"It's fine." He put her down, and she felt his seed drip down her thighs. "It's…" He started chuckling. "We were very loud."

"No, we weren't." She shook her head.

"We were. Very fucking loud."

She made a face. "Oh! Sorry." She covered her mouth with her hand. "I know you don't want anyone to know… about us." Was there even a 'them'? She was getting ahead of herself. The sex had addled her brain.

"It would mean complications, but I wouldn't mind as much as you think." He leaned in and kissed her softly.

Her heart raced. It seemed like Ice might be serious about her. It was looking more and more that way. A phone vibrated from somewhere on the floor. Ice pulled up his pants while he picked it up.

"Everything okay?" Azure asked, noticing his frown.

"My mom. I need to go and see her after work tomorrow. I've been ignoring her the last couple of days." He smiled. "That's all." He typed a quick message. "That should placate her for now."

"Your mom is so nice," Azure said. The older woman had brought the team cookies and cupcakes after their shifts in the past. She doted on her only child.

"She can be a pain in the ass, but I love her anyway." Ice handed her some tissue paper he'd pilfered from one of the shelves.

"Thanks." She cleaned herself up. "That's parents for you. You're lucky your mom cares so much." Azure pulled her jeans on. If they passed anyone in the hallway, they'd be able to smell what she'd been up to. What they'd been up to.

"I *am* lucky. At least I have a mom, and I'm grateful." He reached out and squeezed her hand. "She's a little overbearing at times, but she always has my best interest at heart." He let go of her hand. "Do you want to come to my place? We could—"

She laughed softly. "I know exactly what we would do." She was very tempted, but they hadn't had a decent night's rest in days. "But I think we need sleep more."

"You could come to my place, and we could just sleep." He took her hand again.

"We would not just sleep, and you know it."

"You got me there." He grinned. "We would *eventually* sleep."

"Tomorrow?" She reached up and kissed him.

"Fine." He gripped her hips and kissed her hard.

"We should probably head out separately. I'll wait a few minutes and leave after you," she said as he pulled away.

"No, I'll walk you home. Unless you don't want to be seen with me. You might want to avoid complications." He lifted his brows.

"I don't mind complications. They make life more interesting."

He grinned. "They certainly do." Ice reached over and pushed a few wayward strands of hair behind her ear. "I'm feeling like we might have something here."

"I think so too." This felt too good to be true. Far too good.

"Let's go, then."

There was only one person out in the hallway. The male looked at them strangely before carrying on, on his way. They looked at each other and laughed. Then Ice took her hand. *He. Took. Her. Hand.* She couldn't keep the grin off her face. It looked like she might be in a relationship for the first time in her life. It felt amazing and scary all at once. Luckily, more amazing than scary.

CHAPTER 29

The next day…

AZURE WASHED HER hands using the liquid soap dispenser. It took a couple of minutes and several washes to get all the blood off of them and out from under her fingernails.

Once she was done, she dried her hands. Then she grabbed her dress and pulled it over her head, smoothing her hand over the fabric.

"Azure!" Fog yelled. She turned to where he was standing. He'd just finished skinning the moose he'd bagged earlier. Her eyes widened when she saw who was standing with him. "Summer." She frowned. What was the she-dragon doing here? She thought back to her run-in with Cirrus. Maybe it had to do with that.

Summer smiled as soon as their eyes locked. "Hi," she said, looking sheepish.

It hadn't been that long since she'd last seen this female, and yet everything had changed in that time.

Azure felt like a different person. "Hi," she replied when she realized she was gaping.

"Can you talk for a few minutes?" Summer asked as she walked over.

"Sure, I just finished up here, but I have somewhere I need to be, so I can't be too long." She was meeting Melina to help her unpack boxes in the salon. After that, she'd go to Ice's place. She'd already packed an overnight bag since she was staying over. All night... until the sun came up. No sneaking around. Ice was meeting with Storm right then to let him know that the two of them were dating. It might mean hiccups where work was concerned. She would probably have to transfer to another team but, it would all work out in the end. She wanted to be with Ice. They wanted this. Both of them did. It all still felt surreal. It also felt good. She wasn't just falling for Ice anymore. She was completely in love with him. Head over heels. It seemed like he felt the same way about her.

"All I need is a couple of minutes of your time," Summer promised. "And I'll be out of your hair. We can go for a walk." She pointed at the field of long, green grass that made up the top of the lair. It had magnificent views of the mountains and valleys in the background.

Azure nodded. "Sure."

"How are you doing?" Summer asked. There was a look of concern on her face.

"I'm doing well... great, actually."

Summer looked at her strangely. Like she didn't quite believe what Azure was saying. "I'm so sorry," Summer blurted. She stopped walking and turned to Azure. Summer had this stricken look. "I should never have pushed you away. I was such a bitch. I didn't know." She shook her head. "I didn't know what he had done." She suddenly sobbed. Tears streamed down her face. "You came to tell me that day. You came for support. You needed a friend, and I was a bitch to you. I closed my door in your face."

"I *did* need you, Summer. I understand your reaction, but—" Azure pushed out a breath. Not sure what to say to the crying female.

"I'm so desperate for a child. So desperate. I would've given anything… anything," she pushed out, crying harder. "I was so angry. So hurt that you didn't spend your heat with someone. I was so selfish in my thinking. You're my friend. You were hurt, and I didn't listen."

"What's done is done. Skarn tried… He didn't succeed."

Summer shook her head. "Cirrus told me what happened to you." She shook her head harder. "I haven't been able to think about anything else since I saw him last night." Her voice was shrill. "He overheard your conversation when you had that meeting with Storm. Cirrus won't say a thing, I swear," she quickly added.

Azure suspected as much. Although she didn't care anymore whether what had happened got out or not. She wasn't sure why she felt ashamed about it. What happened was on Skarn, not on her.

"I wanted to see you," Summer went on. "To let you know that I'm terribly sorry. I only hope you can forgive me. What I did was unthinkable, but I still hope you'll find it deep within your heart to forgive me… please."

"Of course I'll forgive you," Azure finally replied. Summer threw her arms around Azure's neck and hugged her tightly. Azure touched her hand to Summer's back, but didn't return the hug. That was the thing; she'd forgive Summer, but they would never go back to being friends like they had been before. That just wasn't possible. Friends... sure. Close friends? No! Too much had happened. Too much had changed.

It took a while for Summer to let her go. "Thank you," she said. "I can't tell you how much that means to me."

"I should get going." Azure pointed at the rear entrance to the lair.

"Do you think it will happen again?"

Azure frowned. "What?"

"Do you think you'll come into heat again?" Summer asked.

It wasn't something she'd thought about. Azure had been having too much fun with Ice, and then there was the whole business with Skarn. It hadn't really crossed her mind. "I don't know. Probably not." She needed to be honest with herself.

"You never know."

"I guess." Azure shrugged.

"I still wake up every morning and pray," Summer said. "Maybe Cirrus would... want more from me if it happened."

To think that this used to be what they talked about all the time. "And maybe it's time to end things with that male."

Summer's eyes widened. "Why would you say that?"

"Because he only spends time with you between stag runs and females like Crystal. You're worth more than that."

Summer shook her head. Azure could see that the female wasn't buying it. "It's because I'm infertile that—"

"You are worth more than your womb," she told Summer. Words that Melina had told her not too long ago.

Summer put a hand to her stomach. Again, the female looked like she didn't buy it.

"You're a beautiful, intelligent female. You have so much to give, and until you start realizing that for yourself, no one else will. You can't let males like Cirrus treat you like dirt."

Summer narrowed her eyes at her. "What happened to you? You seem... different. But in a good way."

"So much has happened." Azure grinned. "My very good friend, Melina, is opening a beauty salon soon. It will be up and running in a week or two. I will send you the details. You would be surprised at what a haircut can do for your self-esteem. She's bringing in a whole range of clothing, too."

"I saw you wearing human clothes last night. You looked fantastic."

"Oh... when was that?" Azure frowned. "I didn't see you."

"Cirrus and I were going to have dinner at Wings and Things, but we decided to eat in at the last minute, and so we left. Cirrus told me what happened. You know the rest." Summer pulled in a deep breath. "I thought you looked amazing. You look... different somehow."

"You should come to the salon when it opens."

"I will go to this human salon. I want some of what you have got because it's working for you."

"I'll let you know more when she opens. Talking about the salon, I must get going. I promised Melina I would help her set it up. That's where I'm headed right now. Humans are so weak." She smiled. Not so long ago, she would have said that as a slight. Now, she was stating a fact rather than putting Melina down. Without looking back, Azure started jogging for the rear lair entrance when she noticed an elderly lady talking to Fog.

"Snow," Azure said, coming to an abrupt halt.

"Oh, hi, Azure." The woman held up a basket. "I brought goodies," Snow said. "Fog just told me that my son isn't here." She looked downtrodden, and even sighed.

"No." Azure shook her head. "He has a meeting with Storm."

Ice's mother sighed. "That boy. He normally visits at least once a week, but I haven't seen him for over two weeks now, and it's making me worry."

"I think he said that he had planned on popping in to see you after he's done with Storm." She recalled how he had mentioned neglecting his mother last night. Azure felt guilty. The reason for Ice's absence probably had something to do with her. He had been busy over the last couple of weeks. Or, more accurately, they'd been busy... with each other. "I'll send him a message letting him know that you're waiting for him at his place." She knew that Ice wouldn't mind. "There," she said, putting her phone back in the pocket of her dress. "Message sent. I can walk with you a little way since I'm headed in that direction."

Snow beamed. "Thank you. I know exactly why he's avoiding me." Snow shook her head and tsked.

"I'm sure he's not avoiding you." It was more a case of being preoccupied than outright avoiding his own mother.

"My son knows exactly what I'm going to ask him when I see him," Snow said, moving the basket to the other arm.

"Can I help you carry that?"

"No, I'm stronger than I look." She narrowed her eyes at Azure and smiled. They were exactly the same glacial blue as Ice's. Quite striking.

"I'm sure you are." Azure smiled back.

"Every time he comes back from the stag run, I ask him the same thing. Whether or not he met someone nice."

Azure's smile widened. "He doesn't like that, I'm assuming?"

"Not at all, since he always tells me the same darned thing. He tells me no, that he hasn't. Then we end up arguing. I tell him that I'm not getting any younger. His father barely even leaves the house anymore. We're old."

"You're not that old." Sure, Snow had gray littered throughout her dark hair and crow's feet around her eyes, but she was still in great shape.

"We are. Ice's father is completely gray. I still think he's a hunk." Snow laughed lightly. "I was so lucky to have had Ice." Her eyes brightened. "I was already an older she-dragon when Ice's father and I mated. I'd had a couple of heats, but none resulted in a pregnancy. I'd given up hope. Then, lo and behold… I had one last heat, and I was with child." She beamed. "We had the most perfect baby. He turned into the most adorable little boy. I'm proud of the male he has become."

"Oh, I can imagine," Azure said. There was a lot to be proud of. Ice was a good male. He was destined for bigger things. She knew it. Azure couldn't hold back a smile.

"He was a lonely little boy, though. He always begged us to have a brother or sister for him to play with. It's difficult to explain such a thing to a child." She shook her head. "And now that we're getting older... we desperately want to be grandparents." She clutched a hand to her chest and got this look in her eyes, which glinted.

Azure felt a tightening in her gut. She felt bad for the other female. The infertility that plagued their people was terrible.

"I know that Ice wants plenty of children; he's always said so. I'm not worried on that note." The clenching feeling grew worse. "I only wish he would hurry up and choose a mate already. His father and I aren't getting any younger. I might not be alive to see my grandbabies born." She giggled. "He always said he wants at least six."

"He's mentioned it once or twice," Azure murmured. Had she somehow forgotten about this? Ice had always maintained that he wanted children. That he looked forward to being a father one day. To having a family. Her heart seemed to slow. It became louder, though, thudding in her ears.

"Oh, good." Snow clutched her chest again. "So, he wasn't just saying it to make me feel better."

"No. I don't think so." Azure had this terrible sinking feeling. It got worse and worse. "He wasn't just saying it. This is where I need to say goodbye." She couldn't bear hearing anymore.

"So, you see," Snow went on as soon as they stopped walking, "that's why he's avoiding me. He clearly hasn't met anyone, and he doesn't want to disappoint me."

"He's probably just been busy," Azure mumbled. "It

was good to see you, Snow. I'm sure Ice won't be long."
She looked at her phone, but Ice hadn't read her message
yet.

"Good to see you, dear." Snow smiled. "Have a lovely
evening."

"You, too," Azure said, her heart beating wildly inside
her chest. She started towards the salon.

Ice had been avoiding his mother because he didn't
want to disappoint her. It wasn't because he *hadn't* met
someone. It was because he had, and the person he had
met was the wrong someone. Namely her. Infertile her.
He'd always wanted kids. Lots of kids. Ice wouldn't get
his wish if he stayed with her. She'd always ignored her
attraction to Ice. Azure had assumed she did it because
he was her superior, her friend, but that wasn't it at all.
She had ignored her feelings for him because he wanted
children. Children *plural.* If they continued down this
path, he might live to regret it. It felt like her heart was
breaking. Azure wasn't the right female for him. She
wasn't. He just hadn't realized it yet.

Azure stopped walking. She sent Melina a text canceling
their plans. She told her friend that she was going to Ice's
place early. Then she sent Ice a text telling him that she was
needed at the salon, that she would try to make it to his
place if they didn't run too late. She was a yellow-bellied
coward because she was going to hole up instead of
breaking things off immediately. Azure needed to plan what
she would say and how she would play this. She couldn't
tell him the truth. That wouldn't work. Her heart felt like it
had splintered inside her. The shards were digging deep.

CHAPTER 30

ICE LEANED BACK on the sofa. He pulled in a deep breath. "No, I didn't meet a nice human on the stag run, Mom." He shook his head.

By scale, he hated the disappointment on his mother's face. Her shoulders sagged. "That's a pity. Maybe on the next stag run." She made a face and wrinkled her nose. "Such a horrible name. Why can't it be called something else? Something nicer. Human females are nice, aren't they?"

"Yes, they are."

"You should have another cookie." She pointed at the plate on the coffee table loaded with various kinds of cookies. His mom was such a nurturer. To make her happy, he leaned forward and grabbed a large choc chip cookie with extra chocolate chips. He'd already eaten too many of the things, but what was one more if it made her happy?

"These are delicious." They were. The best. His mom was the best. She cared deeply for him, and he knew that all of this ultimately came from a good place. It did irritate him at times, and it was worse today since he had found someone. Someone special. Someone he was beginning to think he could spend the rest of his life with. Azure. His mother didn't need to know just yet. Soon. Soon everyone would know. The thought warmed him.

His mom beamed as she watched him eat. "I baked them today. You'll take some to work tomorrow for your team, won't you?"

"I will." Azure would love the peanut butter cookies. His female could have some later when she came around. She was staying the night. He couldn't fucking wait to see her.

"What about that sweet female, Crystal?" His mom was relentless. Ice had to bite back a groan. Just when he thought he'd dodged a silver bullet. *Holy fuck!* "Her mother and I were chatting about it the other day, and—"

"No, Mom. Crystal is not the right female for me." Ice shook his head hard.

"How can you say that?" His mother frowned.

"Have you ever met Crystal? I know you're good friends with her mother, but have you met her daughter?"

"Well, no, but I've seen pictures. And she's fertile. She will be expected to take a mate soon. Why can't that person be you?"

Ice shrugged, getting annoyed. *She means well,* he told himself. "There are other things that are important aside from fertility."

"What could be more important?" His mom sat up straighter, her voice a touch shrill.

"Love."

She narrowed her eyes, which softened. "Of course, love is important, son. It's the most important." She sounded exasperated when she said the last. "I've never said otherwise."

"Don't you think I should put love as the number one requirement when I look for a mate? Not any of that other stuff?"

"Of course, son, and I know you'll find someone who will love you endlessly. That other stuff is important, too, though. I just know you'll find someone wonderful and that you'll be one big, happy family." She smiled broadly. "A house filled with love and the sound of little feet and laughter." Her eyes got this faraway look.

For the love of freaking scales! "Okay, Mom."

"Don't worry, my son, you will find the right female. I know you will." She reached over and patted his hand.

"Me too, Mom." Ice had already found her. He knew that his mother would love Azure when she got to know her better. The fertility thing wasn't important. It might take a while for his mom to accept that, but she would. Especially when she saw the happiness Azure brought him. "Can I get you some more tea? A juice, perhaps? I have peach. It's one of your favorites, isn't it?" Ice asked her.

"It certainly is, but I need to get back to your father. He'll be wanting his supper. What's on the menu tonight?"

"White-tailed deer," Ice replied.

Her eyes flared. "Lovely, your father will be pleased." His mom stood up. "I'd better get back, or we'll end up eating too late to go on our evening flight. There's been this lovely cool breeze these last few nights. Feels wonderful on the scales."

"Sure does, Mom." Ice walked his mom to the door. He hugged her tightly. "Thanks for the visit."

"Don't avoid me again. I know I get on your case sometimes, but it's ultimately because I love you." She took his hands. "I want the best for you, you know that, right?"

"I do." He hugged her again. "I'll come by for Sunday lunch?" he said as he pulled away, lifting his brows.

"That would be wonderful."

"Great! I'll see you then." Ice watched his mom walk away. She turned after a couple of strides and waved at him. Ice smiled and waved back. He was going to tell them both about Azure on Sunday.

It was still a little early for Azure to come by. She would still be helping Melina at the salon. He couldn't wait for her to arrive. He wanted to fill her in on what had happened with Storm. First, though, he wanted to make the night special. He was going to prepare something delicious for dinner. Then he was going to set the table. Go the whole nine yards for his female.

His!

Yes!

His dragon rumbled in agreement. He could feel his beast stretch in satisfaction. *Mine!* Everything had fallen into place for him yesterday. Everything! It had happened when Azure had bitten him. It had felt right. Like she belonged to him, and more importantly, like he belonged to her. Not just him, apparently, but his dragon, too. She had somehow, somewhere along the line, captured his heart… and she'd done so without him even realizing it.

When he looked back, he could see it clearly now. He had broken things off with Crystal soon after Azure started with the team. He hadn't gone on any stag runs. He hadn't hooked up with any of the she-dragons. None of that. He'd enjoyed spending time with Azure. Looked forward to seeing her at work every day. It took her heat for him to realize that he was also insanely attracted to her. She was *it!* She was everything. He was going to tell her how he felt about her this evening. He was going to say those three words. Words he had never uttered to anyone else.

Then he was going to make love to Azure. Something else he had never done before, either. He was going to make love to her and sink his teeth into her. Mating behavior? Hell, yes!

Ice jumped in the shower, scrubbed down, and then toweled dry before dressing in a pair of black pants and a pale blue button-down shirt. He wanted to look good.

Then he got started on dinner. He was making venison bourguignon with baby potatoes and long-stemmed broccoli. Ice had found a recipe online and was following it to a T. Once the food was bubbling away, he set the table using a white tablecloth, plate settings, and even candles. Then he opened a bottle of red wine and left it to breathe, placing glasses on the table as well.

Nearly there.

The food smelled fucking amazing. He couldn't wait to see Azure. With that in mind, she should be nearly there. Any minute now. He absently checked his messages. There was one from Azure. She'd sent it earlier. He felt himself smile as soon as he saw her name. The smile quickly turned to a scowl when he read her text.

Azure: Lots of work here at the salon. Looks like I'm going to be late. You eat without me. I'll probably end up sleeping at home. I don't want to end up waking you up.

What?

They had plans. They had spoken about this today at work.

Ice: I'll help out at the salon tomorrow. Please come over. I want to celebrate with you. Dinner is nearly ready. I opened wine. There are even candles xxx

This was fine. Azure hadn't been expecting a whole romantic dinner. Once she read his message, she would come right over. His phone beeped, and he couldn't read her message fast enough.

Azure: I can't! I'm sorry.

What? This made no sense.

Ice: Why not? What's going on? Are you okay?

This felt all wrong. His gut was going nuts. This wasn't right at all. He paced for five minutes, but Azure never answered his message. She'd read it but didn't respond. He switched off the stove at the wall.

Ice left, walking fast. He needed to know what was going on.

This couldn't wait. Not for a second.

CHAPTER 31

AZURE SAT AT her kitchen table, her head in her hands. She kept on running through every aspect of her budding relationship with Ice, of their possible future together, and what that would look like. Kept on trying to find a way for them to be together *and* for him to get the family he had always desired. The one he had talked about plenty of times since she had known him. Azure couldn't do it. The two futures couldn't coexist.

If she was selfish, she'd hold on to him with both hands, mate him anyway, and as soon as possible. That wouldn't be fair to him, though. He would never truly be happy if he wasn't a father. Azure knew this deep down. If she really loved him, she would let him go before their relationship progressed any further. It could be a clean break if it happened now. Ice would be upset, but he would get over her soon enough. He'd move on and find a nice female, one who could give him what he needed. One who could give him what she couldn't.

Children.

Azure pushed out a heavy breath and then jumped when a knock sounded. She dropped her head onto her arms on the table. Deep down, she knew that Ice would come. Especially after she ignored his last message. This confrontation had been inevitable. It was best to get it over with. She had a plan. One she was sticking to.

Ice knocked again. This time, he called her name. He sounded concerned.

Azure sighed. It had been amazing while it lasted. The best few days of her life. There was a part of her that wished it had never happened. At least, then she would still have had a friendship. She'd have the memories of their time together. Memories she would treasure. Azure would keep a little piece of Ice's heart within hers.

He knocked a third time as she made her way to the door. "Coming," she told him. This was going to be the single most difficult thing she would ever have to do, but she would do it. She had to. For him. This was for Ice, even if he didn't realize it.

Azure opened the door.

"What's going on?" Ice's eyes were filled with concern. He stepped in closer and tried to cup her cheek, but she took a step away from him. He frowned harder. "Are you angry? Did something happen? You're making me nervous, Azure."

"There's nothing to be nervous about," she deadpanned.

"Okay, now you're really worrying me. Can I come inside?" He looked over her shoulder.

She nodded once and moved away to make space for him to enter, closing the door behind him.

"Melina said that you messaged her to say that you

weren't coming." *Oh shit!* He went to the salon. She didn't react. "You apparently told her that you were going straight to me. Then you tell me that you're with Melina. What is going on?" His jaw was tight. His eyes radiated with emotion. "You lied to both of us."

"Nothing is going on." She shrugged, trying to look as casual as possible. "I didn't feel like doing either of those things." She licked her lips, her mouth feeling dry. "I was tired, and I came home. I'll make it up to Melina tomorrow."

"What about me, Azure? Us? We had plans. Don't you want to know how it went with Storm?

She didn't say anything, but only because she *did* want to know. It shouldn't matter. It didn't matter anymore, but she still wanted to know.

Ice rubbed a hand over his face. "Okay, I'll tell you, anyway. Storm was great for a change since he can be such a prick. He congratulated me... us. He was happy for us, Azure. He said it would be better if we were on separate teams if we are going to be in a relationship. He will organize for someone from another team to swap with you. It will take a day or two, and until that happens, he knows that we will behave responsibly. Don't you have anything to say?" He was starting to get angry. Ice folded his arms across his chest and ground his molars. His eyes were stormy. "Anything at all? I made you dinner. There are candles for fuck's sakes."

All she wanted to do was come clean. To tell him what his mother had said. To tell him what was going on so that he could talk her out of breaking up with him. Ice *would* talk her out of it. She knew he would. Azure had to be strong. "I didn't ask for candles," she pushed out.

"Quite frankly, I didn't realize we were this serious. I'm sorry, Ice, I—"

"Didn't realize…?" he snapped, his eyes blazing. "You didn't…" He sighed, shaking his head. She could see that he was trying to compose himself. He looked at the floor, breathing deeply. "What have we been doing this whole time, Azure?" His eyes locked with hers.

"This whole time? It's only been a few days. We've been fucking." She forced herself to say it without a hint of emotion. She did a good job. It broke her inside. "We've been having fun. I thought you were going to let Storm know as a formality until our hookups have run their course." She snort-laughed. "You're making it sound like we were going to mate each other next week or something." She pushed out a laugh that sounded exactly how it was… fake.

"What's going on?" His voice lowered. The look of concern was back. "I know you don't mean all of that."

"Nothing is going on."

"Speak to me. Please!" He took a step toward her.

She held her ground. "There is nothing to speak to you about. I think we got our wires crossed here. I mean, you didn't think this was serious, did you? I'm so sorry if you did, Ice. I really thought we were just fucking around. I sensed that you might be pushing for more yesterday when I chose to go home… alone. It's part of the reason I decided not to go to your place tonight. Looks like I was right." She made a face. "My bad."

"My bad?" He wiped a hand over his face, sniffing once. "My bad. I know there's more to this. I fucking know it!"

She frowned. "Nope. Nothing more. We rutted a few

times. It was good. I enjoyed it while it lasted, but I think it's better if we leave it at that. I didn't think I needed to give you the whole 'this is just sex' speech. I thought you knew. That you knew me. I don't do serious relationships. I never have, and I never will. It's not me."

"*This* isn't you." He gestured at her. "All of what you are saying isn't you. It hasn't just been a few days. I've known you longer. I've… Never mind."

"Just because it isn't what you want to hear doesn't mean it isn't true. I'm sorry for the misunderstanding." She shrugged. "There's nothing I can do."

"You can tell me what the fuck is going on."

"Nothing to tell. I think it might be better if I still swap to another team even though we're over. Not that we were a 'we.'" She made a face. "I'll call in sick tomorrow and stay home until the swap happens."

"You do that." Ice's eyes blazed. His jaw was tight, his face red. He had this vein throbbing on his brow. "I can't believe this." He sounded hurt for just a second. His eyes clouded with emotion. Then it was gone, replaced with anger. He gritted his teeth, pursing his lips. Then he stormed off, banging the door on his way out.

Azure felt the tears roll down her cheeks. Her throat was clogged with pain. A sobbing wail was drawn from her.

CHAPTER 32

Three days later…

T HE DOOR TO her chamber banged against the wall as it opened. "What…? What are you doing here?" Azure asked the human standing in her doorway. "Argh, Melina!" She put a pillow over her head. "Close the door on your way out." Why hadn't she locked her door in the first place? "Close it!" she growled. "The light is hurting my eyes." She took her head back out from under the pillow, squinting.

"I'm sure it is, since you haven't seen light for days." Melina put her hands on her hips. She slammed the door.

Azure started to breathe out a sigh of relief. Then she noticed that the damnable human was still inside her home.

By all that was winged and scaled! "What do you want? I'm trying to watch this movie. The zombies are taking over."

"Screw the zombies!" Melina yelled. She walked over, grabbing the remote off Azure's chest, and turned the television off. Then she walked to the blinds and pushed the button that opened them. "Don't you answer your phone anymore? Since when do you ignore people when they come to your door? I've been trying to reach you for days."

Azure groaned, putting her pillow back over her head and burrowing further under the covers. "Go away. I'm sick."

"More like lovesick. What the hell happened with Ice? Rumor has it that he's like a bear with a sore tooth. Either he's ignoring everyone with this glower on his face, or he's shouting. There's no in-between."

Azure crept out from under the pillow. "Oh, really?" Her voice came out sounding far too soft and needy for her liking. It was the first time she'd heard anything about Ice in days.

"Yes, really, and here you are, Missy. This place is a mess; you're a hot mess." Melina looked her over, wrinkling her nose. "I don't need superhuman senses to smell that you haven't showered in days. Enough is enough. What the hell is going on?"

"Nothing. I haven't been well. I'm recuperating."

"Back to the part about you lying through your teeth. I don't buy it for a minute. Look at this mess." Azure's coffee table was littered with plates and glasses. There were also a couple of empty ice-cream containers and chocolate wrappers. "This reeks—quite literally—of a break-up." Melina started picking up the plates.

"Leave them."

"No, someone has to clean this mess up. Someone needs to clean *you* up. What is going on?" Melina yelled while she walked to the kitchen, depositing the dishes in the sink and the wrappers in the trash. "Speak to me, or so help me…"

"There's nothing to say."

"I had Ice over at my place the other night, looking for you after you told me that you were at his place. He looked worried. He looked like someone who really cared. Here you are acting like he broke your heart, and yet… that can't be. What happened, Azure?"

Azure wanted to tell the female that it was none of her business, but she refrained. Melina had been there for her every step of the way. She owed the female some kind of explanation. "I broke up with Ice," she mumbled.

"Why the heck would you do that? You're clearly in love with the guy."

"I have feelings for him, but I'll be okay. It's no biggie." She waved a hand.

"No biggie, my ass," Melina muttered to herself. "Back to my first question, why on earth would you break up with someone you have feelings for? Someone you pined after for months."

"It wasn't months," she mumbled. Melina gave her this hard look. "Okay, fine…" Azure rolled her eyes, "months." She sounded defeated because she felt defeated.

"Why did you break up with Ice? What possessed you? He's a great guy. He's *your* great guy. He's in love with you."

"No, he isn't." She shook her head. "He has feelings for me, but not like that. Not so soon." It wasn't too soon, but she held onto that belief, anyway.

Melina laughed. "You might not be my best student after all."

"Still your *only* student." Azure sat up, trying to get her hair behind her ear. It was knotted, so she gave up. "It would never have worked between us, so I saved us a whole lot of heartache further down the line and broke things off now."

"That's too cryptic. You are going to have to elaborate."

She pushed out a breath. "Fine. We want totally different things. I'm talking about fundamental things. I may not know too much about relationships, but I do know that there are a couple of pivotal factors that need to be aligned. We diverge when it comes to a major life decision."

"Major, huh?" Melina looked like she wasn't buying it. "What pivotal life decision would this be?"

Why hadn't she ever noticed how nosy Melina was? It was a terrible trait. "He lives for anal, and I like my asshole too much to have it abused in that way."

Melina's eyes pretty much bugged out of her skull for a few seconds. Then she cleared her throat and licked her lips, then cleared her throat again. "That isn't a pivotal life decision." She shook her head, her blond curls bouncing.

"It is." Oh good, she was buying it. Azure hadn't expected that. Maybe Melina would leave her alone now.

No such luck. "It totally isn't. You never know; you might like it more than you think." There was this look in Melina's eyes. "You should at least give it a try before you shoot it down." Her cheeks turned red. A bright blushing red.

"Holy dragon wings." Azure choked out the start of a laugh, but her chest tightened, so she sucked it back. "You have anal with Freeze? I wasn't being serious." She realized too late what she was saying.

Crap!

"I knew you were bullshitting. I wasn't born yesterday. Up!" Melina walked over to her.

"What?" Azure frowned.

"Get up, you disgusting creature. Get up and go and shower right now. You look and smell terrible. You're showering, brushing your teeth, and then your hair. Once you are wearing something clean, you're going to tell me what is going on. I want the truth this time. I want to hear all about this diverging path when it comes to this pivotal life decision. It had better be good."

Actually, a shower did sound nice.

"I'll clean up in here while you're busy. I realize it might take a while to sort all of that out." Her eyes tracked over Azure's face and her hair… especially her hair. The human grimaced.

"Fine," she groaned. Azure was going to tell Melina everything, but there was no way her friend was going to sway her from her decision. Who knew, perhaps she would agree with Azure. She wasn't sure which she would prefer. It hurt to know that Ice was going through a rough time, but he would move on soon. She squeezed her eyes shut for a moment or two until the pain inside her subsided to a half manageable level.

CHAPTER 33

I CE PUT A small piece of roast boar into his mouth. He chewed and swallowed. His mom had dished up a huge plate for him. He pushed the food around before spearing a piece of roasted carrot. In truth, he didn't feel much like eating. He didn't feel much like anything since Azure had blindsided him.

"Do you want more gravy?" his mom asked, pointing at the stainless-steel jug on the table.

"No thanks. I have plenty." Ice stuck his fork into another piece of meat. "This is delicious."

His mother smiled. "You look like you've lost weight. Don't you think he looks like he lost weight, Cyclone?" she asked Ice's father.

"Leave Ice alone, sweetheart. Let the boy eat in peace." His father picked up the saltshaker and shook it over his food.

"I worry, dear. It's okay to worry. That's what mothers do." She shrugged, cutting a tiny piece off of her slab of meat.

"You have nothing to worry about," Ice mumbled.

"It's just that you look…" she scrutinized him for a second, fork poised halfway to her mouth, "sad," she finally settled on the right word, putting the slice of meat into her mouth.

"I'm tired. I haven't been sleeping all that well. I'm not sad." Who was he kidding? He felt like his heart had been pulled from his chest and then stomped all over by a herd of stampeding bison.

"Why aren't you sleeping? Is everything okay? Come to think of it, your eyes are bloodshot." She put her knife and fork down on the plate with a clang.

"Ice said he was okay, Snow. I'm sure he meant it," his father said, putting a big piece of bloody meat in his mouth. "How is work? I heard your team was way down on kills this week." He spoke around his food.

"We were missing a team member for a couple of days. We were only four. Azure is… she's a big part of our team, and we…" he clenched his teeth for a second or two, "missed her." His throat tightened.

"Oh, Azure. Such a sweet female." His mother beamed. "She was the one who helped me the other day when I was looking for you. She walked with me and put my mind to rest on a couple of things that have been bugging me of late." His mother picked up her cutlery.

"Oh?" He looked up at his mother. "What things would those be?"

"This and that." She waved her fork.

He made a noise to urge her to keep talking.

"She might have assured me that you weren't avoiding me, which was nice to hear, even though I knew it wasn't true."

"I'm sorry about that, Mom." Something was pinging on his radar. "What else?"

His mom smiled brightly. "I told her how lucky we were to have you. Isn't that right, Cyclone?"

His father made a noise of agreement.

"We were already older by then... as far as having a whelp is concerned. I told her what a gorgeous baby you were and how you used to beg us for a brother or sister." Her eyes clouded over. "I would have dearly loved to grant you your wish."

"I know." Ice nodded. "I had a great childhood, though. Are you kidding? Two parents who doted on me. I had friends to play with." He shrugged. "Azure was also an only child. Most of us were."

"Oh, and I told her how I knew you were purposely avoiding me because I was going to pester you about a mate. That, and grandbabies."

"What about grandbabies?" The pings grew louder and more frantic inside him.

"Just that your father and I aren't getting any younger and that we hope you have them soon." His mom laughed softly. "That I know it's something you've always wanted. That I wish you'd hurry up, already."

Ice got this sinking sensation. *Holy fucking shit!*

"Azure assured me that you did, indeed, want kids. Apparently, you've spoken about it on numerous occasions. That definitely put my mind at ease. I sometimes wonder if you only say that to appease me." His mom narrowed her eyes. "What is it, dear? You look like you just saw a ghost. Ice... hon'?"

He put his knife and fork down. *No fucking wonder.*

"Everything okay, son?" Even his father looked worried.

"I fell in love with someone," Ice blurted.

"What?" His mother's eyes widened. "That's great... but... what's wrong?"

"Let the boy talk, Snow," his father said, leaning back in his chair.

"I'm in love with Azure, Mom. I'm totally in love." *Shit!* No wonder she said those things. No fucking wonder she pushed him away.

His mother frowned. "Azure, as in...?"

"Yes." He nodded.

"The she-dragon who had the late heat? The one on your team with the pretty eyes. The one I spoke to the other day." She looked pale. "Nice female," she muttered. "But..." Her eyes widened.

"Azure can't have children." There was a growl to Ice's voice. One he couldn't help.

"And you went and told her all of that?" His father was frowning at his mother.

"I need to go," Ice said. "I need to go and see Azure."

"Now? You haven't finished your food. We're still talking."

"I need to see my female. I need to set a few things straight." He was already standing. "I love her, and love is the most important ingredient in a relationship. None of those other things matter."

"But, Ice..." his mother tried.

His father grabbed his mom's hand. "You know it's true, Snow, my love. Look at us as proof of that."

"We didn't think we could have whelps," he heard his mother say behind him.

"And look how we turned out," his dad spoke gently.

"We turned out just fine." Ice smiled when he heard his mother say those words. "Good luck, Ice!" she shouted after him.

"I know you're going to tell me I'm full of hot air. I made my decision, and I'm sticking with it. You can't talk me out of it." Azure pushed some of her still damp hair behind her ear and took a sip of her water.

"I understand where you are coming from, but you have to talk to Ice about this." Azure had told Melina everything. Somehow, she couldn't keep anything from her nosy human friend.

"Not happening." Azure shook her head.

"He deserves to know the real reason you broke it off with him."

"What difference does it make? The outcome will remain the same." Azure shrugged.

Melina shook her head. "That's not true. Right now, he thinks that you don't give a shit, and we both know that isn't true."

"It's better that way. He'll have an easier time moving on if he thinks I don't care. I'm leaving things just as they are," Azure insisted.

"You should—" They both turned to the door when someone knocked on it.

Before Azure could stop her, Melina walked over and opened it. It was Ice. Her heart just about beat right out of her chest. He was even more handsome than she remembered. Those eyes... hauntingly beautiful.

No, wait!

No!

"You can't be here," Azure blurted.

"I'm glad you're here," Melina said. "Come on in. I was just leaving." Her friend turned back to her. "Good thing we got you cleaned up when we did," she whispered, making a face. "Don't you dare take no for an answer," she told Ice.

"I don't intend to." Ice folded his arms, looking at her with an intensity that almost scared her.

"And for the record... there's nothing wrong with anal," Melina threw back at Azure over her shoulder.

Ice frowned, and Azure squeezed her eyes shut, giving her head a shake. Her and her big mouth. Why had she even joked about anal in the first place?

"Um... I'm going to ignore that," he said.

"Please do. You shouldn't be here." She folded her arms. "We said everything there was to say the other day. Again, I'm sorry you got the wrong idea."

"That's bullshit, and you know it."

Azure frowned. "It isn't bullshit. It's how it is."

"Thank you for helping my mother. I was just visiting my parents... having lunch with them, actually."

"How is this even relevant? I don't mean to be rude, but I was watching a really great movie when Melina barged in here earlier. I'd like to get back to that unless you want a quick rut." She huffed out a breath. "Oh yes, we can't because you can't keep your feelings under control." Holy dragon wings, but she was being a bitch. It took every ounce of willpower she had not to throw herself at him and beg for forgiveness. She couldn't! *Could. Not.* She had to be strong.

"Now I'm really worried." Ice narrowed his eyes.

"Why would you be worried?"

"Because the female I'm going to spend the rest of my life with can lie to me with such a straight face."

Her mouth fell open.

"We're going to cut the bull, Azure. My mother told me about your whole conversation. I know everything. I know why you suddenly changed on me. Why you're running. I know."

"You have it wrong." She had to try.

"I wasn't born yesterday. I can see that you're afraid."

Azure swallowed thickly. "I'm not afraid," she pushed out.

"You are!" he insisted, taking a step toward her.

"I'm not afraid." She shook her head. "I don't want you to make a mistake. I don't want you to have regrets. You want a family, Ice. I can't give you one. You need to find a female who can give you what you want."

"I have a female who gives me everything I want." He closed the distance between them, not quite touching her. She could feel the heat radiating from his body. Could hear the steady rhythm of his heart. "Love, Azure. That's what we have... real, true love. What started out as friendship is now so much more. It's everything to me."

"What about a family? You said you wanted one." Her eyes were stinging. Her throat felt clogged.

"I have one. *We* are a family. You and me... we don't need more."

"You want whelps. Don't try to deny it. You've said so on numerous occasions. Your mother told me so. She said that you were a lonely little boy who longed for siblings. Now you won't be able to have children of your own, either. It's not fair, and I won't do that to you." She shook her head.

"That's just it, Azure. I *wasn't* a lonely little boy. I had plenty of friends. My mother wanted me to have siblings. It was her who longed for a brother or sister for me. It was also her who always said I should take a mate and have loads of whelps. She's the one who longs to have grandkids."

She felt everything in her get weighed down. "How can you take that away from her? You should find a nice human, and—"

"I don't want a human, or anyone else, for that matter. I want you, Azure." He took her hands. "I love you and only you. I have for a while. It took a knock upside the head to realize it. You and I will be a family together. You are all I will ever need. You also never know… you could have another heat. Even if…" He cocked his head. "What is it?"

Her blood rushed. For a second, she felt like she could barely breathe. "That's just it, Ice. I don't know if I can ever go down that road. Even if I had another heat, by some miracle, I'm not sure I could go through with trying for a whelp, with becoming pregnant. I'm too afraid." Her lip wobbled. She looked down at the ground. "I'm afraid of dying like my mother. I spent many years with a whole lot of guilt over what happened to her. I couldn't do that to my child. I—"

Azure only realized that she was crying when Ice cupped her chin and lifted her face so that he could look at her. She sniffed. "I'm such a coward," she whispered. "I'm too afraid."

"You're not a coward. You're one of the bravest people I know." She noted that he didn't say female. It warmed her. "I love you. I want to spend my life with you, making you happy because you make me happy. I don't need children. We can adopt a dog or a cat."

Azure choked out a laugh, even though she was still crying. "A pet is not the same."

"I don't need children, but I do need you, Azure. These last few days have been hell. I feel like I've lost a part of myself. If anything, it's solidified my feelings for you. My love for you. I can't be without you. Now say something because I'm not used to being this sappy."

She laughed some more. "I quite like it, actually. I might have to leave you more often."

"No, don't, please—"

She crushed her mouth to his. Kissing him with everything she had. When they finally pulled apart, they were panting. "I love you too, by the way."

"I'm so glad to hear that. Don't you dare scare me like this again."

"I won't," she promised with a hitch in her voice.

They kissed again, tearing at each other's clothes. And then somehow, they were in her bedroom, dropping back onto her bed. Ice crawled over her, caging her in with his body.

"I've missed you so fucking much. Everything about you."

"Missed you too." She nipped at his neck.

Ice growled low, pulling her legs up his body. There was no need for any kind of foreplay. Their desperation for one another was at an all-time high.

"Want you," he growled.

"Yes." She felt his cock nudge her opening. "Rut me," she ground out.

Azure yelled as he breached her opening. Ice grunted loudly. "Missed this too."

"So much." Her voice sounded breathless.

Ice bottomed out inside her on a low groan that had her belly coiling tight. He stayed deep inside her. Then, using small, precise movements, he fucked her, moving fast. Tiny little thrusts, right there where she needed him. He whispered a curse.

Azure groaned. She cried out, yelling, "Yes... oh yes!" Her tight nubs rubbed against his chest as she arched into him. She could feel that her mouth was wide, her eyes too. "I'm going to... Oh, by the gods!" Her voice shook in time with his punchy movements. That coiling sensation was almost too much. "I'm going... I'm..." Her voice dropped a couple of octaves.

She could hear from the noises he was making that he was close, too. That he was trying to hold on. His jaw was tight. His beautiful eyes were glowing. Their bodies made those wet sounds.

He punched a little deeper, and everything inside her stilled for a few moments. Then she was clamping down on him with her pussy as her body spasmed around his thick girth. She felt his teeth sink into her just as she was coming down, and a second orgasm rocked through her. Her eyes rolled back. The air got caught in her lungs. She bit down on him. The skin at the base of his throat was soft and sensitive.

Ice roared.

Azure screamed, her pussy clenching tighter. He gripped her hair, holding onto it. Ice jerked against her. Her orgasm seemed like it was never-ending. She'd have muscle pain in the morning. Ice groaned her name as he unclamped his mouth.

It was only then that she realized she was still biting him. Azure forced herself to let go.

Ice licked her neck. It stung. He was still moving slowly. "Love you," he whispered into the shell of her ear. He was panting hard.

She made a noise of agreement. Somehow, she knew that if she tried to talk, it wouldn't work so well. Not after that.

It was hardcore mating behavior. This was moving fast. It didn't matter. Not now. Not anymore. Ice loved her. The two of them were going to be a family. She smiled, hugging him close. Her eyes closed in bliss.

CHAPTER 34

Six weeks later...

T HE MALE'S EYES flared with shock before he schooled
his features. "Fuck, you gave me a fright." He glanced
at Ice's chest, frowning. "Are you lost? This is a private
balcony. I think you might be in the wrong place. The main
access balcony is a little further down the—"

"Nope, I'm at the right place," Ice said, advancing on
the male.

"What is your name, Air dragon? Why are you here?"

"It's Ice, and you're Skarn." There was no reason to fuck
around.

"Yes." The male frowned. "How did you know?"

"You were abducted by those mysterious creatures, is that
right? I mean, everyone knows that they took you." The
kings had downplayed the fact that there was potentially a
fifth tribe in existence. They were keeping almost all the
information surrounding what had happened a secret. They
had let this prick get away with far too fucking much.

"Yes, that's right." Skarn's expression darkened further. "I must warn you. I have been asked by numerous dragons about exactly what happened, and who took me, but I can't tell you. I risk banishment or cage time. Probably both." His eyes widened with... fear.

"There are stories of a fifth tribe who fled to the caves. It was most likely them." Ice gave a one-shouldered shrug.

Skarn's eyes flashed with shock for a moment, probably because Ice knew more than most. "I can't tell you anything or discuss this further. I'm sorry... what did you say your name was?" The male narrowed his eyes.

Ice put his bag on the floor. "It's Ice. So, the kings threatened you with banishment? Wow, whatever happened... whatever you told them must have been serious. I can't imagine why all the secrets, though. Why not just be open and honest?"

"All I can tell you is that we are safe. There is nothing to fear from... the cave dwellers." That line sounded rehearsed. "That's all I have to say on the matter." He folded his arms.

"Okay, fair enough. That is good to know. I heard you had it rough down there. That you were held captive for close on a week. That they cut off your wings... twice."

Skarn flinched.

Good! Fucker!

"Yes, I had it bad." Skarn's eyes clouded. "It's not something I want to talk about."

"Those bastards pulled you away from a female in her heat. Let's just start there." Ice shook his head. "Fucking savage."

"Yes, they did. It was a tragedy." Skarn's expression

switched again, actually looking upset. Ice felt his blood start to boil. Just looking at this male pissed him the fuck off.

"Azure is hot. I've seen her," Ice commented, forcing himself to sound bored.

"Sexy piece of ass if I ever saw one." Skarn whistled.

"I'm sure you're upset about not becoming a father." Ice shook his head.

Skarn snorted and then smirked. "I wasn't there to become a father. I was there to rut. I've never been with a female in her heat before. I hear that they are like insatiable wildcats."

So, this prick was going to get Azure with child by raping her and then shirk fatherhood. Why was he even surprised?

Ice pretended that what Skarn had just said excited him. "It would've been some ride, especially with a female like Azure. She's so indifferent. Acts like she's better than us… gives all of us the cold shoulder. Must've been amazing having her beg for it."

"There wasn't much begging even though she was gagging for it. I could tell. Sometimes you've got to go for it, anyway. It's funny how quickly a 'no' can turn into a 'yes.' You know what I mean?"

"Absolutely. You're persuasive like that?" Ice chuckled.

"I know how to win them over. I can be very charming." He grinned. "Also, I know how to get the job done! It's as simple as that. If a female makes too much noise, I shut her up." He lifted a fist. The fucker lifted his fist.

Ice couldn't hold back anymore. This prick had almost forced himself on Azure. He'd come to teach him a lesson, regardless of the words that came out of his mouth. It looked like he would need to do more than that, since the words infuriated him.

Bastard!

"Your eyes are glowing," Skarn started to say. "Do you—"

Ice punched him hard on the jaw, and the male went down. He kicked him a couple of times, hearing ribs break. Possibly his jaw too. *Good!* Blood spattered. Skarn groaned. Too stunned and too hurt to do much of anything except roll himself up into a ball.

Ice pulled the male into the chamber, closing the door behind him. Then he pulled him deeper into the chamber. They needed privacy. The male groaned as Ice opened the bag.

"No... please," Skarn choked out, grimacing.

Ice pulled a roll of duct tape out of the bag. "Is that what Azure said when you were trying to force yourself on her? 'No... please.' Did she beg you to stop?" He pulled out one of his hunting knives. "Even more importantly, did you listen?"

Skarn's eyes went wild; he turned onto his belly and tried to crawl, groaning all the while.

Ice kicked him again, the blow turning the male onto his back. "I asked you a question," Ice said, keeping his voice low. "Did you stop when Azure begged you to?"

"Yes," Skarn choked out.

"That's the wrong answer."

"I didn't..." He grimaced, clutching his side. Blood leaked from his mouth. "I didn't do anything. I didn't touch her."

"You would have, though. If those creatures hadn't

taken you, you would have touched and taken." Anger coursed through him. Making him want to beat this male to a bloody pulp. He wanted to kill him. "You feel no remorse. You're scum."

Skarn started to scream. Ice punched the male in the face a few times. Skarn lost consciousness. Using the duct tape, he taped his mouth shut. Ice considered taping the male's arms, but it wouldn't do any good since the tape wouldn't be strong enough to hold him. If Skarn tried to pry the tape from his mouth, Ice would break a couple of bones.

It didn't take long for Skarn to come to. He groaned, his eyes opening. They were fuzzy with confusion and then flared with the realization of his situation. He tried to scream, his hands clawing at the tape.

Ice broke a couple of fingers on one hand. "Enough," he whispered. "Lie still. You need to listen to me very carefully. You can nod your head if you agree. I would strongly suggest that you do."

Skarn nodded, his eyes wide. He was breathing hard through his nose. Clutching his hand to his chest. Ice could smell urine, and sure enough, the male's pants were soaked with the stuff. Typical bully. This asshole peed himself when dealing with an opponent his own size. Cowardly fuck!

"Azure is my mate."

Skarn's eyes widened even further. He tried to say something; he sounded frantic.

Ice waited until he settled down. "I don't want to hear whatever bullshit excuse you have. You and I both know it would be bullshit. I would kill you, but my female would not approve. You see, unlike you, you piece of shit…" He punched the male, unable to help himself. "Unlike you," he continued when Skarn was listening again, "Azure is a wonderful, caring person. She always sees the best in people. If it were up to me, you'd be dead right now."

Skarn shook his head. His eyes were filled with terror. *Great!* That was perfect.

"Now listen up, you raping sack of fucking shit. You are going to pay for what you tried to do. It's that simple. But first, you need to know that if you so much as come near my female again, I will kill you. Do you understand?"

Skarn nodded.

"If you ever so much as breathe wrong on a female again, I will come back and finish the job. Are we clear?"

Skarn nodded frantically.

"My name is Ice. I am from the Air tribe. I am a hunter. If you speak of this. If you breathe a word, I will track you down and kill you. Your death will be slow. I'll gut you and skin you alive." He held up the knife. "I must warn you, I'm very good at my job."

Skarn tried to get away, but Ice pinned him down with his foot. "I will let you live today, but you need to pay the price for what you did to Azure."

Skarn shook his head, trying to talk.

"I'll give you a choice, your cock or your wings." He held up the knife. "Something is coming off today. You tried to force my female… one of our Air she-dragons. You must pay."

Skarn tried harder to get away.

"Your cock or your wings? Decide, or I will decide for you. I might even take them all." He growled low.

Skarn gave a muffled scream.

CHAPTER 35

The next day…

"C OME ON, PEANUT." The little dog ran after her. "In here." Azure tugged on his leash when he tried to keep running down the hallway.

She opened the door to the salon, watching as little Peanut ran in ahead of her.

"Hi." Melina waved. "Who's my favorite doggie?" Her friend picked the fluffball up and gave him a cuddle. Peanut's tail wagged like mad.

"I was going to ask if it was okay that I brought him, but I guess I have my answer." Azure laughed.

Peanut barked. It came out sounding like a cute yip.

"You sure do," Melina gushed, still cuddling the adorable puppy. Azure and Ice had adopted him about a week ago. Ice had gone into human territory. He had surprised her. Many of the humans at the lair had pets. It was becoming a regular thing to do. It was crazy how they had evolved as a species over the last few years, since the males started taking human mates. Azure was completely in love with their little puppy.

"I think I might have a talk with Freeze about getting a little fluffball of our own. I finally picked out a wedding gown." She made a face at Azure. "I still can't believe you decided on a quiet ceremony. You would've rocked a wedding dress."

Azure beamed. "I just wanted to be mated to Ice. I don't care about all that other stuff. I'm a dragon, after all."

"You're telling me. You didn't even want a ring." Melina shook her head.

"I shift daily. I would lose a ring." Azure laughed. "We may have become quite humanized since mixing with you guys, but we're still half-dragon at the end of the day."

Melina looked at her pointedly. "Well, if you think you're getting out of wearing a bridesmaid's dress, you would be mistaken."

"I would never dream of it." Melina had asked Azure to be her maid of honor.

"I went with that gorgeous green dress, the one with the silver trimming."

"It's beautiful. I'm honored you picked me." Azure felt warm inside.

"Look at my new inventory." Melina gestured to racks of beautiful clothing. "This dress has your name all over it." She pointed at a deep blue sundress with thin straps.

"It's lovely. I'll try it on after you do my nails. Peanut can play with his toy or sit on my lap."

"Sit... sit! Peanut will be just fine. Summer will be here soon. She's having her hair cut."

Azure grinned. "I'm so glad. I've been on her case for weeks."

"Oh!" Melina's eyes widened up a whole lot. "I have some interesting news." She flapped her hands.

"I'm intrigued. What is it?"

"Freeze heard this from one of his work buddies…" Melina paused, probably for dramatic effect.

Azure nodded, encouraging her to continue.

"There are rumors flying around that Skarn… you remember Skarn?"

Azure rolled her eyes. "Unfortunately, yes, I remember him."

Melina laughed. Just as quickly, she was frowning, hard. "Of course, you'd remember that sleazebag. Anyway, Freeze told me his wings were cut off again yesterday."

"What?" *By all that was scaled.* She knew something was up when Ice arrived home yesterday with blood spatters on his chest. He had blood under his nails as well. It wouldn't have been a big deal if he'd come from work, but it was his day off.

When she'd asked him about it, he'd muttered something about lending a helping hand. Azure had assumed he was helping one of the other hunting teams. Then Ice had gone and showered, and that was the end of it. "What happened to the male?" Her heart raced. The last thing she wanted was for Ice to get into trouble over this. Skarn wasn't worth it.

"This is where it gets really strange." Melina pulled in a breath. "Skarn wouldn't say what happened to him. He refused. Apparently, he was petrified they would come back and kill him if he whispered so much as a word. Everyone in the Earth tribe is convinced that the cave dwellers went after him again. That the creatures came back to hurt him."

Not hardly.

Azure bit back a smile. It was Ice. She knew it.

"I think it's great." Melina grinned. "The bastard got what he deserved." She winked at Azure. "He's lucky he didn't have his head cut off."

"Very lucky." Azure smiled. It was clear that Melina had a very good idea of what had happened to the Earth male. She couldn't wait to see Ice. Azure was almost tempted to cancel her nail appointment and head straight home. It might make her a little sick in the head, but the thought of Ice standing up for her and going after that bastard like that turned her on in a big way. She loved that male so much. Azure didn't think it was possible to love someone so much or to be loved back in the way Ice loved her. It was in the little things, like adopting Peanut for her or cutting the Earth male's wings off for what he had done to her.

"Your eyes are glowing," Melina said. "They're beautiful. I take it you're proud of your—"

The door opened, and Summer walked in. "Hello! Am I in the right place?"

"Come on in," Melina said. "Oh, the things I can do with this hair." The human said, letting her fingers run through Summer's blond strands.

Summer looked a little shell-shocked. It looked like she wanted to turn and run.

"Trust me," Melina said. "I know exactly what you need. Let's sit you down over here while I do Azure's nails. We can chat about different styles that I think would suit you."

Summer's eyes were wide. She shook her head. "I'm not sure—"

"I'm sure enough for the both of us, hon.'" Melina smiled. "We won't do anything too drastic. I promise you'll love it. You are going to look even more beautiful than you do already."

"You think I'm beautiful?" Summer narrowed her eyes.

"Are you kidding me? With big blue eyes like those. The guys must chase you day and night."

Summer giggled. She sat down next to Azure. "Hey, Azure. Hi… what's his name again?"

"Peanut."

"Such a cute name," Summer gushed, her eyes still on the puppy.

"The staff at the pound called him that. It stuck."

Summer reached over to stroke his soft fur. Her nostrils flared and she sniffed. The other female sat upright abruptly, shoulders square, eyes forward, like she'd just had a big shock.

"What is it?" Azure asked.

"Um…" Summer locked eyes with her. "Don't freak out, but I think you might be going into heat."

"Nah." Azure shook her head. "So soon? I doubt it very much." It was arousal the other female was scenting… since she had been aroused just before Summer entered the salon. Who wouldn't be? After hearing about what Ice had done for her.

Summer sniffed at her again. "I'm pretty sure I can scent the start of your heat. I was with you before, remember? I know what it smells like. It's a different scent."

What?

Could it be?

"Oh… um… oh." Melina licked her lips. "Wow, that is interesting. Maybe you are, and maybe you're not."

"She is," Summer insisted, smiling. "The more I smell

you, the more convinced I am." Her eyes were bright.

"Either way," Melina said, her voice steady. "You don't have to do anything or rush into anything. You can hide out like you did last time. Only this time, you won't be alone. You don't have to—"

"I think I might want to try for a whelp," Azure blurted, her words shocking her for a moment. The thought terrified her, but Melina was right; things had changed since the last time. They had done a full one-eighty. Azure wasn't alone. She had Ice. A male she loved with everything inside her. "Do you think you could watch Peanut for a few days?" She nuzzled his fur.

Melina gaped at her. Then she blinked a few times. "Of course," she quickly said.

Azure's skin was feeling tight. Her nipples were hard. "I have to... um... get home. I need Ice."

"Go already," Melina urged her. "I'll take good care of this guy." She picked Peanut up. "Might as well start practicing my baby-sitting—"

"Don't say it," Summer growled. "You'll jinx Azure and Ice."

"Yes, it's bad luck to say anything until a female is with whelp," Azure warned. "Keep quiet about it."

"Even once a female is with child," Summer shook her head, "one must be careful of what one says."

"Noted! I'm still learning." Melina cuddled the puppy. "I have Peanut. You run along. When you see Summer again, you won't recognize her."

Summer went pale. She looked so worried that Azure had to laugh. "I'll see you guys." She ran from the salon and didn't stop until she was in her mate's arms... where she belonged.

CHAPTER 36

One month later…

ICE MADE A low rumble to signal that he had spotted something. The male picked up the pace, wings flapping almost noiselessly.

Yes!

There was a herd of bison up ahead. It was a big herd, too. Fog felt a rush of energy surge through him. It always happened this way. It didn't matter how long or how hard they had been flying, the thrill of the hunt would hit when needed, replenishing waning strength.

There was a flash of pink in the bushes below.

Pink?

That didn't compute. There shouldn't be anything pink down there. He slowed while the others surged forward, the hunt firing their blood. For just a moment, he was tempted to ignore whatever it was, or might be. He'd probably made a mistake… seen wrong. It was probably nothing.

No!

It wasn't nothing. He'd seen it… whatever it was. It was a glaring pink and it shouldn't be there. One thing was for sure, he was finding out. Fog dove down, turning back as he did. He spread his wings, gliding, slowing his descent. Silent.

Up ahead, he could hear the sound of the bison being spooked, of hooves throwing up the earth, of claws finding flesh. He remained focused on his task, though.

Where are you? Where?

Holy fucking shit!

What?

The human yelped. Her mouth fell open as she took him in. Then she turned and ran. The little thing was pretty quick for a human. *What the fuck was a human doing here anyhow?* She wore jeans and a pink top. The kind of thing a female would wear if she was going on a night out. Not the right attire for a hike in the middle of fucking nowhere.

Fog shifted as his feet hit the ground. Within a few long strides, he was gripping her arm, trying to be as gentle as possible. He could scent fear on her. There was also anger and agitation there.

"Not again!" she shouted, turning and hitting him on the side of his arm. "No, you don't!" she yelled some more. "No, you brute!"

"I'm not going to hurt you," he said.

She kept pummeling him, her eyes wide. "Let me go. Let me go! I won't go with you. I won't!"

"Stop… female." He kept his voice even, releasing her. He could see that holding onto her was doing more harm than good.

The female turned and ran again. Fog rolled his eyes and went after her. "Wait! I'm trying to help you." He jogged behind her for a short while. "Stop! Let's talk." No luck, so he moved in next to her. She tried to lose him, but he kept up with her easily. Even when she tried to suddenly change direction. Hopefully, she would give in soon.

"Leave me alone." He noticed that she wore boots with heels. How was she running without—?

The human tripped and fell in the long grass. Not the best attire, or footwear, it would seem. He tried to help her up, but she swatted his hands away.

"Ash! Ash!" she shouted.

"What are you saying?" he asked. "What ash? How did you get here?"

"I need to get help!" she shouted, her eyes wide with fear.

"I'm here to help you," he said, holding his hands up in submission.

"Not from you," she yelled. Her blonde hair fell in a tumble over her shoulders. The female was quite beautiful.

Fog looked around them. "Um… I think I'm all you've got."

"You're one of them… sort of… not really, but… Ash! They have my friend. They have Ashlyn." She was frantic. Not making much sense.

"Who has your friend?"

"Those creatures! Oh, lordy! They abducted us. They have my friend. Please." Even though she asked for help, Fog noticed that she backpedaled, scooting back on her ass.

"I will help you," Fog said. "I will keep you safe."

The female seemed to relax—just a smidgen, but he'd take it.

"What about Ash?" She was breathing hard. "Can we get her? We have to find her."

"Where is she?" Fog asked. "Where is your friend?" he added when she didn't answer.

"With them. They took her." She backpedaled further, breathing hard.

"Where?" he asked. "Where did they take her? I want to help you." Fog spoke softly and carefully, so as not to spook her.

"Down… they took her down into the caves. I'm lucky I got away."

A shiver rushed up his spine, and his blood turned cold. Those creatures had kidnapped some human females. There was at least one down there right then. *Fuck! This was bad.*

AUTHOR'S NOTE

Charlene Hartnady is a USA Today Bestselling author. She loves to write about all things paranormal including vampires, elves and shifters of all kinds. Charlene lives on a couple of acres in the country with her husband and three sons. They have an array of pets including a couple of horses.

She is lucky enough to be able to write full time, so most days you can find her at her computer writing up a storm. Charlene believes that it is the small things that truly matter like that feeling you get when you start a new book, or a particularly beautiful sunset.

The Chosen Series:
Book 1 ~ Chosen by the Vampire Kings
Book 2 ~ Stolen by the Alpha Wolf
Book 3 ~ Unlikely Mates
Book 4 ~ Awakened by the Vampire Prince
Book 5 ~ Mated to the Vampire Kings (Short Novel)
Book 6 ~ Wolf Whisperer (Novella)
Book 7 ~ Wanted by the Elven King

Shifter Night Series:
Book 1 ~ Untethered
Book 2 ~ Unbound
Book 3 ~ Unchained
Shifter Night Box Set Books 1—3

The Program Series (Vampire Novels)
Book 1 ~ A Mate for York
Book 2 ~ A Mate for Gideon
Book 3 ~ A Mate for Lazarus
Book 4 ~ A Mate for Griffin
Book 5 ~ A Mate for Lance
Book 6 ~ A Mate for Kai
Book 7 ~ A Mate for Titan

The Feral Series
Book 1 ~ Hunger Awakened
Book 2 ~ Power Awakened
Book 3: Hate Awakened
Book 4: Hope Awakened

The Earth Dragon Series
Book 1 ~ Dragon Guard
Book 2 ~ Savage Dragon
Book 3 ~ Dragon Whelps
Book 4 ~ Slave Dragon
Book 5 ~ Feral Dragon
Book 6 ~ Doctor Dragon

The Bride Hunt Series (Dragon Shifter Novels)
Book 1 ~ Royal Dragon
Book 2 ~ Water Dragon
Book 3 ~ Dragon King
Book 4 ~ Lightning Dragon
Book 5 ~ Forbidden Dragon
Book 6 ~ Dragon Prince

The Water Dragon Series
Book 1 ~ Dragon Hunt
Book 2 ~ Captured Dragons
Book 3 ~ Blood Dragon
Book 4 ~ Dragon Betrayal

Demon Chaser Series (No cliffhangers)
Book 1 ~ Omega
Book 2 ~ Alpha
Book 3 ~ Hybrid
Book 4 ~ Skin
Demon Chaser Boxed Set Book 1–3

UNTETHERED

SHIFTER NIGHT

CHARLENE HARTNADY

CHAPTER 1

Ana should never have agreed to coming to a place like this. The restaurant was a hive of activity. Every single table was taken. It was the best place to go to in town, so it wasn't that big of a surprise that even the waiting area and the bar were full. Crystal glasses, linen serviettes, the whole nine yards. It wasn't easy to get a table in here. The Red Mole was normally booked at least two weeks in advance. She'd only ever eaten here once for her best friend Edith's thirtieth birthday a couple of months ago.

Ana's heart beat faster. Her hands felt a little clammy and a knot formed in her stomach. Who was she kidding? The knot had been there the whole day. It had just grown and tightened since walking in. She stopped for a second to catch her breath. Then stayed there, hand resting on the wall, for another five just to be sure.

Was this normal nervousness or… something else?

Was she about to…?

She put a hand to her belly. Her breathing remained a little elevated, but nothing out of the ordinary. *I have this. I do!* Doctor Brenner had given her the go-ahead. It was just a stupid little date. Ana sucked in a deep breath and kept walking in the direction the hostess had pointed her. The table in the corner… to the left and…

There.

Right! Okay!

She could breathe a little easier since he looked just like his online picture. A suit, dark styled hair and a megawatt smile. Her date stood up… good god, he was tall too. In short, he was really good-looking in a neat, professional kind of way. His profile said he was an accountant, he looked like an accountant. It was a positive start. She willed her hands to stop shaking.

He stepped around the table and took a few steps towards her. "Hi, I'm Brett. You must be… Ana."

She said her name simultaneously, a nervous giggle escaped. Brett put his hand out and she shook it. His hand was soft, as was his skin. *Please don't let my hand feel sweaty. Please don't let me embarrass myself.*

Brett let go almost immediately, a smile still on his face. "It's so good to meet you. You look exactly like your picture." He gave her the once over and she could tell he liked what he saw. She had decided to go with a plain black figure-hugging dress. It came to just above the knee. Ana had taken the time to do her hair and to put on a little make-up. In short, she'd gone to a lot of trouble.

"So do you." Her voice was a little high-pitched.

"For a few minutes there, I thought you were going to stand me up." He arched a brow.

Ana smiled and shook her head. "I might be ten minutes late, but I would never not show." At least, not without telling him first. The thought of canceling had crossed her mind once or twice today.

"Here, allow me." Brett pulled a chair out for her.

"Thank you." She smiled at him as she sat down and he smiled back, taking his own seat opposite of her. So far so good. The knot in her stomach eased its hold just a smidgen and she could breathe a little easier.

The waitress came around to the table and took her order. A glass of white wine. Something light and easy, just like she hoped the evening would go.

Ana saw a tumbler of whiskey on the rocks already on the table. It was dripping with condensation. It looked like Brett had not only arrived on time but most likely, he'd arrived early. Another server came to the table with a basket of breads and a plate of different kinds of butter. "Truffle, herb and regular." He pointed at each of the creamy mounds before walking away.

"So, do you do this kind of thing regularly?" Brett asked as soon as they were alone, he leaned forward slightly in his chair.

Talk about hitting her with a difficult question right off the bat. "Um… are you talking about dating, or…?"

Brett chuckled. "Of course not, a woman like you

must get asked out all the time. I'm sure you go on plenty of dates?"

Yeah… no! She smiled, hoping he wasn't expecting a reply. She couldn't tell him that this was her first date in one and a half years. She certainly couldn't tell him what a disaster her last date had been. She hadn't even made it to the one before that. *Not thinking about it!*

"I'm talking about online dating," Brett answered, not picking up on her discomfort. "Do you do this a lot?"

"This was the first time I tried online dating," she answered simply.

The waitress arrived with her chardonnay. "Would you like some ice with that?"

Ana shook her head. "This is perfect, thanks."

"Are you ready to order your appetizers?" She held her pen poised over a pad. "The oysters are…"

"Give us a couple of minutes, please. We haven't even looked at the menus yet," Brett said, pointing at the leather-bound menus in front of them.

The waitress gave a nod. "No problem, take your time."

Ana picked up her menu. It would give her something to do with her hands which ☐ thank god ☐ had stopped shaking.

Brett drew her attention before she could open it. "Yeah, this is my first date where I had to swipe right." He smiled. "I must say, I'm glad it's not something you do all the time. I was a little worried about the kind of women I might meet through this type of service."

Ana wasn't sure what to say to that so she picked up her wine and took a sip. She gave a small nod to show that she was listening.

"Didn't you find it weird having to sift through all the profiles?"

"It *was* a little strange."

Brett picked up his menu but didn't open it. "I guess we live in a world where it's becoming more and more difficult to meet people in the regular fashion. I work twelve-hour days so…"

"I can understand how that must make it difficult."

"Yeah well, one must work hard to get ahead." He opened his menu but didn't look down. "I recently made partner at my firm." He took a sip of his whiskey.

"Oh, that's great. Congratulations!"

"Just last month and four years early."

Ana frowned. "Four years?"

"Yup, I had planned to make partner by forty. I'm only thirty-six so that's sooner than I'd anticipated."

"It certainly is. That's wonderful. You must be thrilled."

"I am." He looked serious for a moment, his brow creased and his lips pursed. "I have a four-bedroom home, with a pool and a big landscaped garden."

"Oh!" If he thought to impress her with money, he was sadly mistaken. "That's great!"

"Complete with a white picket fence." He swirled his glass. "Granite tops in the kitchen and marble finishes in all the bathrooms. It's quite lovely."

She nodded, taking another sip of her wine. "That's wonderful."

"All that's missing is a family." He was looking at her strangely, almost like he was judging her reaction. Maybe a guy like him had women coming onto him for his money.

Ana put down her glass, giving another nod. Maybe he just liked the attention that money brought him. Well, he was barking up the wrong tree. She scanned through the appetizers, a couple of things catching her eye.

"What do you do?" Brett picked up his own menu and opened it, he kept his eyes on her.

"I'm a nurse at the Sweetwater Hospital."

"Oh!" He smiled. "How nice!" The way he said it was kind of patronizing.

"I really enjoy my work, I've—"

"I guess being a medical worker is something that could come in handy." He rubbed his chin.

Ana frowned. "What do you mean?"

"In the home, that is. I'm sure you want to become a mother… have kids one day. Maybe even sooner rather than later?" He raised both brows.

"Yes." Her heart beat a little faster. "I would love to be a mom… one day that is." Her chest tightened. Ana picked up her glass and took a big glug of wine, not sure where this conversation was going. Not liking the direction.

"Shall I order some water?" He frowned, glancing at the wine glass still in her hand. He had a look of disapproval but she knew she must be reading him wrong.

"Yes, that would be nice," she answered, trying to be polite. Ana put the wine glass back down.

He settled back in his chair and smiled at her. "It's good to know."

"What is?" she asked, as Brett flagged down one of the waiters and ordered water.

"Good to know that you want to be a mom." He turned back to her. "It's important to establish these things early."

What was he on about? He must have seen her confused look because he elaborated. "I'm looking for marriage and a family."

Ana took another big sip of her wine, her heart all a-flutter. Her stomach knotting back up. "This… um… this is our first date. It's too soon to—"

"It's never too soon to make your intentions known," he interrupted. "I'm looking for a wife… there, it's out. I know that most women want marriage and security so I doubt I'll have much trouble. I just don't want to waste my time, is all. I realize that not everyone is looking for the same thing. Not everyone wants kids." He paused. It was like he was waiting for her to interject if she had something to say. "That's why I was a bit worried about using a dating app. I'd heard that the people you meet… the type of person… some of them are just out for a good time…" He pulled a face. "Hey, are you okay? You look a little flustered."

"I'm fine." She tried to control her breathing. *I can handle this. I can!*

Brett gave a small nod. "So, you're not just here for sex, are you?"

"No," she blurted. "Not at all." *It's fine! It's all good.*

"Well, then we can relax and enjoy our date." He narrowed his eyes, leaning forward in his seat. "Are you sure you're okay?"

Ana gasped for air, her throat closing quickly. *Please no! No!*

"Can I pour you some water?"

Ana nodded. She was way beyond water. Way beyond trying to talk. *Shit! This isn't happening. It isn't!* The room was hot… that's why she felt flushed. That's why she couldn't breathe. *Damn! Dammit all to hell!*

Brett hurriedly poured water, some of it sloshed over the rim of the glass, his eyes were filled with concern. "You're sweating."

Gee, I hadn't noticed.

She grabbed the glass and tried to drink some but it gushed over her lips and down her neck. *Cold!* Ana swallowed the little bit she could. It felt like a rock trying to go down a straw. Her throat was officially closed. The room was both spinning and crystal clear, all at the same time.

Around them, waiters carried beautifully prepared meals and expensive bottles of wine. Diners chatted, drank and ate their meals, oblivious to the turmoil in the far corner of the room.

"What can I do?" Brett was out of his seat. "Are you having an allergic reaction? Do you have medication in your purse?" He lifted her purse from the chair next to her. "Is it in here? Try to breathe slower."

Gee, why hadn't I thought of that?

Ana realized that she was being a bitch but couldn't help it. She needed to get the hell out of there. She pushed her chair back, eliciting a hard scraping noise on the gleaming wooden floor. *Oh shit!* Now the people from the table next to them were gaping at her and one of the servers was making her way over, eyes wide.

Out!

Now!

She had to leave. If she made it outside and to the safety of her car she would be okay. It was a pity, but she didn't feel like that was going to happen. She was beginning to feel light-headed. Her stomach seemed to clamp and unclamp. Stars were beginning to flicker in and out of her vision. She felt dizzy… no, she felt… ill. Her legs might not work anymore but she needed to try.

"Out," she managed to somehow moan the word. She planted her hands on the table and used it to leverage herself up into a standing position. Well sort of. She was hunched over the table. Her glass of water tipped over, clanging as it hit, water soaked into the beautifully crisp white tablecloth.

"Ana," Brett kept calling her name. He clasped her elbow tightly. "Sit. You shouldn't be—"

Ana twisted around, trying to push past him… trying hard not to… her stomach gave a heave and out it came. The apple she'd munched on before coming here and the wine, her vomit was sour… it was disgusting and it was all over Brett's shoes, all over his left leg. He let go of her, taking a frantic step back. Then everything went black as she passed out.

CHAPTER 2

A sh put his nose into the air and sniffed deeply. His already pointed snout elongated even more. His nostrils widened. He sniffed again, lumbering from one side of the clearing to the other, eyes shifting from left to right. His heavy fur bristled. The big male rose onto his muscular hind legs and gave another exaggerated sniff. The sound of his snuffling filled the clearing. The rest of the sounds of the forest seemed to become drowned out.

Winston could see that the male was agitated. He growled, landing heavily onto all fours before walking back to the spot he had just vacated. Winston sniffed the air as well and got... the edge of something... maybe... he ultimately got nothing. Crisp air, the scent of the nearby river. He could smell the earth, a squirrel that had recently run across this particular patch of earth. He could scent the daisies growing on a patch of moss nearby.

He could scent many other things as well that were of little importance. What had gotten his friend so rattled?

He watched as Ash ripped up the earth with his heavily clawed paws, frequently stopping to sniff some more. Then there was the familiar sound of bones cracking, of tendons reshaping.

Ash's low bear growl became less animal and more human… straddling the line between the two. He crouched down, fingers sinking into the earth. His body covered in a thin sheen of sweat. Ash looked his way and gave a quick lift of the chin.

It seemed his buddy wanted to have a little chat. Winston pictured his human form, feeling his wolf retract, starting with his fur. It pulled into his skin, his limbs folding in on themselves. It hurt but it was a good kind of pain. "What is it?" he said, as soon as he was shifted enough to talk. His voice still held a guttural edge, his vocal cords still remembering those of his wolf.

"Not sure." Ash was still agitated. "Something… and yet, I can't put my claw on what exactly."

Winston chuckled. "It's a known fact that wolves have a better sense of smell than bears. I didn't pick up a thing."

Ash sniffed again, even though there was no way he would pick anything up in his human form, despite the fact that his sense of smell was far superior to any mere human.

Winston chuckled at the male. Ash was his best friend. Even though they were different kinds of shifters. Even though Ash was older and an alpha. It didn't matter in the least. They had still become fast friends from the word go. "Let's change back and head home," he suggested.

Human skin or not, Ash bristled, the male still on high-alert. "Call it a gut feeling… something isn't right."

Winston paced to where Ash was standing.

The male seemed to be listening for something, his brow heavily furrowed. "I wish I knew what the fuck was going on."

"Something is definitely up. Herds of game don't disappear into thin air. At this point though you're just hungry. We're all hungry… for meat."

Ash's nostrils flared, his eyes were focused on the canopy up ahead. "I'm hungry but that's not it. Something spooked the game. I sensed something out here. Something's wrong!"

Winston shook his head. "If there was something in these woods, we'd know about it."

"Make no mistake," Ash paused. "There is something in these woods. With thousands of square miles, it would be easy for them to hide."

"From us? We're shifters for fuck's sake. They can't hide from us." Winston shook his head. "Now that's crazy talk."

Ash shrugged. "You're probably right but I'd still be willing to bet my right nut on it."

Winston laughed. "You're on. I'm sure it's a simple case of the herds migrating though. Something to do with the solar system and the way the planets are aligned. Or maybe global warming. It's fucking with nature in the worst of ways."

The big male shrugged, his agitation from earlier all but gone. "What happened to you on Saturday?"

"What do you mean, what happened to me?" Winston folded his arms. "Nothing happened."

"You're right, nothing happened," Ash chuckled.

Winston fought an eye roll and lost. *Here we go again.*

"You took a female back to your hotel room but didn't touch her." Ash grinned. "My sources tell me she was not too thrilled when she left. Made a ton of noise and called you a limp dick." Ash choked out a laugh. "Limp dick," he muttered to himself, still laughing.

Winston rolled his eyes a second time. "Yeah, yeah, it's 'Pick on Winston' week. Why can't a male just change his mind? Why was it that my dick immediately got a bad rep? Why can't a male walk away from sex without being ridiculed?"

"There was nothing wrong with that female." Ash shook his head. "Trent told me it was the blonde with the hair all the way to her ass. She's a little noisy, but—"

"My point exactly." Winston blew out a breath.

"Are you still banging on about how you've had it with fucking around?"

"You have no idea." Winston narrowed his eyes. "You've only been at it for a couple of years."

Ash's eyes darkened, pain caused his features to pinch.

"Hey, bro…" Winston kept his voice soft. "I'm sorry. That was out of line." *What the fuck is wrong with me?*

Ash shook his head. "Nah!" He rolled his shoulders. "I'm fine. Don't worry about it."

Winston could see that he wasn't. What male would be?

"So, no more Shifter Night for you then? No more going to the 'Dark Horse'? No more females? No more fun… fuck! I'm glad I'm not you."

"Who says I can't still go to Shifter Night? Who says I can't spend time with the females? Who says that sex equates to the only form of fun to be had?"

Ash barked out a laugh. It was deep and throaty. "You

have got to be fucking kidding me. You still plan on hitting town?"

"Sure," Winston shrugged, "why not? I don't plan on fucking around but I can still go and enjoy myself."

"We're meat to those human females, plain and simple. Meat. They don't want us for anything other than our dicks," Ash palmed his cock as he said it.

"You're wrong. Humans want nothing more than to spend more time with us. I've had numerous females beg me to meet with them again, or to take them back with me. They *wanted* a relationship with me. Begged me for a chance."

"They wanted more cock. It's always about the sex, trust me. They don't want to take you home to meet daddy. They don't want you to take them out to dinner or to go dancing. They want you because they know you have a big dick and you know how to use it. That's it, end of story."

"Cynical much?"

"Nope." Completely deadpan.

Winston shrugged. "I guess I'm just better relationship material. Females definitely want me for more than just sex."

"How do you figure?" Ash narrowed his eyes.

"I'm better looking and I'm easier to talk to."

Ash choked out a laugh. "So full of shit."

Winston grinned. "You know it's true."

"I'm better in the sack. The other stuff means fuck all to me," said in true Ash style.

Winston nodded. "Yeah well, I'm sick of being used. Sick of using females right back. I guess I want more, that's all."

"Said like a true pussy."

"Who the fuck are you calling a pussy?" he growled.

"Pussy wolf," Ash lowered his voice. His canines were longer than they had been a few seconds ago.

"Fuck you, bear." He felt his own teeth erupt, his hairs stood up and his muscles bunched.

"Plenty of fucking for me; for you," he laughed, the sound rough and raw, "not so much." Hair sprouted from his chest. His jaw elongated.

"Fucking around! Huh!" Winston felt his own fur begin to sprout. He felt the cords in his throat tighten. "It's meaningless, emotionless and not for me. Not anymore." So deep he could barely understand himself. "I want something more."

Ash changed back. The male breathed deeply, even hunched over the middle. It took effort to shift. He pulled himself upright, eyes on Winston. "Something more." He was breathing deeply, his eyes on the ground. "You don't want love... trust me on that. Love can destroy a male." His friend took in a deep breath and shifted.

It was exactly what Winston wanted. It was what he craved.

Printed in Great Britain
by Amazon

27770643R00178